Blinded By The Brass Ring

PATRICIA SCARLETT

Blinded By The Brass Ring

THE JEWELLE JOSEPH SERIES

Baraka
Books

Montréal

ISBN 978-1-77186-314-8 pbk; 978-1-77186-322-3 epub; 978-1-77186-323-0 pdf
Cover by Maison 1608
Book Design by Folio infographie
Editing and proofreading: Blossom Thom, Elizabeth West

Legal Deposit, 2nd quarter 2023
Bibliothèque et Archives nationales du Québec
Library and Archives Canada

Published by Baraka Books of Montreal

Printed and bound in Quebec

Trade Distribution & Returns
Canada – UTP Distribution: UTPdistribution.com

United States
Independent Publishers Group: IPGbook.com

We acknowledge the support from the Société de développement des entreprises culturelles (SODEC) and the Government of Quebec tax credit for book publishing administered by SODEC.

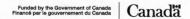

When we revolt it's not for a particular culture. We revolt simply because, for many reasons, we can no longer breathe.

—Frantz Fanon

Contents

Foreword

Simple Stories, Complex Characters

It seems like yesterday that Toronto, and Canada, were mono-chromatic in colour and culture, and the media landscape reflected the city and its suburbs. Minority media professionals were few and far between. In the late 1960s it was still cause for comment when a non-White face appeared on TV (as a presenter) and young media professionals of colour complained.

Then things changed. By 1970 to be trained in television or radio did not seem as quixotic as it once did. Young visible minorities began graduating from professional schools. Youngsters graduating from community colleges and going to seek work in the United States was one option.

It still wasn't easy, but it was easier. A job in media didn't seem as impossible anymore. Of course, there were obstacles, but they were surmountable. It's still not easy. Media professionals of colour have to work hard to prove themselves but it's worth the effort. In front and behind the camera, at radio microphones, in executive offices, the media reflects the country. It's not perfect. There is some way to go, but for a lot of young media professionals, there is hope and optimism and that's a lot better than the decade of the 1960s.

Roger McTair, Writer, TV/Film Producer, Mentor
11 July 2020

PART I

One

TV3

"Mother," Jewelle whispered nervously into her phone. "Did I wake you?" Adele rubbed the sleep from her eyes and slowly turned to check the time on the alarm clock.

"It's six o'clock in the morning. Is everything okay?" asked Adele, her lilting Jamaican accent more pronounced than usual.

"Yes, everything's fine. I got home very late from the office so I couldn't call you back yesterday." As usual, Jewelle's workday had infiltrated her personal life.

"So, Miss Jewelle, let me understand this. It was too late to call me last night, but it's not too early to wake me up!" Adele's tone and use of "Miss" signaled her displeasure and her battle readiness. Jewelle took a deep breath to calm herself.

"Mother, you know work has been really busy and ..."

Before Jewelle could finish, Adele snapped, "I don't care how busy you get at work; how many times have I told you family comes first!? How many times, Jewelle? I'm your mother. When I call, I expect you to call me back on the same day. What if I was having a heart attack?"

Jewelle felt her blood pressure soar. She took another deep breath.

"Well Mother, what medical crisis were you in the throes of?"

"Miss Jewelle, I hope I don't hear nuh rudeness in yu voice. Look here," Adele's voice softened, "ah just wanted to hear your voice."

3

Jewelle also lowered the temperature.

"Mother, I'm sorry I didn't call yesterday. I promise I'll return your calls on the same day."

The two women paused, allowing the silence to soak up the lingering tension.

"Alright then," Adele said, her voice getting syrupy, satisfied that she had won this round. The woman had always reigned supreme over her children and refused to see them as adults.

"I was also calling to let you know that your father is trying to reach you," said Adele, now barely containing her rancour.

"Did Daddy say why he was trying to reach me?" asked Jewelle cautiously.

"He didn't say, and I didn't ask. The less I say to him, the better."

Adele's divorce from Jewelle's father, Radcliffe Joseph, was bitter. He had tried unsuccessfully to hide his assets to lessen the financial blow of the divorce settlement. He had underestimated Adele's doggedness as she fought for what she felt she was rightfully entitled to. She has never forgiven him for his "worthless behaviour" and the fact that he left so that he was free to chase and capture the hearts and bodies of nubile young women. Nevertheless, she always encouraged her children to respect, if not love their father because he loved them and had provided for all their material needs.

Radcliffe Joseph was a reckless eyeballer and prolific lover who zeroed in on every attractive young woman who crossed his path. They were drawn to his clean-shaven good looks and dapper style, and his fat wallet was a bonus. Radcliffe's other passion was dominoes. He played regularly and often with his band of merry men, friends he made shortly after migrating to Canada and who had become lifelong buddies.

"Well, I will give him a call tomorrow," said Jewelle breezily.

"Don't rush to call him, though," Adele warned. "I'm sure it's nothing important. Anyhow, you are an adult. I can't tell you what to do," added Adele, oblivious to the fact that she was telling Jewelle what to do.

"Mother, thanks for passing on Daddy's message. I have to go now."

"I know you have to get ready for work. Have a pleasant day and don't let that scrawny, troublesome woman ... whatever her name is ... work your nerves. Love you."

"Love you too." Jewelle gently returned the telephone to its base, savouring her mother's last words.

Jewelle stretched, got up, and moved into overdrive: a hit of Bob Marley to feel no pain, a quick bowl of muesli, a three-minute shower, rapid make-up application and a slate gray cotton suit brightened by her shapely curves and a cherry red silk blouse. She felt like a movie character in fast motion.

Before heading out the door, Jewelle took one last admiring look around her stylish and tidy condominium apartment and quickly double-checked to make sure she didn't leave files behind. The gleaming hardwood floors were bare except for the red Bokhara runner in the hallway. Sunflower yellow walls displayed paintings of tropical landscapes; portraits of African men, women and children; African masks; and hand-woven African and Aboriginal baskets. Furniture was minimal. In the living room two tall wooden bookcases were lined with hardcover classics—Balzac, Camus, Zola, Baldwin, Morrison, Ellison, Wright, Du Bois, art books, paperback chick lit, and somber looking business books. A royal blue suede sofa accessorized with striped silk cushions was flanked by an end table on one side and a large leafy green plant on the other. An antique brass lamp anchored a glass-top end table. A dark brown rectangular coffee table with a large crystal bowl in the center faced an entertainment unit with a stereo system. The dining room's round teak table was encircled by four white, slip-covered chairs.

Satisfied that she had everything she needed, and the apartment was in order, Jewelle locked the door and walked down the hall to the elevator. Amid the morning rush, she flashed back to the unhurried and joyful summer holidays with her maternal grandmother in Gordon Town, at the foot of Jamaica's Blue Mountains. Jewelle remembered her grandmother's insistence on rules and order, that everything in her little four-room house had its "rightful place." Granny made sure that her children, Adele and Constance, lived by adages like cleanliness is next to Godliness. Her yard matched the sense of order in her house with its mango, avocado and lime trees, rainbow-coloured crotons, leafy ferns, and licorice shrubs surrounded by brilliant bougainvillea hedges robed in cheerful pink, orange and white. Adele passed the love of "order" on to Jewelle and her siblings, Deeana and Ryan. Her older sister Cass embraced chaos.

Dew glistened on the grass and brightly coloured flowers swayed in the fresh morning breeze when Jewelle walked briskly past the garden beds out front of her condo. Out on the street, she hailed a cab and told the driver which route to take. She wasn't about to be driven all over the city so that the normal ten-dollar fare would be jacked up to a small fortune. As the car turned north on Yonge Street, she commanded, "Step on the gas."

"Do you want me to run the red lights?" cracked the driver.

"Of course not! But amber is fair game," Jewelle replied with a mischievous grin. Looking out the cab window, Jewelle watched the morning light nudge the dawn from the sky as the city slowly came to life. On this stretch of Yonge Street, the longest street in the world, soulless glass and steel office towers loomed over overpriced restaurants and condominiums, ornate heritage buildings, and upscale antique shops and boutiques. A few early morning joggers commandeered the empty sidewalks, construction workers hurried along with their lunch boxes, and security guards, whose shifts had ended, scurried to the subway. A few of the homeless had already begun panhandling; the sight of their daily grind saddened Jewelle. She quietly thanked God for her many blessings.

TV3 occupied five floors of a glass and steel clone of all the other towers built during the 1980s. The tenants were a mix of telecommunications and mortgage companies, a few restaurants, and a bar where many frustrated TV3 employees could be spotted sipping on drinks that they hoped would lower their stress levels, if only for a few hours. A few high functioning alcoholics spent more time at the bar than at their desks. Jewelle thought a few of them channeled Norm, the ever-parched sitcom character on *Cheers*. The nonchalant uniform—T-shirt, jeans, running shoes—of those who worked in production set them apart from those in TV3's executive suites, and from the strictly dress-coded employees of other companies.

"Which floor are you on?" asked the moon-faced security guard looking up from his video monitor.

"Fifth floor, TV3, Sales Department," snapped Jewelle Joseph, walking over to the elevators where she stopped to rummage through her handbag for the elevator key. A frown creased her forehead as the key eluded her. The security guard got up from behind his desk in the cavernous lobby and waddled over to the elevators eyeing Jewelle suspiciously. His large round head sported a five-strand comb-over that rivaled René Lévesque's, the legendary, chain-smoking, nationalist premier of Québec. A pompous mid-section protruded from the guard's stocky frame.

"Where's your ID?" he demanded, walking closer to Jewelle.

"Where's Phil?" Jewelle shot back as she fished out her wallet and quickly flashed her company ID.

"Phil called in sick. I'm filling in. Hold on a minute. Let me have another look at that." The guard's steely gaze probed her.

"Sure," she replied testily, holding up the ID long enough for him to verify that the photo was a close facsimile of the flesh and blood original standing in front of him.

"Thanks. You're in early," he observed, as he turned to make his way back to his desk, clearly disappointed that the ID proved to be authentic.

"Yah, some of us have to work for our money," she said dryly and continued searching for the key. Finding it, she hit the up button, the elevator doors opened immediately, and she stepped inside. As the elevator climbed to the fifth floor, Jewelle wondered why she was subjected to this crap. It's six thirty in the morning, she thought. Do I look like someone who's up to no good, a felon he saw on last night's news, a loser dangling precariously from the lower rung of the economic ladder? Jewelle inhaled deeply then exhaled to pull herself back from mounting her soapbox.

Studying her reflection in the mirrored elevator walls, Jewelle saw an attractive heart-shaped face, warm mahogany complexion, large, dark brown eyes rimmed with long black lashes and invitingly full lips staring back at her. Girl, you look good for a woman in her mid-thirties, she thought—no wrinkles, still a perfect size eight, the girls and the booty still firm. What more could she ask for? Perhaps an inch or two on the five feet six inches she had been allotted, not to mention adjustments to her splayed out feet that made fitting stylish shoes tricky, and what about that wide mouth of hers? She tried to comfort herself with the fact that the beautiful singer Sade's mouth was as generous as hers.

The sound of the elevator bell pulled Jewelle back from her reverie. When the elevator doors opened on to the fifth floor, she stepped out briskly and wondered aloud, "What fresh hell awaits me today?" No doubt, the resident demon, her rival Chantal Mercier, a fellow international sales executive, would be dispensing her customary torment. Jewelle grew agitated. Within weeks of settling into her office, the newest member of the international team, Chantal had pit herself against Jewelle seemingly on a mission to undermine her at every turn. Chantal's tall, slender, booty-challenged frame owed as much to genetics as her obsessive daily workouts and relentless consumption of green salads, green juices, and specialty water.

To ensure that she had all the ingredients for the foul-looking raw cocktails she made at work, she grew wheat grass on her office windowsill. Given her French River, a.k.a. Rivière des Français, Northern Ontario roots, the greening of Chantal amused and amazed Jewelle and her colleagues. By her own account, Chantal's father used to be an avid hunter until a hunting accident dampened his enthusiasm. Chantal, on the other hand, was undeterred. She wasn't a bad shot with a rifle and proudly displayed a photo of herself and one of her kills on her office wall.

Jewelle was sure Chantal's restricted diet was the cause of her perpetual bitchiness and deviousness. Privately, Jewelle thought she could easily deliver master classes in both and that the woman's demeanour could be greatly improved by an injection of carbs (good carbs of course). At certain angles and in a certain light, Chantal's face reminded Jewelle of aging, relentlessly tanned Hollywood stars, specifically George Hamilton when he was still considered hot. But when she applied her makeup, Chantal forgot to camouflage her neck. It revealed the true nature of her complexion—pale and pasty. Chantal's long, well-toned and tanned legs reminded Jewelle of baguettes. Her no booty body did appeal to more than a few men, including clients with whom she engaged in textbook flirtations. What she lacked behind she more than compensated for up front, making her an ideal hire if she applied for a job at Hooters.

Chantal dressed well but had no "style" per se as she invariably succumbed to the prescribed trend du jour. Whatever she wore, somehow, always seemed borrowed. Her not-a-strand-out-of-place, currently blonde hair made her look Fox News ready. Hooters and Fox ready. Chantal seemed oblivious to the fact that her look made her a walking cliché. Of course, she had the intellectual curiosity of a mink.

Jewelle walked down the long, nondescript corridor. The walls on both sides were covered with framed promotional posters of TV3 productions and grinning headshots of on-camera personalities. Finally reaching her office, she unlocked the door and walked in. She took off her coat, hung it up, and turned to look around the tidy workspace, her eyes landing on the ever expanding to-do list in the middle of her desk.

Jewelle settled into the comfortable, ergonomically designed desk chair and gazed blankly at the walls of her office decorated with groupings of scenic postcards of the places she had visited over the years, family photos, framed images of select TV3 documentaries, and mounted posters of Martin Luther King and Malcom X. When she hung the King poster it went unnoticed. This was not the case for the Malcom X. Many of her colleagues nervously asked about its "meaning," and Jewelle's stock response was that Malcolm X was historically more important to the advancement of Blacks in North America than any other person. She would then add with a wisp of a smile crossing her face, "Of course you understand that that was an arguable statement." To her way of thinking, he wasn't simply a hot head racist as he was often portrayed. Her position led her co-workers to wonder if they had a revolutionary in their midst. The most conservative of the lot, particularly Chantal, became increasingly suspicious after she started wearing dreadlocks. What they didn't know, or couldn't begin to understand, was that she had simply grown weary of the tyranny of her blond ghetto fabulous, sadistic hairdresser—and so had her hair. Jewelle no longer wished to accept the interminable wait for the hairdresser to "look after her hair" as her blood pressure took flight. If the wait wasn't enough, her poor scalp had been complaining about the relaxer burns. Whenever Jewelle dared to seek relief by asking her hairdresser to wash out the nasty chemicals, her request was met with, "Mi dear, yu hair tuff, di relaxa have to stay on longa." Jewelle was fed up with this physical and emotional torture. Locks provided a natural, relatively low maintenance solution.

Chantal Mercier had been hired two years after Jewelle. Within months of her arrival, it was clear to Jewelle and everyone else that Chantal was ruthlessly ambitious, prepared to step on and over anyone to advance her career. She was a bounder who gave new meaning to Malcolm X's rousing maxim By any Means Necessary with her outrageous behaviour and covert manoeuvrings. A mutual dislike instantly sprang up between them. However, for the sake of her career, Jewelle managed, most of the time, to maintain a frosty politeness towards Miss Machiavelli.

Like many other corporations, TV3's senior management was nervous about the year 2000 and all the forecasted technological collapse. Overpaid Y2K consultants of every description camped out at TV3 dispensing their sage advice that was speculative at best and outright lies at worse. Rumours were running rampant that all the apocalyptic advice cost a princely sum, enough to sink the company. The sales department had been abuzz for weeks, anticipating that the company's financial woes would land squarely on them with a thud. They would have to eke more dollars out of their tired program catalogue to keep the network upright. The situation was intensified by management's confirmation of rumoured layoffs and voluntary severance packages. Market consolidation through mergers and acquisitions was dramatically changing the television landscape. Small channels like TV3 were losing audience share to their competitors and no longer had need of a large, underworked, and overpaid staff. Lean and mean was designated the way of the future. The rumour mill throbbed.

Jewelle's colleagues gathered daily around the photocopier or the fax machine to predict who would stay and who would go. When the salaried women of the sales department weren't fully preoccupied by their prognostications, talk of Barb Winter's, the Manager of Sales, sudden and mysterious resignation filled the gap. Hourly, or so it seemed, they met to speculate and concoct ever more outlandish scenarios to explain Barbara's speedy departure. Jewelle stayed out of the fray, preferring to take it all in from the periphery. Besides, she had more pressing matters to take care of. MIP-TV, the annual Cannes gathering where self-important high-powered, low-powered, and barely powered television executives from around the world bought, sold, and traded television programs, was two weeks away. The ritual planning, packing and logistics of getting ready for a television market felt like a small-scale military operation. Like most Cannes regulars, Jewelle both dreaded and looked forward to being in the home of the famous film festival, a place of glamour, intrigue, and sunny beaches where some sunbathers displayed bodies well past their prime, a place where handsome (and not so handsome) males and beautiful young female media types wined, dined, and played musical beds as they worked their way into bigger executive offices.

Jewelle was more than a touch irritated that Chantal wasn't pulling her weight on the MIP-TV preparations. She never seemed to have time to complete tasks like proofing the program catalogue pages, a task that had now landed on Jewelle's desk. Chantal was now working on a special project with a few of TV3's board members. Somehow, she always managed to get by with not doing her full share. Her shameless flattering and flirtations with the geriatric white males in the executive office provided a shield from any reprimand.

Glancing at her watch, Jewelle noted that it was already seven. Obsessive about time and punctuality, her father's mantra, Better an Hour Early, Than a Minute Late, looped in the back of her head. Now it was time to shift into execution mode if she was to get a few things done before her colleagues arrived. She scanned her to-do list but was momentarily distracted by the small Kosta Boda glass sculptures sitting on her desk. She reached over, picked up the one in the shape of a mountain range and held it up to the light to better see and appreciate its colours. This sculpture, titled *Perseverance in the Face of Adversity*, had been sent to her anonymously. She suspected the sender was her Swedish client and admirer Johann Eriksson since the sculpture was made by Kosta Boda, a renowned Swedish glassware company. When asked, Johann denied that he was the sender. This sculpture was a constant reminder to Jewelle that she would prevail if she worked hard.

Jewelle turned her attention to the to-do list. At the top of it were phone calls to overseas clients, including TV3's agent in France, Thérèse Cartier, to finalize meetings during the market. Jewelle and Thérèse had become friends over the years and always got together for dinner during MIP. They first met when Thérèse visited TV3 to execute her agent agreement. The first things that Jewelle noticed were Thérèse's lively bright blue eyes set in a compelling, symmetrical face. She looked trim in her impeccably tailored St. Laurent suits, which were always accessorized by a striking ruby and pearl brooch that Jewelle later learned once belonged to her mother.

As she reached for the phone to call Thérèse, she noticed the flashing red light signaling messages. She replaced the phone on the cradle, punched in her password, hit the speaker button, and listened. The first message was from her "posse," a group of many-hued, self-confident, opinionated girlfriends. Apart from family, these women supported Jewelle through the highs and lows of her life. Bernie, the alpha female of the pack, never hesitated to tell Jewelle the unvarnished truth about herself.

"Jewelle, you still on this planet?" demanded Bernie. Maxine chimed in, "You may be out of sight but not out of mind." Melanie added, "Girl, you work way too hard. You trying to match James Brown's claim that no one in the biz works harder than him?"

"Camilla here, I might as well add my two cents. I've discovered a new designer that you need in your life."

"Of course, only when the sales are on," contributed Joy. They laughed in agreement then shouted in unison: "We miss you. Don't make us have to come find you!"

The second message was from Anthony, Jewelle's long-suffering boyfriend. A warm smile spread across her face as she listened to his mellifluous voice. Nice vibe, she thought. Anthony had called to wish her a pleasant day and to tell her he loved her. Jewelle was very fond of him but sometimes he could be too clingy, which made her want to escape.

Jewelle met Anthony one snowy winter evening when she discovered that her car battery had died. Angry with herself for leaving the car lights on again, she trudged through the snow in search of a boost. She spotted Anthony hurrying towards his car and approached him. "Hello. Can you help me?" Jewelle hesitated. "My car battery has died and ..."

"Where are you parked?" Anthony asked commandingly.

"Well, why don't you just follow me in your car, and I'll lead you?" Jewelle smiled tentatively.

Anthony, paused, cocked his head roguishly to one side and repeated, "You'll lead me ... Then, I guess I'll follow! You could just get in the car and drive with me," he added.

Jewelle felt the inklings of a feeling that went beyond a need for a battery boost. And when she felt something so fast, she attributed it to destiny. Maybe.

"I'd prefer not to," said Jewelle flashing him a warm smile as she allowed herself a moment to drink in the fine brother that she'd be leading. Anthony's ruggedly handsome lightly tanned face with its strong jawline, wide-set eyes, and short curly hair made him magazine cover worthy. She allowed herself to be swept up in the magic of the moment and quietly wished that his bulky coat was hiding a well-toned body, that he had good teeth and manners, and was seriously ambitious. In her mind these were just a few of her requirements for a personal relationship. Once the boost was done, they traded phone numbers. Their first date followed quickly.

On the surface Anthony and Jewelle were a match. They looked great together. But their first date revealed their differences. During dinner, they discovered that they both loved to swim and enjoyed good food. However, it was also clear that Anthony's interest in literature was limited to the newspaper, specifically, the sports section. Further, he had no desire to climb the corporate ladder. Anthony was content in his position as a systems analyst and was happy with the toys it afforded him, particularly his cherished hot red Audi. He had no interest in moving into management. This puzzled Jewelle as she was raised to be all that you can be. Anthony's apparent lack of ambition irritated Jewelle, but she consoled herself with the fact that he adored her and had a decent job. It was a start, and besides, she had enough ambition for the two of them. Ambition was embedded in her DNA, according to her father Radcliffe. She saw herself climbing to the top of the heap in television sales and was prepared to work hard to make it happen.

Anthony was clearly the introvert in the relationship, a quiet, stay-at-home kind of guy with a few very close friends. Jewelle, on the other hand, did not mind the quiet nights occasionally but relished the social scene and was not shy about being in the spotlight. She also enjoyed playing the role of the gracious hostess from time to time. Together she and Anthony had managed, over the course of two years, to arrive at a harmonious balance. Jewelle, however, still had lingering doubts about marrying Anthony, which clearly, he wanted to do.

Jewelle grabbed her phone and quickly punched in Thérèse's number. After several rings, she answered.

"Oui, allô."

"Thérèse, ici Jewelle. *Ça va?*" Jewelle's French was effortless. Thérèse's voice brightened. *"Oui ça va très bien et toi?"*

"Bien, merci," Jewelle said. Switching to a mixture of English and French she continued, "Time to set up the ritual meeting and dinner during MIP. *Est-ce que tu seras libre, le 15 à 13 heures pour une réunion et 20 heures* for dinner?"

"Oui," Thérèse enthused.

"Great." Jewelle relaxed slightly now that some business was done. "Looking forward to catching up face-to-face."

"Enee changes wid Chantal?" inquired Thérèse.

"Non, toujours pareil."

"Oh là là!" Thérèse chuckled.

"I'll fill you in when we meet," Jewelle murmured. "Enjoy the rest of your day. *Au revoir. À bientôt.*"

"Au revoir, Jewelle." The static of the overseas call cut into the dial tone. Jewelle always got a kick out of speaking French with Thérèse and particularly liked her *oh là là*s when something surprised or outraged her. All those years of French immersion were not wasted after all.

Jewelle made many more quick calls. By nine, people were filtering through the halls, and she was about halfway through. She felt good about successfully linking with people, for it wasn't uncommon to play telephone tag for days on end before connecting with a live person. Booking appointments for MIP-TV, or any other television market, could be frustrating, but this morning, her schedule was filling, and she was pleased. She had thirty confirmed meetings with the possibility of ten more walk-ins during the market.

The next item on Jewelle's list was the preview DVDs of the new programs that would be screened by TV3's clients. She rifled through a pile of papers on her desk to find the approved preview list. Grabbing it, she headed out the door and down the hall to the preview video library. Once there, Jewelle pulled select DVDs that would be screened by TV3's clients and prospective clients. Meticulous as always, she checked them off her list, placed them alphabetically in two shipping containers, and cross-checked the list and the DVDs, running her perfectly French-manicured fingernail down the sheet of paper to ensure that all the units were there. Jewelle felt a little jolt when she realized that screening DVDs of two new series, featured at MIP, were missing. She frowned slightly and pursed her lips when she suddenly remembered the dubs were not going to be ready until later that day. Heather, the Sales Coordinator, would deliver them to her after she picked them up from the Dubbing Department.

Heather, a quick-witted, self-effacing Newfoundlander, joined TV3 shortly after Jewelle. She was a breath of fresh air, comfortable in her skin, seemingly hang-up free. She did, however, like to indulge her appetite for candy. She especially loved peppermint knobs, which were a favourite she picked up regularly from the Newfoundland store on Victoria Park near St. Clair. Heather was a buxom beauty, large blue eyes, thick shiny dark brown hair and a peaches and cream complexion. The painter Rueben would have delighted in her. Every chance she got, Chantal made it her business to inform Heather of the latest fad diet she discovered. Heather would counter with news of some delectable dessert she recently sampled and gushed in her Newfoundland-accented English: "Yes, b'ye, it was some good." From time to time, she'd even offer to share a calorie or two with Chantal who adamantly said no thanks. Heather savoured digs levelled at Chantal, a lightweight she could take down easily.

Pleased that all the required items were in place, Jewelle sealed one box, left the other open, and returned to her office where she focused her attention on the next item on the to-do list—sell sheets, the mini-posters used to promote TV programs and movies. She sighed as she examined the sheets stacked in piles in front of her desk. As she stood up to walk over to them, there was a loud knock on her door.

"Jewelle, are you in there?" chirped Chantal. Immediately, Jewelle sensed that Miss Chantal was up to something. She could read the woman like the top line of an eye chart.

"Good morning to you too, Chantal," replied Jewelle walking over to open the door. Chantal stepped into the office quickly, her inquisitive eyes darting about like Mrs. Kravitz's, the nosy neighbour who tormented Samantha and Darren on the old sitcom *Bewitched*.

"You must have camped out here last night," Chantal commented matter-of-factly.

"In fact, I just rolled up and tucked away my sleeping bag," said Jewelle, wishing hard that Chantal could be beamed up to some other galaxy populated solely by A-type personalities like herself.

"There's really no need for sarcasm this early in the morning, dear," poked Chantal.

"Really? I am not your dear," Jewelle said, eyeing Chantal as she tried to figure out the reason for this visit.

"I know when I am not wanted," said Chantal, flicking her long, blonde-for-this-week locks over her shoulder as she bolted toward the exit. Just before closing the door behind her, she poked her head through the opening, "By the way, there's something I've been meaning to ask you."

"What?" bristled Jewelle.

"Isn't it great news about the new sales and distribution company that is being created," oozed Chantal. Before Jewelle had a chance to answer, Chantal revealed what she *really* wanted to know. "Are you planning to apply for the VP of Sales and Distribution job?" asked Chantal, barely concealing a smug grin.

"Perhaps," Jewelle replied coolly, making her way over to the door where she now stood a foot away from Chantal. "You have your answer and I have work to do," said Jewelle curtly moving closer to shut the door. Immediately, there was another knock. Jewelle jerked the door open and glared at Chantal's smiling face. "Did you forget something?" she asked.

"As a matter of fact, I did!" Chantal smirked. "Forgot to mention that I have already submitted my application. May the best woman win!" the little backstabber purred, savouring Jewelle's agitation.

"You're just full of news this morning!" said Jewelle in a flat steady tone. "Run along and spread your joy elsewhere," she cracked, slamming the door behind Chantal. Chantal knew full well that Jewelle had applied for the VP of Sales and Distribution position. Confidentiality was a foreign word at TV3, its meaning, an impenetrable mystery. If you wanted something known to all and sundry, all you had to do was *confide* in one of the HR counselors. Otherwise, you kept it to yourself.

Chantal's petty provocation annoyed Jewelle more than usual. She was feeling vulnerable now that Barbara was no longer around to look out for her. Barbara, who hired Jewelle, later became a friend and mentor who encouraged her to upgrade her skills, particularly in the areas of marketing and TV production. Barbara had approved all her requests for professional development seminars and training courses. Despite her success at the network, Jewelle worried that her application might not be successful with Chantal also vying for the position, buttressed by her dubious connections in the executive offices. The little bounder's sudden announcement shook her more than she cared to acknowledge. Jewelle felt she was better qualified for the position based on her experience and enviable sales record over the past five years. However, she wasn't so naive as to believe that skills, ability, and education were the determining factors. The thought vexed her. She would never stand for Chantal playing boss with her. If it came to that, she would have to weigh her options.

In the frantic weeks before MIP-TV, Jewelle did her best to get the shipment out on time and prepare for the market. But, increasingly, she had become aware that Chantal was deliberately waging a cold war against her. It began with the disappearance of requisition forms for broadcast masters. This odd kerfuffle resulted in the late delivery of master tapes to broadcast clients. A few missed their air dates and went ballistic. When the second set of broadcast masters disappeared, Jewelle charged into Chantal's office, kicking the door shut behind her and knocking a small plant from its stand. Soil scattered everywhere. Jewelle stopped right in front of Chantal's desk, legs apart, glaring down at her.

"Where are my broadcast masters?" Jewelle demanded.

"You knocked over my plant," sputtered Chantal.

"I don't give a damn about your plant. Dubs, now!" demanded Jewelle.

"How dare you accuse me of stealing! It's not my worry if you can't do your job," hissed Chantal. Jewelle ignored the dig.

"The technician in Operations told me that you picked up my dubs yesterday. Are they lying?" Before Chantal had a chance to answer, her phone rang. She grabbed it.

"Chantel Mercier. Please hold." Chantal put the caller on hold.

"Jewelle, this is an important call. Get out. Good luck finding your dubs."

"I'm not leaving until you give me what belongs to me," insisted Jewelle.

"The Chairman of the Board is on the line. Should I fill him in on your accusation?" Jewelle glared at Chantal for a few seconds before retreating to her office. Shortly after this incident, Jewelle was summoned to the HR Department where she met with Marg Hunter, the head of the sales department, and an HR counselor.

"Jewelle, based on your reviews, you've been an exceptional employee to date, but lately you have been making careless and costly mistakes. Is there something going on that we should know about?" asked the HR counselor.

Jewelle took a deep breath. She was tempted to spit out her suspicions about Chantal but refrained from doing so because it could be viewed as professional jealousy without tangible proof. "I'm really sorry. It's just that I've been working long hours and am exhausted," said Jewelle. The HR Counsellor and Marg Hunter were sympathetic but told Jewelle that there had been one too many mistakes and they were now compelled to place a warning in her personnel file. Jewelle was devastated, but not defeated. It was now time, she decided on the spot, to put her own plan in action and take the offensive. She also indulged in fantasies of giving Chantal a few body slams like the ones female wrestlers enacted.

Jewelle began by keeping copies of all requisition forms in a locked drawer. She also instructed the dubbing department that all her orders were to be delivered directly to her or Heather. Chantal soon caught on. More things started to disappear in increasingly creative manoeuvres—Jewelle's PowerPoint presentation for a group of visiting television buyers, her galley proofs for the program catalogue, and PAL masters she had picked up from the tape library. Jewelle complained: "Okay Barbara, since you agree that these disappearances are not random, what would you suggest I do?"

"Jewelle, I wish I had an easy answer for you," Barbara said with a sigh, shifting in her chair. "You need proof that Chantal is the person behind all this. Wish I could be of more help. From their first meeting, Jewelle and Barbara connected. The first thing Jewelle noticed was her exceptional style, wholly original. She could make anything look fabulous on her less than perfect body. She mixed and matched one-of-a-kind whimsical pieces that only Barbara could pull off: a short kimono with pajama linen pants, plaid skirts with floral blouses that would come off as a miss rather than a hit if worn by anyone else.

Jewelle later learned that Barbara had moved to Barbados after she married James, a Bajan businessman. James had found it difficult to find work as an engineer in Canada, so he returned home where he and his skills were appreciated. When their marriage ended, Barbara returned to Toronto. She understood the nuances of West Indian culture, which meant she got Jewelle and her ancestry in a way that her other colleagues never could.

Since Barbara couldn't help, Jewelle decided that another confrontation was in order. She was about to knock on Chantal's door, but it was wide open, a symbol of her "transparency." Miss C. was seated in front of her terminal staring blankly at the screen. Jewelle marched right in and closed the door quietly behind her. She studied Chantal's reaction as she strode over to her desk and looked down at her.

"What do you want?" snapped Chantal.

"What do you think I want?" Jewelle shot back, the Mandinka in her threatening to surface.

"Haven't you ever been told it's rude to answer a question with another question," said Chantal through clenched teeth.

"I certainly didn't come here for a lesson in manners," Jewelle said, trying to control her outrage. "What I want is for you to stop interfering with my work. Your schemes are child's play compared to what Black folk have had to overcome for centuries. I'm a living testimony to overcoming and surviving. Think about that!" hissed Jewelle before she turned around, walked over to the door, threw it open and stepped out into the corridor.

Outside the office, Jewelle paused and turned slowly to eyeball a speechless red-faced Chantal and said calmly, "May the best woman win!"

On the walk back to her office, Jewelle's emotions were a mixture of dread at what she'd done and delight for having done it. She'd put Chantal on notice and felt strengthened by her defiance.

Within minutes of settling back into her chair, Jewelle's phone rang. She allowed it to continue a few more times before picking up.

"Hello, Jewelle Joseph," she answered with a smile in her voice.

"Jewelle, it's your mother. Do you have a few minutes?" asked Adele Joseph breathlessly.

"Mother is everything okay?" asked Jewelle, nervously.

"Well, no one has died, and no one is sick if that's what you mean.

But ..." said Adele, allowing her voice to trail off.

"But what?" insisted Jewelle.

"Ryan is going to ask Keisha to marry him," Adele blurted out, gasping for air.

"This is great news!" gushed Jewelle. "I've always liked Keisha. Besides, they've been dating long enough!" There was dead silence on the other end of the line, except for Adele's heavy breathing. "Mother, are you still there?" asked Jewelle.

"Of course, I'm still here," said Adele sharply. "I guess I made a mistake calling my daughter about an important matter."

"Mother, what do you want me to say! Ryan loves Keisha and that's good enough for me. Sorry you don't feel the same way!" said Jewelle forcefully. She hardly ever challenged Adele.

"Well Keisha may be a nice girl for some other man but not my Ryan. She's far too bossy and demanding," said Adele fighting hard to maintain a level tone.

"What you mean, Mother, is that she's got a mind of her own and o-pin-i-ons," countered Jewelle.

"Miss Jewelle, yu really think dat I want Ryan fi marry some birdbrain who can't talk for herself? Mek I tell you something, I have been on dis planet much longa than you. I know ah ting or two. One of dem is dat Keisha is not right for my Ryan."

"Well, your Ryan is a thirty-two-year-old man."

"You don't need to tell me his age. I gave birth to him!"

"Mother. Honestly, I'm glad Ryan is standing his ground and defending his queen. You need to accept *his* choice," said Jewelle evenly. She waited for Adele's comeback.

"So, you now think you are old enough to tell me what I *need* to do?" thundered Adele. "Well, I know what I don't need from you and that is disrespect."

"Mother, no disrespect given or intended. I just do not share your opinion about Keisha. That's all," said Jewelle coolly, pleased that she had spoken her mind. Score one for Jewelle. The silence sagged between them under the weight of their disagreement.

Adele broke the silence. "Anyway, when are you coming home for a visit?" she asked softly.

"In a couple of weeks, right after I get back from France," answered Jewelle. Hoping to change Adele's mood, she asked, "What would you like me to bring for you?"

"Surprise me. On second thought, I wouldn't mind another Guerlain perfume. You decide which one," said Adele, relaxing.

"Consider it done! Mother, there's someone at my door," she whispered into the mouthpiece. "I have to go. Love you!" She hung up the phone.

"Come in, Heather," said Jewelle. She had been expecting her co-worker, who walked in carrying a handful of DVDs.

"Here are the dubs of the new shows you ordered—*World of Wonder* and *Peter's Playroom*. This set is for your hand luggage and the other's for the shipment. Should I go ahead and box them?"

"Sure," Jewelle said, then paused a moment, considering. "Why don't I come with you so that we can do a final check?"

"Okay," said Heather.

They walked in collegial silence down the empty corridor to the preview library. A pall had been cast over TV3 since the announcement of upcoming layoffs. Staff had grown über-protective and fearful. Everyone seemed intent on keeping their head down to avoid notice. Once in the tape library, the two women double-checked the preview DVDs in the boxes. As they were about to seal the second box, Chantal breezed in.

"Hi, Jewelle, hi Heather," Chantal clucked. "Just realized that I haven't pulled the stationery kit together, and I have to head down to Stores to get some missing items. Please leave one box open. I'll seal it after I put the stationery kit in." Jewelle was suspicious.

"Against my better judgment, I'm going to leave the box open. Heather will be my witness should anything go missing!" said Jewelle in a firm voice.

"You really are becoming quite paranoid, Jewelle. You should get some help with that!" Chantal hurled back. Sensing that Chantal was trying to pull her into an argument, Jewelle walked away. She wasn't about to allow this to lead to another warning in her personnel file.

Jewelle was concerned that her application for the position of VP of Sales and Distribution might be unsuccessful with Chantal, who was intimately connected to the powers that be, as competition. Chantal's sudden announcement rattled Jewelle more than she liked acknowledging. She felt she was better qualified for the position, based on her experience and enviable sales record over the past five years. But she also knew, and all too well, that experience and ability weren't always enough. Jewelle would never stand for Chantal lording it over her.

The intercom rang, breaking Jewelle's train of thought. It was Marg on the phone, asking for a meeting in her office at five thirty. Jewelle wondered what Marg wanted to see her about. She checked the time: four forty-five. Jewelle tried to work but could not focus. She grew anxious. Every five minutes, she checked her watch. Time slowed to a crawl; she wanted the meeting over and done with. At five twenty-five she headed down the hall to Marg's office. Jewelle knocked gently on the door.

"Come in, Jewelle," said Marg. She motioned for Jewelle to sit in the chair in front of her desk. Marg looked uneasy.

"Well, Jewelle, there is no easy way for me to say this, so I'll be direct. It has been decided that Chantal will take over Germany," Marg said rapidly. It took Jewelle a few moments to process what she just heard, or what she thought she heard.

"Marg, did you just say that I'm losing Germany?"

"Yes, Jewelle," replied Marg wearily.

"I've worked very hard to build that territory. Why am I losing it?"

"Jewelle, we all recognize your contribution. But Chantal's connections in Germany have the potential to take sales there to the next level."

"This is not fair!" Jewelle shouted angrily.

"Jewelle, it's not a question of what's fair. It's a question of what's best for the company's bottom line. TV3 is in the red and we are desperately trying to stop the hemorrhaging," said Marg, sounding crushed under the weight of her responsibilities.

"What about my contributions to the bottom line over the last two years. What about that?" Jewelle asked heatedly and stormed out of Marg's office.

Back in her office Jewelle felt betrayed and hurt. She had been sacrificed for how many pieces of silver. She started to cry, and through her tears, she tried to force herself to concentrate on what she still could do, but she found herself unable to focus on anything but how much she hated Chantal and the system that supported people like her.

The phone rang and Jewelle let it go to voicemail. It was well past six o'clock. She turned to look out the window and allowed her thoughts to meander through the ribbons of pink clouds stretched out across the sky. Nature's beauty teased a smile from her and reminded her that tomorrow she'd be back on the French Riviera.

On her way home, she stopped at the nail salon for a mani-pedi. It was important to look the part of the successful international sales executive even if she didn't feel like one currently. Jewelle tried to shake off the events of the day. While waiting for her nails to dry, she made a mental note to call Anthony before she finished packing her suitcase and trunk.

Shortly after she returned home, Jewelle continued her beauty regimen. Before applying her clay mask, she put on a Nina Simone CD and hummed along to "I've Put a Spell on

You." There was a gentle rapping on her front door, rat-a-tat-tat, rat-a-tat-tat. She knew it was Anthony. It was their special knock so that she'd not be frightened if he used the key to let himself in. She opened the door momentarily forgetting about the mask on her face. Anthony let out a scream pretending to be terrified.

"Where's my woman?" he gasped. "Have aliens abducted her?" Stepping into the apartment, he cast about frantically in search of Jewelle before erupting into laughter.

"Very funny, Anthony Brown. That performance is Oscar worthy," she laughed. Anthony walked over to her and pulled her towards him and wrapped her tightly in an embrace. She momentarily yielded to his muscular body and freshly shaven scent before noticing that there was something in his jacket pocket poking her.

"What's in your pocket?" she asked. Anthony reached into his pocket and pulled out a small box of Godiva chocolates and handed it to her. He looked at her intensely with his warm brown eyes. She couldn't help but take in his handsome face. Any woman would be happy to have him. "Thanks. That's very sweet of you," Jewelle said half-heartedly while lightly running her hand along his face.

"Anything wrong? Didn't you get my message that I'd be dropping by?"

Jewelle took a step away from him. "I didn't listen to the last couple of messages before I left the office. More problems." And she went on to explain. By the time she was done, any thoughts of a romantic evening with his woman slowly faded from Anthony's mind like a dying flower.

Two

Airport Shuffle

Jewelle hurriedly took one last look around her apartment. George would be there shortly to pick her up as he had for the past three years. When the doorbell rang, she told him through the intercom that she'd be right down. She stopped to change the message on her voicemail: "Gone to Cannes. Yes, it's that time of the year again. Back in eight days. Talk then."

Five minutes later, the black town car lurched through the heavy afternoon traffic on the 401. No matter the time of day, the highway was packed with cars and trucks racing from one end of the city to the other. Jewelle allowed herself to get comfortable in the soft leather seat, blocking out the past weeks of drama. Chantal had been insufferable, needling Jewelle with her sarcastic remarks at every opportunity. Jewelle gave as good as she got but was growing weary of having to engage in this interminable battle.

"It's all under control, so relax. All that hard work is bound to pay off," she told herself as she stared out the SUV at a man negotiating a lane change while engaged in a hand-waving conversation with his driving companion.

"It's now two o'clock and we'll be about twenty more minutes to the airport in this traffic, Jewelle," pronounced the chauffeur.

"No rush, George," she replied. "My flight isn't until six. We've got plenty of time." George Mason, a pleasant middle-aged man with a full head of thick white hair, had come highly recommended by a friend who said his attentive and personal limo service provided a relaxing atmosphere for stressed out executives.

"Are you off to France again?" George inquired in his friendly manner, glancing at her admiringly through the rear-view mirror.

"Yes," she answered, hoping her short reply signaled that she did not wish to chat. Normally, she was happy to regale him with tawdry tales of the goings-on in the television industry, but with all the extra hours she had put in over the last two weeks, and the mayhem that awaited her, these few minutes were undoubtedly going to be the last peaceful ones she would know until MIP-TV was over. "Hope, I'll be able to visit there someday," George commented. He steered the car off the main highway and onto the road leading into the airport.

Lapsing into silence, George weaved through the cars, buses and other limos approaching the terminal building.

"Here we are, Ms. Joseph," he said formally, hoisting her luggage from the trunk. "Have a great trip! What time would you like me to pick you up when you return?" he asked as he set Jewelle's vintage Goyard trunk and suit bag on the curb. The trunk was not a very practical piece of luggage, but Jewelle loved it, the craftsmanship, its history, and its style. Her mother, Adele, had inherited a few pieces of Goyard from a friend who had been a seamstress for a German socialite. Adele kept one piece for herself and passed on the others to her daughters.

"I won't need your services this time around. My boyfriend is going to pick me up."

"But you'll need a trolley, Miss Joseph. Wait here, I'll get one for you," said George.

"Thank you, George," said Jewelle, smiling at him. He certainly is a man with old-world manners, she thought. She liked this about him. George returned with the trolley, placed the trunk on it and lay the suit bag on top. As he turned to go, Jewelle pressed a tip into his hand then quickly entered the terminal where organized chaos threatened any kind of order—trolleys overflowing with luggage, parents trying to calm crying kids, a convoy of wheelchairs, a family chasing a dog that was enjoying his freedom and people in search of the correct airline counter. Jewelle's fantasy of simply gliding elegantly through the airport straight to the ticket counter and then into the plane abruptly ended when she was assailed by an avalanche of suitcases. She let out a squeal. The owner of the suitcases released his trolley, rushing to her side.

"So, sorry Miss ..." the gentleman said, pausing to get a name. As Jewelle didn't offer one, he asked, "Are you alright?"

"Barely! Had they landed on my feet, I certainly wouldn't be boarding my flight," she replied, still a little shaken.

"I'm glad you weren't hurt," said the gentleman sincerely.

"That makes two of us!" retorted Jewelle before continuing her walk towards the Air France check-in counters to join the long economy class line.

She felt guilty that she hadn't been more gracious. But in that moment a vision of her weeks of hard work being wiped out had flashed before her eyes. The stranger quickly gathered up and returned the fallen suitcases to his trolley, then quickly made his way to the Air France counter. He spotted her in the line and wheeled his trolley over to where she was standing. Jewelle caught sight of him out of the corner of her eye but pretended she didn't see him, keeping her head straight.

"Hi," said the stranger. "I didn't have a chance to introduce myself back there, I'm Charles Dalton," he said, extending his right hand.

"Hello Charles Dalton," said Jewelle coolly as she shook his hand. "I'm Jewelle Joseph. I've got to get to the counter before the line gets any longer," she said as she pushed her trolly ahead. "I'm fine. Don't worry about it."

Charles had now turned his trolly around and was trailing behind Jewelle.

"Glad to see that you're fine. Perhaps, I'll see you after you're checked in."

Jewelle didn't comment. She just kept moving.

Charles, a fit-looking middle-aged man of average height, pushed hard on his trolley that he was having difficulty keeping straight. But he managed to catch up to Jewelle.

"Just one more thing Ms. Joseph, I'd like to give you one of my cards," said Charles. He reached into his pocket and pulled out a stack of cards. He peeled one off and handed it to her. Jewelle paused to read the information on the card aloud, "My Way Productions, Charles Dalton, President." She glanced at Charles who had a satisfied smile on his face. She was now certain that she would see more of him, realizing that he was heading to Cannes for MIP. "Thanks for the card. I really have to go now!" said Jewelle, growing exasperated.

"Okay. Good luck checking in!" said Charles cheerfully. He was obviously thinking of asking her for a card, but it was a gamble he didn't want to take.

When Jewelle arrived at the Air France counter, there was indeed a long queue. As the line inched along slowly, Jewelle spotted a few industry colleagues who were on the same flight. She immediately recognized the cadences of sales-speak, and her guard went up. A documentary producer she knew quite well was chatting loudly to a colleague as he pushed the trolley ahead. Deal a minute Dan is making waves, thought Jewelle. He'd better be careful, or a tsunami might just take him out.

"Yeah, we've got a dinner meeting with the Discovery UK buyer on Saturday, followed by drinks at the Majestic bar with a potential co-production partner. If we get a deal, we'll send them chocolates or cigars after the market." Dan paused to let his companion get a few words in but quickly jumped back in.

"Stan, I didn't tell my girlfriend that I'm going to Cannes. So, if you see her after the market, I wasn't there. You know what I mean?" Stan nodded, acknowledging that Dan's secret was safe with him. Privately, Jewelle thought if she knew Dan's girlfriend, she'd personally fill her in on his whereabouts and arouse suspicions about his after-hours plans in Cannes.

As the caterpillar of travelers inched a few feet closer to the head of the line, an elegantly dressed woman and her husband swept past to the business class counter, followed by Gordon Douglas, a distributor who used to represent TV3's catalogue in Eastern Europe. Gordon enjoyed a reputation as a self-proclaimed A-Lister who spared no expenses when wining and dining his clients. Jewelle recalled some of the dinners he hosted at the Palme d'Or. The champagne flowed and the caviar was abundant. Rumour had it that Gordon's company was going through a hard time, yet here he was traveling business class. Perhaps, he had a good quarter, Jewelle thought, or maybe some poor producers simply weren't getting their royalties. The latter is probably the case, she thought. Finally, it was Jewelle's turn.

"Bonsoir, Madame" the agent uttered wearily.

Jewelle handed him her ticket and passport. "Bonsoir monsieur," she replied, already switching into "Cannes mode."

"Just the one bag tonight, Madame?" the agent asked.

"Yes."

"And you are continuing to Nice?"

"Yes. Please check the bag straight through to Nice."

"Will you be staying in Nice?"

"No, I'm on my way to Cannes."

"*Oh la, la!* You are fortoonate," he smiled broadly as he tapped the keyboard. "Uh, Madame Joseph, there has been a small change. Azz dere have been a change in the airplane, your seat is no longer available. I will ave to poot you at a window. Iz dise a problem?"

33

"Monsieur, I really would prefer an aisle seat but ..." she trailed off, when she noticed that Charles Dalton was now standing at the back of the Air France line. "I am sorry Madame, we have none left, but I will give you a seat in Espace Affaires on your return flight to Toronto. *Ça va?*" he asked, smiling. Jewelle nodded as he struck a key to spit out her baggage tag and boarding passes.

As she collected her documents and carry-on bag, Jewelle noticed an African family scrambling to re-assign some of their belongings to meet the weight restriction. The woman had become quite agitated as she explained to the agent, in rapid-fire French, they couldn't leave anything behind as many items were gifts for family members they had not seen for years.

Jewelle wished there was something she could do to help. This was a scene she had witnessed many times when her family made the annual pilgrimage to Jamaica. Occasionally, they were asked to check in a bag for a fellow passenger, and her mother Adele had obliged against her father Radcliffe's wishes. He would chide her during the flight that someday she'd get into more trouble than it was worth. Adele let his words fall on deaf ears.

Jewelle slipped away, leaving the verbal battle in full swing and sitting down for a few minutes in the departure lounge, the full impact of the last few weeks began to hit her hard. Jewelle was tired and stressed out. The long hours phoning and arranging meetings, pulling promotional materials together and coaching Heather to ensure that she could manage things had really taken it out of her. She was grateful for Heather's diligence in putting together a binder containing checklists, waybills and content lists of each box shipped to Cannes a week ago. Without the help, Jewelle would have been lost.

While Jewelle was out for lunch, the day before her departure for Cannes, Heather caught Chantal in her office.

"What are you doing in here?" demanded Heather.

"I'm just checking to see if you scheduled the dinner meeting for our Japanese clients," Chantal answered breezily.

"If you want that information, I'm the person you need to speak to! I'd suggest you get out of this office now," Heather snapped.

"And if I don't?" taunted Chantal.

"Chantal, you wouldn't want to find out, now would you?" answered Heather menacingly.

Chantal sensed danger and made a speedy exit from the office. As soon as Jewelle returned from lunch, Heather filled her in on the incident. Jewelle was upset because she knew Chantal was up to no good. Chantal had her own clients to manage, so Jewelle's clients shouldn't be of any concern to her unless she had ulterior motives.

The week before the Cannes departure, Chantal kept pestering Jewelle for a copy of her schedule. Finally, she agreed to sit down with her to compare and review their itineraries. During their meeting, Chantal made no comment except to remind Jewelle that she was responsible for arranging the dinner for their NHK clients. It was just like Chantal to zero in on the one thing that Jewelle had not yet done. She had not forgotten about the dinner but was holding off until Johann Eriksson suggested a date and time for their ritual dinner, and his fax didn't come through until the day she left for Cannes.

Jewelle first encountered Johann three years ago at the Martinez Hotel in Cannes. It didn't seem that long ago. She was standing alone observing some of the "beautiful people" milling about at the opening night party. Johann spotted her as he was coming down the winding staircase which led to the lobby. He walked over and gently tapped her on her shoulder. She spun around and found herself gazing into a pair of striking green eyes set in a handsome, deeply tanned face under thick salt and pepper hair, stylishly cut to make the statement "I'm still in the game."

Feeling his eyes studying her, she said, "Don't you know it's rude to stare?"

"I think, I should be the one asking that one," he stated jokingly.

She tried to look away but felt a powerful pull towards Johann even though he made her nervous and uncomfortable. Jewelle wished she was still wearing her badge as she would have held it up for him to read her name. She reluctantly told him aware of the instant romances that sprouted each year.

"Jewelle Joseph" he said in a low voice. "That's an unusual name. Jewelle, that is. Maybe not! You're obviously a gem." Johann's smile was broad and mischievous.

Mmmm! Jewelle thought. What's with these men and their tired pick-up lines? Despite her misgivings, she continued chatting with him and found him to be charming and witty. She let her guard down. The awkwardness she felt initially dissolved.

The increasingly friendly chat over, Jewelle walked through the lobby. The self-important were, as usual, on parade—preening, strutting. The famous emperor of birthday suit fame had nothing on them. It was a badge of honour that every second of their day was booked with meetings, many of which would amount to nothing more than talk. Two colleagues walked by, and she overheard the younger one breathlessly rattling off to the other, "So I booked a table for four at the Gray d'Albion Plage for lunch. The BBC buyer and her assistant will meet us there on Tuesday, and the commissioning editor from the Austrian channel can't make it for drinks until Thursday evening at the Majestic Hotel bar." The young man clearly hoped to impress anyone within earshot that he was the major player he imagined himself to be. Jewelle recognized the older of the two, a slippery character known for selling shows that he was not legally authorized to hawk.

"Pierre ... Pierre! Viens ici!" A young mother called after her escaping toddler, who squealed gleefully as she chased after him. Jewelle stepped into his path and caught the little guy who giggled loudly as she scooped him up and delivered him to the arms of his winded mother.

"Merci, Madame. Il est vraiment un petit coquin. Viens mon petit." The mother smiled at Jewelle as she lowered her son to the ground holding his hand firmly.

"Pas du tout Madame. Plus, il est fatigué avant le vol, mieux il dormira," Jewelle replied. The women shared a smile before the mother returned to her seat with her son.

Other people were filling up the lounge as they waited for their flights. Jewelle scanned the room looking for friendly faces and noted the range of passengers: a group of students herded by their teacher, elegant Europeans, Canadian holidaymakers underdressed and sloppy by European standards, and Julie Katz, a friend of Jewelle's who used to work at TV3. Their eyes met, and the two women came together in a warm embrace.

"JJ, how are you? I haven't seen you in months," Julie said, calling her by the nickname used by friends, family and some colleagues, taking her in from head to toe. "Have you lost weight? You look thinner."

"Julie, I have been working like a dog. You know how it is before the markets. I probably burnt off a few pounds."

"You don't have much to spare!" Julie smiled knowingly. "I take it you are off to MIP. Glad I'm not on that treadmill anymore."

"What do you mean? The last time we spoke you were still in sales with the CBC," asked a puzzled Jewelle. It made her think fleetingly about her own escape from TV3.

"They were offering voluntary severance packages, so I volunteered to fire myself. The bureaucracy was starting to choke the life out of me. Anyhow, Isaac and I are off to Rome to have a second honeymoon. Fun, fun and more fun!" Julie giggled as she fired a wicked wink at Jewelle. "Let's get together at the end of the month when we're both back and settled. I'd better go find Isaac before he spends all our money in the duty-free store," said Julie. She crushed Jewelle with her mama bear hug and turned to go: "I'll call you at the end of the month to set up a get-together."

"I hope the two of you have a great time," said Jewelle.

Julie spun around quickly, blew Jewelle a kiss and waved goodbye before resuming her search for her husband, Isaac.

As Julie turned away, Jewelle imagined herself with Anthony, enjoying his charm, and wished he was there with her. She had asked him many times over the years to travel with her to the market, but he had always found a reason not to. Thinking about it now, she reviewed how this had been a big disappointment to her, but she consoled herself with the thought that he was good to her in many other ways. And sometimes, she thought, better than good, as the corners of her mouth unconsciously curled into a smile.

On board the flight, passengers settled into their seats. Jewelle watched in amusement as successive passengers searched in vain for space in the overhead bins to stow their carry-ons. So much for the airline's effort to discourage excessive baggage on board, thought Jewelle. Flight attendants nimbly tried to get the passengers and their belongings to the right seats, delicately steering one member of the African family out of seats assigned to another family. A few passengers registered their annoyance as the flight attendant helped to find assigned seats.

As Jewelle settled in the window seat, she quietly prayed that the two other seats beside her would remain empty or occupied by people who weren't heading to Cannes to buy or sell TV shows. She just didn't want to start the market small talk so soon; there would be plenty of time for that in Cannes. Optimistic that she would soon claim the empty seats, Jewelle pulled a few magazines from the pocket in front of her and placed them on the seat beside her when she heard a familiar sounding male voice say, "I think your magazines are on my seat." She looked up to see the owner of the seat with his boarding pass in hand. She gasped when she looked up into the smiling face of Charles Dalton.

"Guess we are going to be neighbours," he said, ignoring her shock at seeing him again. "Don't worry. I'll be careful with my bags. Most of them have been checked in." Still reeling from the feeling of intrusion, Jewelle removed her magazines from the seats to allow Charles sit down. As he sat down, Jewelle muttered under her breath, "This is going to be a long flight!"

"Did you say something," Charles asked.

"No, I was just talking to myself."

"Guess that's alright, as long as it doesn't become a dialogue."

Great! thought Jewelle, now I have a comedian beside me.

After the final announcements, the aircraft pushed back from the terminal and the in-flight safety video droned on. Newspapers rustled throughout the cabin, and quiet conversations started up. The big 747 taxied to the runway, turned, and with the roar of the engines began its *unsticking*, as the French describe take-off, gaining speed and lifting into the evening sky. Jewelle sighed as she watched Toronto the Good slip away.

Three

Market Madness

From her first market in 1995, Jewelle fell in love with the spectacle of the Riviera: the wonderful restaurants, the outrageously expensive shops with their stunning window displays, the men—their daring sense of style and colour, their ease with expressing their appreciation of the female form—the women of a certain age dressed to look like their daughters (in some cases grand-daughters), and rich men holding hands with their latest barely legal plaything teetering precariously on five-inch stiletto heels.

Yes, for Jewelle, the Riviera, particularly Cannes, was pure theatre. It was impossible not to be affected by the beauty and magic of this place, its clear blue skies, the beaches, the royal palms, and the beautiful flowers. Much as she enjoyed Cannes, at the end of the workday she preferred to be in one of the small nearby towns where she could quietly stroll about and unwind after a long day of non-stop pitching and listening to blah blah. There was also less chance of encounters with market participants who invariably greeted her with the question, "So, how's the market going?" She often felt like replying, "Same answer as the last time you asked." Instead, Jewelle smiled and said, "Great, so far. But that could change in a heartbeat," leaving them to ponder what could possibly bring about such a dramatic change. A part of her pleasure, this game of market speak, was leaving them guessing.

"Madame, pleeze open your bags" asked one of the smiling nubile sentinels stationed behind the rectangular tables at all the entrances to the Palais. When Jewelle unzipped her bags, the young woman gingerly looked through each of them, barely shifting any of the contents. Satisfied that there were no concealed weapons of any kind, the search quickly ended with "Merci Madame." Jewelle was then directed to one of the indifferent metal detector wielding security guards who carelessly flashed his wand up and down the length of her body, front and back. No metals detected here. "Merci, Madame."

As was her custom, Jewelle quickly unpacked as soon as she got to her hotel, La Residence Maeva, a nondescript hotel nestled at the top of Rue George Clemenceau. She had grown friendly with the hotel manager as well as the night watchman, Jacques, who never missed an opportunity to engage her in conversation and to pay her a compliment. She neatly placed some clothes in the dresser drawers, hung up her suits, blouses and dresses. She lined up her shoes in a straight row at the bottom of the closet. When she looked around, she sensed that something was missing: the photo of Anthony. She took the small, framed photo from her handbag, smiled warmly at the image that gazed back at her then and placed it on the night table. Gratified that everything was where it needed to be, she washed her face, re-applied her make-up, changed into a fresh kelly green T-shirt, paired with black jeans and black leather running shoes with white rubber soles.

Jewelle walked down from the Suquet to the Croisette, the main street in Cannes bordering the Mediterranean Sea. As she strolled along the Croisette to the Palais to pick up her identification badge, Jewelle could feel herself transitioning to Cannes mode, re-orienting herself to the sounds, smells, peculiarities, and routines of this place. Little had changed since the last market six months earlier—undulating brick-coloured sidewalks striped with cracks, colourful flower beds, the majestic palm trees in the centre island of the street, the weather-beaten chairs looking out at the sparkling azure blue Mediterranean. The only noticeable change was the closure of a few restaurants. All the high-end designer boutiques—Chanel, Paco Rabanne, Lacroix, Dior—were still standing where they've been for a long time.

Leading off the Croisette were narrow streets where motorists regularly cursed each other in their attempts to squeeze through. As Jewelle got closer to the Palais des Festival, she could see the mayhem taking place out front as it did year after year. Everywhere you looked, large transport trucks (clearly not designed for the narrow streets of Cannes) were being unloaded by fit young men from all over Europe, a cacophony of languages as they called out instructions to each other. Their cargo of electronic equipment, exhibition stands, and furniture would soon transform the inside of the Palais into a television market. There would be nobody hawking their wares like the vendors in local fruit and vegetable markets. The hustling would be left to the eye-catching posters, sell sheets in display racks, and the army of fast-talking sales people capable of selling anything, including the flops in their catalogues.

Jewelle looked at her watch and saw that she had only a few minutes to collect her badge before heading off for her first dinner meeting of the market. She quickened her steps to get to the registration hall and was pleased to find that it was almost empty. She'd be processed in no time at all. After Jewelle collected her badge, she walked over to the Palais and wandered up and down the aisles casually observing the designs of the booths, each one featuring an array of promotional fliers of TV programs available for acquisition, and others still in the planning or production stage. Scraps of conversation floated above the din, like smoke rising and swirling in the air. She quietly wondered how she and many of her colleagues managed to license anything given how much content was available.

Competition was fierce. Nevertheless, TV3 and other broadcasters and producers had managed to carve out a niche in an industry overstuffed with great and not so great programs.

It's the first day of MIP-TV. The air is charged with the anticipation of the next multi-million-dollar, multi-territory deal that would set tongues wagging and heads spinning. Jewelle had just arrived at the TV3 exhibition stand and was thankful for this brief period of calm. For soon the main arteries of the Palais des festivals, an enormous concrete pyramid-shaped building, home to the legendary Cannes Film Festival, and many other TV and film events, will be choked with anxious, cigarette-smoking buyers in search of the next big hit; fast-talking sellers seeking the next early retirement making deals; and cash strapped producers ever hopeful their latest production will recover their missed fortunes. All rushing to their first appointment of the day, many already running late. A few of the curious pause to examine a sell sheet or two or a poster of the latest and greatest (or worst) in television and film.

Sometimes Jewelle felt smothered by the clamour of the Palais. By coming in early, she had avoided the crush of the morning crowd at the main entrance and bought herself a little time to bask in the calm before the storm. However, she didn't escape the perfunctory security search by guards who first checked her identification badge before performing the body scan, front and back. The search ended without the discovery of any objects intended for dastardly deeds and a "Merci Madame."

Now free to roam wherever she willed, Jewelle made her way to TV3's stand. She was often asked about her country of origin. When she replied Canada, people often restated the question, "Where are you from originally?" Matter-of-factly, she would again reply, "Canada. I'm first-generation Canadian."

Surely, by now, Jewelle thought, people must have known that Black Canadians really existed and weren't figments of people's imagination. Hadn't they heard of Oscar Peterson or Dan Hill? It struck her too, that nobody ever asked the question of Irena Dumitrescu, the coordinator in the Audience Relations Department, who had a thick Romanian accent. For it didn't seem to matter. The same couldn't be said for her poor parents. It seemed that every time Adele and Radcliffe opened their mouths, their country of origin would be questioned. No one seemed to notice that their English could rival an Oxford don's. Their accent was a wall that most seemed unable and unwilling to scale.

TV3's twenty-by-twenty foot stand was located on the corner of aisle seventeen in "The Bunker," an airless, windowless section of the Palais. It had a black and white colour scheme with royal blue accents and was divided into two meeting areas that were separated by a partition, allowing for some semblance of privacy. There was also a waiting area for early or late arrivals. Each meeting area was furnished with a multi-standard playback machine atop a cabinet that houses the screening DVDs, a small round white table with a black ashtray on top, encircled by four black molded plastic chairs with chrome armrests. Black plastic wastepaper baskets lurked in each corner, and a chrome coat rack stood guard at the far-right corner of the outer meeting area. The black backdrop, brightened by several colourful posters, featured some of TV3's most successful children's programs. At the front of the stand stood the reception desk, enlivened by the vibrant floral arrangement set in a royal blue vase at one corner and in the other, a uniform row of business card holders displaying the cards of TV3's three representatives: Jewelle Joseph, Chantal Mercier and their boss Marg Hunter. Ten plexiglass racks, displaying sell sheets and mini-posters hawking different programs, were affixed to the front of the reception desk and others were arranged in a vertical column on the edge of each wall of the meeting areas. Behind the reception desk to the immediate left, a four-shelved display case housed various children's merchandise—plush toys, notebooks, pencils, schoolbags, and dolls.

To still first day jitters, Jewelle busied herself arranging and rearranging the sell sheets and double-checking the screening DVDs. As she went through the alphabetically ordered discs, she noted two were missing, the two new programs being high-lighted at the market. She was certain that she had included them in the shipment and made a mental note to check with Chantal as soon as she arrived. For both their sakes, she hoped that Chantal wasn't behind the missing DVDs. Shaking off her concern, Jewelle stepped into the aisle to get a better look at the stand. Overall, she was pleased with the look, but made a few adjustments to the front desk. Pleased that everything was 100%, she walked over to the corner meeting area, placed her appointment schedule on the table before returning to the front desk where she took the MIP-TV directory from her bag, wrote her name on it and placed it under the front desk. There would be some wandering soul who would stop to borrow the directory to locate the number of the stand for their next appointment.

Jewelle returned to the meeting area where she reviewed her schedule and made a few notes. A smile brightened her face when she noticed that she would be meeting with Johann Eriksson at ten o'clock the following day. Their meeting and dinner were always one of the highlights of the market.

When they first met at the Martinez Hotel, she found out that Johann was a buyer with a Stockholm-based station. Prior to joining it, he had toughed it out as an independent producer of drama programs. They talked easily, sharing information about their family backgrounds, interests, and dreams. Their conversation had ended with him asking for her stand number. She gave it to him. He was most definitely her type—tall, slim, bordering on rangy with some flair in his dress and manner.

The following day, Johann turned up at the TV3 stand to schedule a formal meeting for later. When they met, Jewelle asked Johann about his station's schedule and his immediate programming needs. When he said he was looking for documentaries and children's programs, she was thrilled as TV3 had plenty of both to offer.

As Jewelle walked Johann through TV3's catalogue, giving him a synopsis of the titles that were suitable and available for Sweden, he stared at her, and she returned his gaze. Sparks flew. But she put up her guard. She asked if he wanted to screen a few programs. He said yes, as it would allow him to be in her company a while longer. She ignored the comment, popped a disk into the player, handed him the headset and sat quietly trying not to look at him. Johann screened segments of many titles and asked that she send him previews of all of them. At the end of the meeting, she thanked him and extended her hand to shake his. Johann looked at her quizzically, pulled her close to him and gave her a kiss on each cheek. Jewelle reeled. As he was about to walk off the stand, he turned and asked her to have dinner on the last evening of the market. She accepted. Since then, they met at each market to discuss business and share a meal.

Jewelle had made it clear that there could be nothing more than a friendship as she was in a committed relationship. Johann listened but didn't hear. He persevered.

High heels clicked into the stand area, jolting her from her reverie. Jewelle looked up. It was Chantal. There was an awkward silence before either of them spoke.

"Hi, Jewelle. What time did you get here?" asked Miss C. in a disinterested tone. "I thought for sure, I'd be the first one in." Before Jewelle could reply, Chantal turned and walked over to the front desk to check the master schedule where all the confirmed appointments were listed. As she turned away, Jewelle took a deep breath before she spoke.

"Chantal, when I checked the DVDs this morning, I noticed that copies of the two new shows, *Peter's Playroom* and *World of Wonder* are missing. Do you have them?"

Without a moment's hesitation, Chantal shouted, "Jewelle, are you telling me that you left the new shows behind?"

Jewelle replied in a soft, measured, and icy tone, "Chantal, I remember placing them in the box myself. Heather was with me when I did so. You were the last person to have contact with the box before it was sealed."

"What are you accusing me of, Jewelle? Don't try to blame your incompetence on me."

"Incompetence!" Jewelle exclaimed. Wild with fury, she wanted to grasp Chantal by her hair and give her what Jamaicans call a good lick that would rattle her teeth. But she held herself in check.

"Don't start with me today, Chantal! I simply asked if you have the DVDs. A simple yes, or a no, will do!" Jewelle was trying her best to keep her temper in check but thought, If this tired woman pushes me today, I may just have to unleash Nanny on her. Nanny was Jamaica's ancient Maroon warrior queen. She destroyed battalions of British soldiers.

As they were facing off for the next round, Marg Hunter, TV3's Marketing Director, arrived at the stand pulling a fabric covered shopping cart with boxes of wine in one hand and stuffed Monoprix shopping bags in the other. The bags contained peanuts, and various cheeses and crackers that would be greedily consumed, particularly the wine, during TV3's reception later that afternoon. Some of the goodies would go to freeloaders like the infamous Canadian gate crasher "Payless," whose radar zeroed him in on every industry event where he could load up on free drinks and hors d'oeuvres.

"Good morning, ladies. You're both in early. Did you come through the main entrance?" asked Marg.

Chantal quickly replied. "I thought it was important to get here early to make sure that everything is in place. We are all set. Let me give you a hand with those bags."

"Thanks Chantal."

Chantal and Marg walked over to the storage room, located behind the waiting area, opened the door, and started to put away the groceries in the small fridge hidden there. As they unpacked the bags, they chatted and exchanged a few laughs. Jewelle was irritated that Chantal gave Marg the impression that she was the first person on the stand. Not only wasn't she the first one in, but she also hadn't even troubled herself to help with the set-up. Where was Chantal yesterday when she was unpacking all the boxes only to discover that three of them hadn't been delivered, resulting in her having to make the trek to the basement to seek the assistance of one of the shipping company's representatives? When she arrived at the Martini Technotrans' office, two young men were engaged in an animated conversation, hands flying in every direction. Jewelle stood patiently waiting for them to acknowledge her. As this wasn't about to happen any time soon, she spoke up.

"Messieurs, je m'excuse de vous déranger. Est-ce que vous pouvez m'aider?"

The elder of the two men looked directly at her, clearly annoyed at having been disturbed. How dare she interrupt their conversation. Couldn't she see that they were busy attending to important things?

"Oui, qu'est-ce que vous voulez?" demanded the younger.

Jewelle explained that three boxes had not been delivered to the stand. She presented him with the waybill which he took grudgingly. Without another word he walked off leaving Jewelle standing for a full twenty minutes before returning.

"Mademoiselle, I found dem. I weel deliver dem to your stand soon."

Did he know the meaning of the word *soon*, wondered Jewelle as she headed over to the elevators that would take her back to the level where TV3's stand was located? Ms. Chantal can go on pretending that she is "working,'" thought Jewelle, but we both know the truth and others will in time.

Marg Hunter was a rare sight at these markets—a mature woman with natural silver hair. Tall, elegant, and confident, Marg wore her crown of hair with grace and style. The lines etched on her beautiful face told the story of a life of tragedy and triumph. Marg had not embraced the illusion of eternal youth offered by cosmetic surgery, exercise, and a low carb diet. At heart, she was still a spirited young woman who enjoyed a good laugh as much as she did a few glasses of wine. Marg treated the employees in the sales department like extended family. She could be tough but was always fair. If anyone ever needed a sympathetic ear, Marg could be counted on. Over the years, Jewelle had developed great admiration and respect for this woman who wore her many hats—mother, wife, career woman—well.

The stand now fully staged, Marg took a seat in the waiting area, lit a cigarette and started leafing through the *MIP-TV Daily Magazine* to check out the competition, TV3's ads, and any press on new programs.

As Jewelle was about to resume her latest Chantal altercation, Chantal walked over to the waiting area and sat down purposefully beside Marg. Jewelle heard her tell Marg that screeners of the new shows were missing. Marg's look of surprise switched to displeasure. She asked Chantal to double-check that the missing discs had not been mislabeled. When the search proved pointless, Marg signaled to Jewelle to join her and Chantal in the waiting area.

"Jewelle, I'd like to meet with you and Chantal after your meeting with Ben. He just arrived. He's early. Go walk him in."

Jewelle walked back to the reception to greet Ben Herzog, who was one of her long-standing Israeli clients. They greeted each other with the customary air kiss to each cheek, then she walked him over to the corner meeting area. Jewelle inquired if there were any changes to his network's broadcast schedule and if so, what were they and finally, what new shows, if any, he was seeking at the market. Since he was seeking children's and documentary programs, Jewelle pitched him TV3's two new series, *World of Wonder* and *Peter's Playroom*.

"Now, let me show you the synopsis of our new series," Jewelle said, turning to the marked page in TV3's new catalogue. She placed it in front of Ben Herzog, who quickly read both synopses and asked to screen the programs. Jewelle explained the DVDs had been left behind but that she would send him previews when she got back to the office.

Ben was understanding. "These things happen," he said. Yes, they do, thought Jewelle, but not to me.

She gave him copies of the sell sheets of the new shows and again promised to follow up with previews. Business out of the way, they chatted collegially about the industry and the challenges for broadcasters and producers alike. Jewelle found it difficult to be fully present as she was worried about the meeting with Marg and how the missing DVDs might spoil her application for the VP of Sales and Distribution position. Ben finally got up to go as he had another appointment. Jewelle walked him to the edge of the stand, and they parted with a market kiss.

"Don't forget to drop by at five thirty for a glass of wine," Jewelle reminded Ben as he walked away.

"I'll try but I can't promise anything. You know how it is, meetings often run late." Nearby, Charles Walker, one of Chantal's Australian clients had arrived for his ten thirty appointment. Chantal stepped out from behind the reception desk to greet him.

"Charles. Good to see you," she said as they exchanged three air kisses, the third for good luck.

"When did you get in?" asked Chantal

"Late last night," replied Charles in a richly textured New South Wales brogue.

"Well, you wouldn't know it. You look great. We'll sit over there at that table."

Jewelle thought to herself, Why would a man who exuded so much warmth and character want to spend any more time than necessary in the company of a snake? With her diary in hand, two copies of a license agreement, and a bottle of Badoit sparkling water, Chantal guided Charles over to the meeting area. Within seconds of sitting down, Chantal offered Charles the bottle of water which he gladly accepted. Many market participants seemed to have an unquenchable thirst. They couldn't drink enough water, or wine. As it was too early for wine, water, Badoit avec gaz, would have to do. Chantal gave one copy of the license agreement to Charles for review. Prior to the market, he had licensed twenty-six half hour children's programs from her. He quickly reviewed the agreement and commented that all the terms reflected his offer except for the license fee.

"Charles, I am certain that we had finally agreed to a per episode cost of $1,500 US."

"That's not quite right, Chantal. I offered you a 1K per episode and your counter-offer was $1,500. I subsequently explained that my budget could only accommodate $1,000 per episode but that I was prepared to take twenty-six episodes."

Chantal listened intently with a contrived look of confusion on her face. "Charles, my mistake. With all the faxes going back and forth, I must have missed something."

She then leaned in and gently stroked his hand. Jewelle, looking on at the scenario thought, well, I guess he is going to be tied up later exfoliating a few layers of skin. Chantal crossed her legs at just the right moment exposing her finely toned calves and asked in a syrupy sweet tone, "I know money is tight, but do you think you could manage $1,250.00?"

Charles chuckled before replying. "Chantal, you drive a hard bargain. How about $1,200?"

"I'll take it!" she said cheerily. "I'll write in the new figure, and you can initial it." Chantal quickly made the changes, passed the agreements on to Charles who initialed and countersigned both copies.

"Thanks Charles, *really* appreciate your business. Here's your copy. Will send a fax back to the office this afternoon to request the BSP PAL broadcast masters."

Inside, Chantal was laughing as her "oversight" had played out exactly as she planned it—a higher license fee. But she wasn't through with him yet.

"Charles, we have one new pre-school children's series, *Peter's Playroom*, that I think would work for you. Do you have a few minutes to screen?"

"Yes, I have time," he replied cautiously, wanting to avoid any more misunderstandings between himself and Chantal.

Chantal pulled her chair close to the cabinet and pretended to look for the DVD, knowing full-well that it wasn't there. A look of concern registered on her face as she pushed back her chair and turned to face Charles.

"Charles, the DVD doesn't seem to be there. Jewelle must have left it behind," she said loud enough for Marg to hear.

"Sorry about this. I'll send you a preview when I get back to the office. In the meantime, here's a copy of the sell sheet."

Chantal wrapped up the meeting with Charles, thanking him again for his business and walked him out. She then walked over to Marg and handed her a copy of the signed license agreement.

"Marg, Charles just signed off on the deal. I managed to push up the license fee by $200 US per episode. See, they *always* have more money than they claim."

"Congratulations Chantal. Well done!"

With Ben and Charles off the stand, Marg called the meeting. All three sat in the waiting area.

"Now ladies, please explain to me why the DVDs of our two new shows are missing?"

Jewelle looked at Chantal and Chantal glared back at her. The tension between them was palpable.

"I am certain ..." Jewelle began before being rudely interrupted by Chantal.

"Marg, Jewelle is trying to blame this on me. The fact is *she* was the one who ordered these DVD copies, and *she* was the one who packed them. I had nothing to do with it," Chantal said heatedly.

"How right you are that you had nothing to do with them. The fact is you did precious little to get the shipment out on time," huffed Jewelle. "What Chantal said is true. I put the DVDs in the box myself. They were double-checked by Heather. I have a copy of the checklist that she signed off on in my binder. What Chantal failed to tell you is that she was the last person to put materials in the last box before it was sealed."

Marg sighed wearily.

"Ladies, all I know is the DVDs are missing. We have placed ads in several trades to promote these programs and we have nothing to show. You are both responsible. Jewelle as the more experienced of the two, you should have hand-carried the backup set. What happened?"

Jewelle's frown flipped into a smile that rapidly spread across her face as she remembered that she did indeed have a set of the DVDs. They had been rolled into two large scarves to avoid detection at Customs and were still in the front pocket of her carry on.

"Marg, I could kiss you. Thanks for reminding me. They are back in my room. I had forgotten about them. I'll get them during lunch."

"Well, that takes care of that!" snorted an angry Chantal. Her plan had been foiled.

Throughout the day, there were many more meetings. The same questions asked, and the same answers repeated: When did you get in? How are your kids (to those who had children)? What are you looking for? Although, the answers varied slightly: Yesterday. This morning. The kids are fine. I am looking for lifestyle and documentaries. Not sure what I am looking for, pitch me. By the end of the day, Jewelle was suffering from physical and mental exhaustion but had to bear up for TV3's wine and cheese which attracted some one hundred parched prospective clients and passersby in need of a boost.

Jewelle felt maxed out. Back-to-back meetings, an overpriced lunch swallowed down quickly after rushing back from the hotel with the missing DVDs. Seated at the table in the meeting area, she gathered her notes and daytimer together, locked them in the video cabinet, and tried to find the determination to carry herself back up the winding path of the Suquet to her hotel. Slipping her shoes back on Jewelle grabbed her purse and an armful of industry magazines to take back to her room.

Colleagues and fellow delegates looked equally tired as they exited the Palais. Jewelle's eyes briefly connected to a senior broadcast executive who she felt was free of the milk of human kindness. She turned away quickly to avoid him. All the glamour that is show business gets crammed into this space for a few weeks each year, but this is the part the public never sees. The hawking and horse-trading of second-hand sitcoms, the hyped-up promotion of the next big thing and the sad little souls wandering back and forth with their DVDs and cheaply printed flyers trying to get somebody, anybody, interested in their "masterpiece." Back out in the fresh cool air of the Croisette, Jewelle breathed in the sea air and thanked God that day one, in the Palais, was now a memory.

The moment was disrupted when her eyes landed on the self-assured Senegalese vendors hawking their wares—knock off designer sunglasses, umbrellas, and other trinkets. Their efforts were usually not rewarded much. However, if it rained, their pockets would be fattened with euros from the sales of cheap umbrellas. Jewelle often wondered how these men made their way to Cannes, and how they maintained their dignity in the face of their invisibility and the contempt directed at them. This was also the sad reality for the Romany women who creeped around Cannes discreetly telling fortunes. Their beautiful, tanned faces revealed the hardships of their lives and their determination to overcome. Jewelle was pulled back from this contemplation when she heard someone call her name.

"JJ, honey!"

Jewelle turned, looking amid the sea of people milling around out front of the Palais.

"Over here Jewelle!" A woman waved, her arm protruding from a carefully tailored Chanel jacket.

"Oh, hi Britt. How are you?" Jewelle answered, as they weaved through the crowd to each other.

"Fine darling, fine. Had a monstrous day. I'm heading over to the Majestic with some movers and shakers from Channel 4. Come and have a drink with us. You look absolutely shattered!" Britt gushed, her Gucci sunglasses pushed back as a hairband, perfectly manicured blood red tipped fingers clutching a delicate designer purse and the latest Samsung cellphone.

"That's very sweet of you, Britt, but my dogs are barking. If I don't go put 'em in some cool water, I'm going to be a wreck."

"Oh, you poor dear. Come with me, we'll sit by the pool." Britt took Jewelle by the elbow and steered her across the road and past the luxury boutiques to the steps leading onto the Majestic Hotel's bar terrace. Each step bore a plaque displaying Cannes Film Festival winners from days when glamorous starlets wed minor European royalty. Gliding elegantly between the tables of chattering, chain-smoking distributors, Britt delivered Jewelle to a chair adjacent to the reflecting pool and took a seat opposite.

"Now darling you just slip your tootsies in that water and cool off," Britt instructed, her posh British accent carrying the authority of someone accustomed to having her words obeyed. Jewelle eased out of her shoes and delicately slipped her feet into the pool, hoping not to attract attention. A smile of satisfaction and relief spread across her face.

"Feel better, darling?" Britt asked.

"Yes," Jewelle answered, savouring the moment.

"Now don't you worry yourself by being self-conscious. I'll bet £20 some rather exalted people have fallen in drunk or cavorted in here in a far more shocking way. What are you drinking?" Britt asked as the waiter stopped by their table.

"I'll have a Kir Royale," answered Jewelle decisively.

"Very good. Same for me. Monsieur, *deux* Kirs, s'il vous plaît." Britt ordered then stood and waved her friends over to the table.

Jewelle sat with her feet in the refreshing water sipping the rich cranberry red cocktail of champagne and cassis as she made pleasant small talk with the big wigs from Channel 4. One of them took more than a passing interest in her, but he was not her type. Still the attention and flirting were always fun. She knew of or suspected a few women who used their feminine wiles to secure big sales or promotions, Chantal among them. Hard work and tenacity had been instilled in Jewelle since childhood by her Jamaican parents—values that she lived by.

When the throbbing subsided, Jewelle used a couple of cocktail napkins to dry her weary feet before slipping on her shoes. She bade farewell to Britt and her friends and walked down to the grand sweeping forecourt of the hotel to grab a taxi. An elegantly uniformed footman waved the car over and held the door for her as he gave her an admiring glance. She pressed a couple of euros into his hand and settled into the seat. The unmistakable new car smell hit her as the Mercedes readied itself for take off.

"Où allez-vous Madame?" the driver asked hurriedly.

"À la résidence Maeva, s'il vous plaît," she informed him.

No one drove Mercedes taxis in Canada, especially not the way the French do, aggressively and with unforgiving confidence treating their vehicles, like airplanes speeding down a runway. Both vehicular and pedestrian traffic was heavy going past the Palais and towards the *mairie*, the town hall where the buses deposited and picked up passengers. Amongst the plane trees, in the park, a few weather-beaten old men were still playing *boules*, a scene so quintessentially French. It always gripped her that only men played the game.

The car screeched to a halt. A coach, the local transit Bus Azur, had cut in front of them without signaling. Horns blared as Jewelle lurched forward and slammed against the front seat. Her driver leapt out of the car and began shouting and hurling insults at the bus driver. Unwilling to let his pride be bruised, he climbed down and the two grown men stood inches apart cursing and gesturing while bystanders gathered. Jewelle hunkered down inside the taxi trying to avoid being seen.

After an animated exchange of verbal abuse and threats, the passengers implored the driver to get back behind the wheel. The bus soon moved off, and Jewelle's driver climbed back into his seat.

"*Voilà* Madame. He izz not right and everybody knows it. Le transport public, think they own the road. Incroyable!" he ranted as he threw the car into gear and pulled away, resuming his runaway speed.

Passing the sailboats and luxury yachts in the distance, Jewelle noted the queue of people from the market outside *La Pizza*, an over-hyped pizzeria with equally over-hyped prices. Its enduring popularity remains one of life's unsolved mysteries, especially in a town dripping in expense account dinners and where equally good Italian food can easily be found. Jewelle had been taken there for lunch, on her first trip to the market, and sworn off it ever since. Moreover, in Jewelle's opinion, the over-priced restaurant was more about showing yourself off than fine dining.

Up a narrow street with cars parked on both sides, the taxi had to pick its way carefully to avoid locals who were carrying their baguettes and *pâtisseries* home for dinner. Jewelle's stomach growled at the thought of food. So different from Toronto, she thought. Shuttered windows thrown open to let in the light, palm trees, flowering vines and a riot of bougainvillea climbing over the walls. A television flickered in one apartment as the taxi turned a corner to the hotel. She paid the fare and, before she could blink twice, the taxi had disappeared.

Wearily Jewelle forced one foot in front of the other and got into the tiny *ascenseur* to her room on the third floor. She turned the key and pushed the door open. A fresh clean lemony scent greeted her. The apartment sparkled. The cleaning woman had gotten her "clean on." Jewelle dropped her bag by the front door and walked into the living room where her eyes landed on the vase of colourful, cut flowers sitting in the middle of the coffee table. There was a small white envelope leaning gently against the base of the vase. Jewelle hurriedly walked over to the coffee table, picked up the envelope and pulled out a small card of handmade paper decorated by a red heart. She opened the card slowly and read the handwritten note:

> *Precious Jewelle, dinner tomorrow?*
>
> *Johann Eriksson*

A smile hoisted the corners of her mouth. She re-read the note before placing it beside the vase.

On the second day of the market, Chantal was sitting at the front desk when Johann Eriksson arrived. He was Jewelle's first appointment of the day. Jewelle noted his arrival but decided to wait until Chantal informed her that her first client was there.

"Hello, I am Johann Eriksson. I have a ten o'clock with Jewelle Joseph."

"Hi Johann, we met last market. Chantal Mercier", she said, holding out her badge so Johann could see the spelling of her name.

"How have you been?"

"I am well, Chantal, and I can see that you are too."

"That was a nice little deal you made with Jewelle last year," said Chantal, winking conspiratorially at Johann.

"I'll get Jewelle for you. Have a good market."

"Thank you, Chantal," said Johann.

Jewelle had been quietly taking in the exchange between Johann and Chantal. She wondered what Chantal was up to as she approached and said, "Mr. Sweden is here for his ten o'clock."

Jewelle thanked Chantal before going over to the front desk to walk Johann in.

There was much talk and speculation amongst her colleagues as to what was the exact nature of their relationship, particularly after he licensed a package of twenty hours of programming from her. If that wasn't enough, the deal was concluded at the top of their scale, the maximum paid for acquired programming. It was Jewelle's first sale in Sweden and TV3's largest sale in this territory. She was grateful because now she would surpass her sales targets.

"Hello Johann, it's great to see you. Come on in!"

As he stepped on to the stand, they exchanged a hug and a kiss. With Johann it was not the customary air kiss exchanged by colleagues. He liked to hold her gently by the arm and pull her close to him as he kissed her firmly on both cheeks. This had become their greeting.

Jewelle guided Johann to the inner meeting area. Before he sat down, he noticed Marg sitting in the waiting area, walked over, and greeted her with a handshake. They exchanged a few pleasantries before he excused himself and returned to Jewelle.

Jewelle seated Johann so that his back faced the main aisle. This way she would have his undivided attention as many clients were often distracted by passersby who might wave or simply stop in for a chat.

"So, how have you been JJ?"

"How do you think I have been? Don't I look well?" she asked flirtatiously.

"You look great as you always do. Nice suit. Another Montreal find?"

"How did you know?"

"I remember the things you share with me. Last market you mentioned that you prefer to buy clothes in Montreal as you could find items that were more original than in Toronto."

"Yes, I did say that." She laughed. "Time to talk shop."

"Not so fast, Jewelle. Are we on for dinner tomorrow?" asked Johann warmly.

Jewelle thought about the way he pronounced her name, stretching out each syllable that made it seem like he was addressing royalty. She returned his warm smile.

"Yes, to dinner." A smile played on her lips as she recalled her dinner with Johann during MIP-COM, six months earlier. "I guess you didn't receive my fax confirmation before you left Stockholm."

He arrived in a taxi at seven thirty out front of the Residence Maeva where he got out and met her in the lobby. They greeted each other with their kiss. She was wearing a black silk cheongsam, the straight dresses worn by Chinese women, covered in a pattern of silver and gold swirls. "You look beautiful, Jewelle." She could feel her face grow warm and was thankful that her rich melanin concealed her blush.

"Thank you," she replied quietly.

"I love the dress. The pattern reminds me of Van Gogh's *Starry Nights*, the design a perfect balance that conceals as much as it reveals."

Jewelle ignored his comment and simply told him she had the dress made during her last visit to China.

They walked out the front door to the taxi where they slid into the back seat. Jewelle asked where they would be dining, but Johann wanted to surprise her. When the taxi headed down R. J. Dulfus and turned right at Hotel Belle Plage, onto Boulevard Jean Hibert, Jewelle knew that they were heading to La Napoule. However, she wasn't sure which restaurant they would be dining at.

During the drive out they exchanged pleasantries and talked about the "foolishness" of the industry. They laughed about the gatecrashers who tried in vain to get into the parties hosted by the likes of Warner and HBO. Johann reminded her about one incident where a man, who should have known better, kept shouting "What do you mean, I'm not on the list. What list? I'm with HBO, you are going to be sorry big time that you didn't let me in." Jewelle, like Johann, had no time for the self-importance of many of their colleagues. Many of them had very little, in their estimation, to crow about.

The taxi arrived at the main entrance of the Hotel Ermitage du Riou. Jewelle was delighted as this was one of her favourite restaurants. The waiter greeted them cordially and led them to their reserved table, which gave out on an excellent view of the Riviera and the setting sun. A spell cast over them as they absorbed the magic of the moment and their spectacular surroundings. It was broken by the arrival of the waiter who asked what they would like to start with. Jewelle deferred to Johann. He ordered two Kir Royales, remembering that this was one of her favourite cocktails. The waiter soon returned and carefully placed the champagne glasses in front of them.

"What shall we toast to?" asked Johann eagerly.

"Friendship," replied Jewelle with a wry smile. Noting Johann's disappointment, she added, "We all need a friend to survive in this industry. Not so?"

"True enough. Let's toast to friendship and possibilities," said Johann with a mischievous smile.

The two of them ordered sole meuniere. Jewelle asked that hers be "*bien cuit*" because she did not like to see the sinews and veins in the fish when she cut into it.

They enjoyed their meal and each other's company, unaware that the restaurant had become empty and quiet as they talked late into the evening. Finally, one of the waiters approached their table to let them know it was closing time.

After Johann dropped her off, she quickly changed into her nightie and got into bed. The dinner played over and over in Jewelle's head like a loop tape. She felt a faint stirring of affection for him, more than she cared to admit, and wondered if Anthony would consider this to be cheating. She resolved not to go out with Johann again. If she did, it would have to be strictly business.

She was slightly intoxicated from the Kir and the wine as she drifted off to sleep, wishing that Anthony was with her.

In the morning, Jewelle discovered a message from Thérèse: she broke her ankle and would not be attending the market. She asked that Jewelle give her a call.

"*Oui, allô!*"

"Thérèse, ici Jewelle. So sorry to hear about your accident. How are you feeling?"

"*Beaucoup mieux.*" Switching to English, "I wuz een a lot of pain but I am taking peels zat are helping me. How eez zi market? Did you see dee Swede?"

"The market was great. Yes, I saw the Swede. In fact, we had a lovely dinner together in La Napoule at Ermitage du Riou."

"*Oh là là.* Dis sounds serious. Est-ce qu'il est libre?"

"I think he is. But it doesn't matter. I'm sticking with Anthony."

"*Oh là là. Fais très attention* … I think you both like each other. But remember what I told you about market affairs. Dey don't work. How are things with Anthony and your family?"

Four

Family Matters

It was early Friday afternoon when Jewelle returned from MIP-TV. Pearson International was busy as usual, weary travellers everywhere, seniors precariously perched on slow-moving carts, others in the wheelchair convoy, the sturdier set hurtling down the corridors and on the walking sidewalks. Surprisingly, Jewelle cleared customs without the routine interrogation. Having vaulted over this first hurdle, she anxiously headed to the baggage carousel to await her luggage.

As suitcases slid down the ramp onto the baggage carousel, she silently prayed that her luggage would be amongst the early deliveries. Her prayer was answered. She hoisted her trunk from the conveyor belt to a few curious stares. As she struggled to place the luggage on the cart, a gentleman came over to assist her. She thanked him, headed towards the exit, turned in her immigration card and exited Customs in search of an Aerofleet Limousine as Anthony couldn't pick her up as planned.

Within minutes, a shiny black town car pulled up in front of her and parked. The turbaned Sikh taxi driver jumped out of the car, made his way to the other side, held the door open for Jewelle and placed her luggage in the trunk. Back behind the wheel, the driver quietly asked for her address, signaled left and joined the line of cars heading out of the airport. He must have sensed her fatigue as he made no effort to engage her in conversation except for the usual inquiry, "Did you have a good flight back?"

She muttered, "Yes," and then rested her head on the back of the seat and closed her eyes.

As the limousine inched along, Jewelle looked out the window and wondered where all these people were headed at this time of the afternoon. When the limousine finally pulled up and parked out front of her building, the driver took her luggage out of the trunk and huffed and puffed it into the lobby. Jewelle tipped him handsomely before turning to walk into the lobby of the building where she was warmly greeted by Peter, one member of the team of concierges. It felt good to be back. She stopped to check her mailbox, which was filled with the usual assortment of bills and flyers. She slipped them into the outer pocket of her handbag and walked over to the elevators. Alone on her way to her floor, Jewelle was thankful that she did not have to engage in small talk. She was talked out from back-to-back meetings during the market.

Jewelle exited the elevator on the third floor, turned left and took a short walk to her front door. On entering her suite, she parked her belongings by the front door and quickly walked over to the telephone table where the flashing red message light beckoned. She quickly punched in her password and put the phone on speaker. The voicemail was full. Her Auntie Constance had left several messages asking her to call. There were also messages from Anthony, her sisters Cass and Deeana, her mother, as well as a few of her girlfriends. She called her sisters and her mother to confirm that she'd be heading for Montreal on tomorrow's midnight train. This would give her a chance to start the post market follow-up in the office. Her last call was to Aunt Constance, her mother's older sister, a well-upholstered woman whose opinions matched her heft. After several rings, Constance picked up the phone.

"Hello Auntie," said Jewelle.

"Jewelle Joseph, is yu dat?" asked her aunt in her inimitable Jamaican patois. From Auntie's tone, Jewelle knew she was in for a lecture and hoped it would be one of her shorter ones.

"How yu went away widout even so much as a word to me?"

"Auntie, I am sure I told you I was going to France. You know, I make the same trip every April and October," said Jewelle, struggling to maintain an even and measured tone. Any hint of her exasperation with having to perform this dance for her aunt Constance could erupt into an unpleasant confrontation.

"Yes, Miss Jewelle, me know yu always flying all bout di place. Me keep remindin' yu dat yu not a bird. How yu expect mi to remba when yu a cum an when yu a go?"

Sensing that this could escalate into a battle of words, Jewelle sweetly cooed, "Auntie, if it did slip my mind, I'm really sorry."

"Yu betta be sarry. Anyhow, ah glad yu reach back safe and sound. Yu nuh see any lookable French men who might like a pleasingly plump Jamaican woman?" she asked, chortling. "Me know dat French cuisine suppose to be delicious, but dis Kingston Technical School old girl could certainly whip up a ting or two to please even di most delicate and discerning palates of dem Frenchmen."

Here we go again, thought Jewelle, as always, amused by her aunt's bulletproof confidence. Constance embraced her Rubenesque body, convinced that her figure was far more appealing than the skinny, insubstantial bodies promoted in fashion magazines. She had had her fair share of lovers, and three husbands. An avid, pioneer, extreme recycler, Constance gleefully told friends that the only thing she threw out were husbands who wanted to control her and/or her money. She thought of her lovers as mighty fine specimens who could best be described as having been crafted by God's own hands, unlike the run-of-the-mill variety off the assembly line. Constance fully owned ALL of her appetites and was quick to chastise the women who pretended they didn't need or want anything ... not even a good steak.

"Well, I didn't run into any gentlemen that meet your specifications," said Jewelle. "They weren't quite tall enough. I know you like them tall and slim. Next trip, I'll send out more scouts," said Jewelle, smiling to herself.

"Allright den. Mi counting on yu."

This exchange between Jewelle and her aunt Constance played out every time she returned from a business trip. Jewelle had learned to play along. She felt like she did when she re-watched an episode of Columbo that she had seen many times before, hoping to discover something new.

"Did anything exciting happen while I was away?"

"Nuting I would call exciting but a few ah fi wi people decide fi walk in front of di law and di police bag dem. Mi waan know why dem just caan behave demself. Every time mi see dem on TV mi shame."

"Why are you ashamed? It's not only Black people who commit crimes. Do you think White people are hanging their heads in shame every time a serial killer who looks like them is flashed across their TV screens, or some high-powered executive embezzles the company's money, or some country decides to steal the resources of an African nation?" Jewelle could feel her temper rising but kept it in check as she was too tired to engage in a quarrel with her aunt.

"Miss Jewelle, yu fully entitled to yu own opinions and fi feel di way *yu* wan feel. But mek ah tell yu something. Is nat one or two ah wi people sacrifice suh dat yu and yuh generation can av a betta life and look wha some of dem ah do!"

Knowing full well that her Aunt Constance was not going to budge from her narrow and rather simplistic analysis of the matter, she moved the conversation elsewhere. "Auntie, I am going to Montreal late tomorrow evening. Do you have anything you'd like me to bring for mother."

"Yu barely land, and yu off again? Wha Anthony av to say bout dis?" she asked pointedly.

Jewelle took a deep breath before answering. She often wondered why her aunt thought she had to consult with Anthony on all her decisions. Perhaps it's a generational thing.

"I told him before I went to France."

"Oh, suh Anthony know all bout yu plans, but I av fi wait to hear bout dem. Yu a big woman and mi nah interfere inna yu life, but likkle considahration would be appreciated. Anyhow, me ah go bake a cake and send fi mi sister. Drop by an collect it suh dat mi can bless mi eyes on yu. Hope yu nah starve yuself. Di last time mi see yu, yu look tin."

Sensing that her aunt was gearing up for a full-on scolding, she quickly assured her that she had been eating well, and that she'd come by around eight o'clock so that they could spend some time together. It would also give her time to go to the office to put in a few hours.

The hours passed quickly as Jewelle finished unpacking and sorting clothes that needed to be dropped off at the dry cleaners. Next, she did some light dusting before heading to the office. While walking down the hall to the elevator, she remembered that she had to return her father's call. Jewelle waited until she got into the taxi. Radcliffe picked up after a few rings.

"Hello."

"Hello Daddy. How are you?"

"Glad you found some time to call me back. I am well."

"That's good. What's up?"

"Does something have to be *up* for me to call my daughter?" asked Radcliffe testily.

"Well, it shouldn't be but …"

"I'm not looking for any kind of an argument this evening," Radcliffe interrupted. "I just wanted to let you know that I am going to Jamaica on business. On the way back, I plan to over-night in Toronto and wondered if I could stay with you," said Radcliffe hurriedly.

"Oh, so that's what's up! Well, I don't think it should be a problem. Just call me the day before you leave Jamaica. Bon voyage."

Naturally, when Jewelle arrived at the office, Chantal was lurking. She did an end-run and went directly to her office where she unpacked the tote bag filled with trade magazines. Quickly, she scanned through the pile and selected a few that she'd take with her to Montreal. She'd read through the rest in the coming weeks. Jewelle checked her watch then sat down to type up a lengthy email with instructions for Heather since she wouldn't be back in the office until late Monday afternoon. She also drafted the outline of her MIP-TV report. Pleased that she had used her time well, she tidied her desk, grabbed her tote and handbags, and quietly locked the door behind her. Just as she passed Chantal's office, she heard her door open brusquely.

"It's good to see you, Jewelle."

Without turning around, Jewelle replied, "I wish I could say the same, Chantal," and kept walking.

The next day when Jewelle arrived at TV3, it was 7:00 a.m. Phil, the regular security guard, was on duty. He warmly wel-comed her back. She was happy to see him and stopped to chit-chat with him before giving him the bottle of wine that she had brought back for him along with the tchotchkes for his children. This exchange was repeated many times over the years. It had become their "thing." Jewelle bade him a hasty goodbye and made her way to her offce.

Back at her desk, Jewelle resumed working on her sales report. When she tired of this task, she returned a few phone calls then created the list of screeners requested by clients and prospective clients. Before leaving the office at 6:00 p.m., she placed the list of screeners in a box in the storage room and sent Heather a text to let her know where to find it. There was no sign of Chantal anywhere. She was pleased that she did not have to expend time and energy on an encounter with Miss C.

Jewelle arrived at her Aunt Constance's door at 7:50. She was pleased with herself that she was early—better an hour early than a minute late. Jewelle rang the doorbell and waited for Constance to open the front door.

"Hello Auntie" she said, stepping forward to give her aunt a hug.

"Hello Jewelle. Good fi see yu and feel yu. Mi can feel every last one of yu ribs. Think yu tell me dat yu been eatin'. Yu certainly don't look or feel suh. Well, mi av some nice oxtail and rice."

"Auntie, I'll have a little bite."

"Wha kind a likkle bite. By di look ah tings, yu need a big bite. Haffi put some flesh pon dem bones. Mi mus have a chat wid Anthony di next time mi see im."

"As you wish. He's not complaining."

"Dat's what yu seh but I *know* dat men like likkle bit ah flesh on dem women, particularly, *our* men. Don't mek nobody fool yu bout dat! Mi hope yu treating im right; yu know. Im is a nice young man. And im easy on di eyes. Annada plus."

"Doing the best that I can under the circumstances."

"Wat circumstances, Jewelle?" demanded Constance.

"Work. Most of my time is eaten up by work."

"Well, yu betta do something bout dat. If yu fall sick and need a cup a tea, work caan do dat fi you. If yu lonely, work caan comfort yu. Trust me on dat. Me on yah a lot longa dan yu."

For all their differences, it was in moments like this that Jewelle was reminded of the similarities between her aunt and her mother.

"Auntie, I appreciate what you are saying but at this stage of my life and career, this is how things are. I'm working towards creating a more balanced life."

"Yu betta. Time nah wait fi no man or no woman fi dat matter. Before yu know it, yu reach old age," Constance pronounced
in full fight.

Jewelle and her Aunt Constance spent the next hour chit-
chatting about family matters. Constance inquired about her
father, and she told her that Radcliffe was going to Jamaica to
sort out some business. To which Constance drily remarked,
"If, I know yu father, an mi *know* yu father, is nothing more dan
skirt chasing."

Jewelle remained silent. This was her cue to get going before
things turned ugly. She thanked her aunt for the cake and
assured her she'd get it safely to Montreal.

Blaring horns and shouts filled the air as cars, taxis and trucks
jostled for space at the curb in front of Union Station. It was
a frenzied dance between vehicles, pedestrians, and luggage.
People streamed in and out of the majestic building. Its tall
Greek Doric columns served as a reminder of the grandeur of
the age of steam. In its early days, thousands of new arrivals first
entered the city here. Today, tens of thousands of feet tread its
marble floors as people rushed to catch commuter trains to the
suburbs or the subway, without a thought to the history that
passed under its vaulted ceiling.

Fighting its way to an open spot, Jewelle's taxi pulled up to
the curb. The driver quickly jumped out to remove her small
suitcase from the trunk. Eager for a new fare and to escape the
chaos, he hurriedly took the money from her hand and climbed
back into the car. She grabbed her case and headed inside.

A few minutes after eleven, Jewelle entered the building.
The relative calm inside was a stark contrast to the mayhem
out front. The cathedral-like great hall with its coffered ceiling
of Guastavino tiles soared sixty feet above. Lights hanging,

seemingly by a thread, were suspended in mid-air, and the familiar loudspeakers chimed before a robust reassuring voice announced departures for cities, towns and villages stretched thousands of kilometers along the tracks. On the walls of the station were the names of the towns the railway served. Under the gold lettered destinations, a few people queued up to buy tickets. An ugly plexiglass awning supported by painted steel pipes overhung the polished granite counters. The queue for the ticket counter was long but moving steadily. The midnight train, also known as the milk run because it stopped in all the small towns along the route, was the last train to leave the station.

Jewelle bought a return ticket and then walked, over to the stand where two porters stood idle over their carts while a red light blinked intermittently above their heads. Her suitcase wasn't heavy, but Jewelle wanted to treat herself. Besides, she remembered her Aunt Constance's words, "Everybody has to eat." The porters needed the work.

"Excuse me," she said, attempting to get one of the porters' attention.

"Yes, ma'am," he said springing into action, dolly at the ready.

"I'm on the midnight train to Montreal. Can you put my suitcase on the train, please?" she asked.

"Certainly," he replied.

Jewelle showed him her ticket and he made a note in chalk on her case, assuring her that it would be in the luggage rack in the first-class car. She passed him a few dollars, and he wheeled away across the great expanse of the booking hall and down the ramp to the trains.

Jewelle followed on his heels making her way to the departure lounge. Instead of going into it, she seated herself on one of the benches in the waiting area where she could observe her fellow travelers standing in one of the long snaking queues. There was always something amusing and interesting to see.

As usual, the Montreal line was the longest. Every so often someone would come along and ask her, "Is this the Montreal line?" When she said yes, a look of alarm registered on their faces as they processed the length of the line which stretched all the way back to the ticket counters. Invariably, they grudgingly made their way to the end. Canadians are so orderly, thought Jewelle.

"Train 50 is now ready for boarding. Le train cinquante est maintenant en gare," the PA system announced.

Great! thought Jewelle as the first-class passengers boarded ahead of those with economy class tickets. Jewelle hated to wait in line—for anything.

She, along with the other passengers, took the escalator to the platform where the train was waiting. She climbed aboard and quickly settled into a seat and placed her hand luggage on the seat beside her, signaling that she wished to be alone.

As the train slowly pulled out of the station, Jewelle breathed a sigh of relief. She felt as though she had been on a treadmill for the past couple of months. She was exhausted. As soon as she returned from the market, she had spent part of the weekend at TV3 working on her sales reports, returning phone calls, and reviewing the list of DVD screeners requested by clients and prospective clients. Thankfully, she could rely on Heather to complete and submit the DVD requisition forms for the screeners.

Jewelle managed to squeeze in Anthony for a few hours. It was a tense get-together as she was still jet-lagged and focused on work. It wasn't easy to turn her thoughts and attention away from it, but she did fold herself into Anthony's arms and nibbled tentatively on his lips. She started feeling warm and aroused, but she couldn't really let go. Anthony had accused her of sacrificing their relationship for her career. She denied it but in her heart knew it was true.

Jewelle soon grew tired of looking out the window and took a well-worn copy of Earl Lovelace's *The Dragon Can't Dance* from her weekend bag. She had started re-reading it on the flight back from France. Like many of the novels by the Caribbean and Latin American writers she loved, each reading brought with it fresh insights and nuances about the honesty and humour of Caribbean people who took intimate and interactive to another level. Where else would you find a character like Taffy, the town's madman, who is quickly brought back to his senses when one of the townspeople answered his plea to "stone me with stones as you stone Jesus!" Certainly, not Toronto or Montreal where people are, generally, intentional in their blindness to the suffering of the people around them.

When Jewelle read these books, she entered worlds that were sometimes magical, sometimes painfully real—where people knew how to laugh, grieve and love despite their mean circumstances. The adventures helped to make her grateful. After reading a couple of chapters, Jewelle inserted her bookmark and closed the book. She then closed her eyes and allowed her thoughts to drift into a deep slumber.

When the train pulled into Gare Centrale, Jewelle got butterflies in her stomach. She always anticipated seeing the city of Montreal as much as she did seeing her family. It was so much a part of her, like a dear friend that she knew intimately. This was the city of her childhood. She loved the evocative architecture of its old churches, the restaurants, the tree-lined avenues, the city's style, its history for better or worse. As soon as she exited the train, she made her way to rue Sainte-Catherine.

Warm sunshine and a gentle breeze carried the smell of spring down the street. People were moving purposefully on the sidewalk, trucks and cars forming a seamless thread on the road—she drank it all in, her eyes darting from image to image. She would forget to look where she was going and occasionally bump into someone who would give her a hard look or admonish her.

Every year, since Jewelle could remember, she welcomed the first buds on trees as the sign that spring had finally shrugged off winter. You could see and feel the joie de vivre of her fellow Montrealers. Montreal winters were bone-chillers; four-foot snow drifts and treacherously icy streets were commonplace. Jewelle shuddered as she thought about the bitter cold and the many winters when she and her siblings trudged to school, arriving frozen stiff, wishing that spring would come early. On this April day she felt like Audrey Hepburn strolling down the avenue, peering into the shop windows.

Years ago, rue Sainte-Catherine was a chic destination, the heart of Montreal's shopping before suburban malls and big box stores drew people. Outside Ogilvy's, that bastion of Anglo respectability, Jewelle feasted on the beautiful window displays. She remembered buying hats and gloves with her mother during a time when it was fashionable for ladies and girls to do so.

She continued her march up rue Sainte-Catherine until she arrived at Metro Atwater. Here, she hailed a taxi to finish the last leg of her journey.

"*Où allez-vous?*" asked the Haitian taxi driver.

"Rue Old Orchard, le 5627," replied Jewelle. Feeling happy to be back in *La Belle Province*, and speaking French, she exchanged a few pleasantries with Pascale, the driver.

As Jewelle climbed the stairs leading to the front porch, she began to feel a little anxious about fresh family drama lying in wait at Joseph Manor. She paused on the porch to gather her thoughts while enjoying the babbling birds and the unseasonably warm breeze on the quiet, tree-lined street before opening the front door. Mouth-watering aromas of Adele's cooking welcomed her, and she hoped that it was her favourite, ackee and codfish, Jamaica's national dish.

As she quietly made her way down the long hallway decorated with a red Bokhara runner, she stopped from time to time to examine and admire one of the familiar oil or watercolour paintings of Jamaican landscapes. She could now better appreciate that this was her parents' way of always keeping their homeland with them.

When Jewelle reached the large brightly lit kitchen, with its black-and-white tiled floor, Adele was standing in front of the stove gently stirring the contents of a large skillet. Not wanting to give her mother a start, Jewelle quietly whispered, "Mother."

Adele let out a cry and dropped the large spoon spilling some sauce on the kitchen floor.

"Jewelle, you startled me! Why didn't you ring the bell or call out when you came through the door? I wasn't expecting you until eightish," said Adele, picking up the spoon, dropping it into the sink, and then wiping the floor.

"I guess I should have but I wanted to surprise you," said Jewelle taking a few steps towards Adele.

"Surprise you did! Well, aren't I going to get a hug?"

Jewelle and Adele embraced and clung to each other. Adele's slim frame carried more pounds than it should. She had finally called a truce to end the war she waged against her body. Now, she simply dressed to camouflage the bits that she didn't want displayed. As always, every hair was in place and her make-up was hardly noticeable.

Adele let go of Jewelle, took a few steps back and took a long look at her from head to toe.

"You look and feel a little thin. Do I have to remind you again that you need to eat to keep up your strength?" inquired Adele.

"No mother, you don't have to remind me. Aunt Constance already did. I am eating. It's just that I'm also working very hard."

"Please be reminded that it's NOT true that hard work never killed anyone." She let her words hang in the air for a moment. "Just look at some of those Japanese businessmen and this Karōshi business. You don't need to take up their style."

"Alright Mother," said Jewelle, fighting hard to control her irritation.

"Well, you are an adult and I have said what I have to say on the matter," said Adele. A silence fell between them as they reflected on their exchange.

"Aunt Constance sent an apple cake for you."

"Great. Anything she bakes is always good. We'll have it for dessert. I'll give her a call later to thank her."

"Don't forget or you'll never hear the end of it."

"You don't have to tell me. I know my sister."

Jewelle walked over to the stove and lifted the lid off each pot and peered inside. Her smile widened as she investigated.

"You've made all my favourites! I can't wait to eat. Thank you, thank you," said Jewelle doing her happy dance, and asking "What's all the news? The short version before the others get here."

Adele took a deep breath and allowed the words to tumble from her mouth. "Well, I will start with Miss Cass. It seems that marriage number three is falling apart. She hasn't said anything to me, but your brother Ryan updated me. Besides, I am not blind, deaf, or dumb. Deeana has quit her job yet again. This time around, she claims the boss's body odour is more than she could stand. Lord only knows what she'll come up with next. Ryan seems to be doing well at FedEx. He's now in middle management."

"Well, it's great that there's nothing too dramatic. Any developments on the Keisha and Ryan front?" Jewelle noted a change on Adele's face.

"Yes, I'm told wedding plans are in the works, and no one has mentioned one word to me," said Adele in a flat disappointed voice.

Adele had expressed her disappointment in Ryan's decision to "play dolly house" with Keisha rather than marry her, and she was equally disappointed that Keisha allowed this "arrangement" to go on these many years even though she was thankful that they did not have children.

"That's great news!" exclaimed Jewelle.

"I wish I shared your enthusiasm," said Adele, allowing her voice to trail off.

"Mother, you don't sound pleased. Isn't this what you have been praying for?"

"I shouldn't have to be praying about this, the two of them were raised to know better!"

At that moment the windchimes-sounding doorbell rang in quick succession. Saved by the bell, thought Jewelle.

"Who is ringing like they trying to mash up the bell?" asked an irritated Adele.

"Who else but your son!" replied Deeana as she made her way down the hallway followed by her brother Ryan.

"Ryan, what ...?"

Before Adele could complete her sentence, Ryan picked her up and twirled her around the kitchen kissing her on both cheeks. She made a fuss, but they all knew that she loved this special attention from Ryan.

"Hello Mother," said Deeana and Ryan in unison.

"Hello," replied Adele, beaming from ear to ear. Then, "Alright, alright, Ryan, you can put me down now so that I can get the dinner on the table. Jewelle, please give me a hand. The rest of you go in the dining room," Adele commanded.

The oak double French doors, with crackled glass and brass-ringed glass doorknobs, opened to the long narrow dining room with mint green walls. A rectangular Duncan Phyfe mahogany dining table, dressed in a white cotton lace tablecloth, sat on a red Bokhara rug. Above the table, a glistening crystal chandelier, to the right, a sideboard displaying framed family photos and a large mirror with an ornate gilded frame. On the opposite wall were vibrant groupings of watercolour and oil paintings of Caribbean landscapes.

Below, the table was set with green Denby earthenware dishes, white napkins with a delicate green floral pattern, stainless steel cutlery and plain crystal glasses. Each sibling sat in their child-hood spot, Cass would sit in the still-empty seat beside Jewelle, Deeana on the other side of the table, Ryan at one end facing the seat reserved for Adele.

Jewelle ferried dishes between the kitchen and dining room. First she came in with a large bowl of ackee and codfish, fol-lowed by a bowl of yellow yam, green bananas, sweet potato, and boiled cornmeal dumplings. Adele carried in piping hot bowls of callaloo, fried plantains, oxtail, rice and peas, and coleslaw. She then stepped back to survey the table to make sure everything was in place. As she was about to sit down, she noticed that the pitchers of water and homemade ginger beer were missing. Adele fetched them from the refrigerator and then took her place at the head of the table.

"Where's Cass?" asked Jewelle.

"You know she'll get here when she gets here," quipped Ryan.

"Mother, I hope you don't plan to wait until she arrives for us to eat," said Jewelle.

"I second that. I'm starving," said Ryan.

"No, Jewelle, we'll say grace and get started. Cass will join us when she gets here. Will someone please say the grace?" asked Adele.

Ryan looked at Deeana as if to say you do it. Deeana ignored his gaze and in turn gave Jewelle the same look.

"Well, is anyone going to say the grace?" asked Adele, emit-ting a sigh. Jewelle said, "I guess, it's going to be me—*again.*"

"Just remember to make it short, we want to eat this even-ing," said Ryan.

As Jewelle was about to start the grace, Cass arrived.

"I'm here," called out Cass making her way to the dining room. She plopped herself down in the seat next to Jewelle.

"Cass you are forever late but somehow always make it in time for the food. Not that you couldn't stand to miss a meal or two," chuckled Ryan.

"Ryan don't start. My weight is not a problem to me, and it shouldn't be to you."

"I don't want any quarrelling this evening. Let's just enjoy each other's company. Jewelle, please say the grace."

Jewelle asked everyone to link their hands, lowered her eyes and prayed, "Father God, thank you for the blessing of this family and this meal that has been prepared for us. As we partake of it, we ask that you bless the food and the provider. May we all be truly grateful for your daily provisions. We ask now that you bless this food to our bodies. We ask all this in the name of Jesus. And the people said?"

"Amen," they answered in unison.

"Short and to the point," said Ryan. "Please pass me the ackee."

When dinner was over, Jewelle and her sisters gathered in the kitchen to clean up and gossip amongst themselves. Adele and Ryan moved to the living room. When the girls arrived, Jewelle noticed that Adele looked tense and agitated. But she refrained from making any inquiries. Instead, she took a seat on the comfortable overstuffed sofa next to Ryan. Deeana and Cass stood at the end of the sofa where Adele was sitting. Cass was the first to speak.

"What's going on?"

No sooner had Cass asked the question, Ryan got up and stretched.

"I ate way too much," said Ryan. "Let's see if I can move some of this food down into a leg."

Adele glared at him.

"Well, I have some good news, in fact, great news that I wanted to share with all of you," Ryan continued. He paused, glancing at his mother before continuing. "I've asked Keisha to marry me, and she has accepted, and we have begun to plan the wedding."

A heavy silence fell over the room.

"Congratulations," said Jewelle beaming from ear to ear. She then ran over and gave her brother a big hug. "I am sooo happy for you!"

Cass and Deeana and Adele were slow to offer nothing more than lukewarm congrats.

"Have you set a date?"

"Next July," replied Ryan. "Keisha wanted to make sure that we had plenty of time to plan the wedding properly."

"I don't have to check my calendar. I wouldn't miss it for anything in the world."

Cass and Deeana had joined their mother on the sofa. The girls seemed to be consoling Adele, who was clearly not jumping for joy. Adele hesitantly got up and walked over and offered her congratulations to Ryan without asking one word about the wedding date or plans. The truth is, she had misgivings about Keisha and the thought of "losing" her son made her sad.

"Anyone for Scrabble?" asked Ryan. "Mother, are you going to play?"

"Not tonight. I want to divide up the leftovers for you all to take home."

Adele headed back to the kitchen, and her children walked in single file, one behind the other, down to the family room in the basement. The large airy room had two small windows that looked out on the sidewalk, a couple of sofas, a large TV, and a sound system with two large speakers. In one corner, board games were stacked close by an acoustic guitar on a stand. Family portraits adorned one wall, and Ryan's basketball trophies were displayed on shelves.

Jewelle and her siblings spent the next couple of hours in a competitive game of Scrabble. The dictionary was referenced often as they accused each other of making up words. In the end, Jewelle emerged the victor. The rest of the evening they reminisced about their upbringing, enjoying more than a few laughs about their father, Radcliffe Joseph's pronouncements and insights: No TV on weeknights. ("Lots of books on the shelf *begging* to be read. Remember, no one can take out what you put into your head.") No sleepovers. ("I don't know what goes on in other homes and I don't want to.") No excuse for poor hygiene. ("Water is almost free in this country.") No this, no that. Now, they could all laugh about "Radcliffe's Rules." Back then, they weren't funny. They recalled their experience of being the first Black family to move to Old Orchard Street, situated in a well-established WASP area of Montreal. The family was welcomed with curious stares. From time to time, they would catch a neighbour pulling back their curtains to see what was happening over at Joseph Manor, particularly when they had visitors, which was often. Family, friends, and who would become friends often just turned up—West Indian style. The evening ended with Ryan strumming a few folk songs on the guitar. Then he went upstairs to see Adele.

"Mother," he called out.

"Yes, Ryan".

"I know you are not crazy about Keisha but I love her and she loves me. It's going to be alright. Please be happy for me. After all, the new *arrangement* will be to your liking. Can I get a smile?"

Adele gave him a weak smile and a tight hug. "She had better take care of you or she will have me to answer to, not to mention your sisters."

"I is scared of you all," scoffed Ryan pretending to be shaking with fear.

"Why don't you join us for a few songs?" Ryan knew his mother would never pass up an opportunity to sing. She was blessed with a melodic voice that could scale multiple octaves.

"Would love to. How about something we can all sing?"

Leading Adele by the hand, Ryan returned to the basement. He resumed his perch on a sofa and picked out the chords for "Day-O!"

"Come mistah Tally Man, tally mi banana. Daylight come and mi wan go home." Ryan motioned to the group to join in on the chorus. And everybody went full blast: "Day-O!, Mi seh, mi seh day-o! Daylight come and mi wan go home."

They sang many more Jamaican folk songs including, "Linstead Market," "Cordelia Brown," and closed with "Jamaica Farewell." Adele performed a solo. "Down the way, Where the nights are gay, And the sun shines daily on the mountain top ..." On the chorus they all sang.

Ryan remembered the "little girl" he left behind one summer holiday. Warm memories of Jamaica flooded in.

Five

Back to Reality

The train was full. Jewelle found a seat next to a navy-blue suited businessman who turned his legs to the side to give her extra room for access to her window seat. As soon as she settled, he took a book from his briefcase. Jewelle noticed that it was Stephen Covey's *7 Habits of Highly Successful People*. "Good read," she said to her fellow passenger. He smiled at her and then searched to find the page where he had left off reading. It was clear that he did not want to engage in conversation, and this was just fine with Jewelle. She turned to stare out the window as the train slowly pulled out of the Gare Centrale. The downtown skyline of nondescript concrete and glass towers, beautiful old European-style buildings built to last, the old Redpath sugar factory building, the oatmeal-coloured concrete silo, and the Pont Jacques Cartier made her sentimental. She thought about her childhood in the city and was flooded with many warm memories. Whatever her differences with her siblings, she loved them and wished she saw more of them. She ached for her beloved Montreal and all its charms. To take her mind off what she was leaving behind, she pulled out her battered copy of *The Dragon Can Dance*. Inside these pages she would once again time travel to Trinidad to find out what Taffy, the local madman and all the other characters were up to. She read until she was interrupted by the service attendant who came by to let her know the meal options

The train was now moving at maximum speed. The hypnotic sound of it rumbling down the track, melding with the light conversations throughout the car, lulled and relaxed her. Jewelle's eyes closed and fluttered open when the polite service attendant came by to take her order. Jewelle chose chicken instead of the filet mignon that was the other offer, figuring that rare chicken could kill so the chef had to cook it thoroughly. Besides, she was suspicious of any red meat that was not cooked by herself or her mother—too bland or undercooked. She often felt queasy when she saw people eating meat that still seemed to show signs of life.

As the tall, slim male service attendant walked away, Jewelle's eyes drifted closed again, and she fell into a reverie about being on the Orient Express, one of the experiences on her bucket list. A sudden flash of railroad history jolted her from her fantasy. The reality of exclusionary practices of railroads crept into her thoughts. She wondered if the service attendant's father and grandfather had also worked for the railway, and if he knew or cared about racism and poor working conditions that black railway porters tolerated for decades to provide for the families they left behind weeks on end. Missing their wives and children, these proud and hardworking men who rode the rails with little or no sleep, put on big smiles, warmed up their voices, and attended to the whims and needs of privileged passengers, many of whom could barely mask their contempt. Her aunt Constance had described the porter's precarious employment situation as, "What they could not cure, they had to endure." Jewelle conjured up thoughts of a few brave souls who had cast off their armour of endurance to fight for racial equality and respect. It was a long time coming. Jewelle quietly thanked the heroes on whose shoulders she stood. She recommitted herself to being all that she could be to make her ancestors and her family proud.

Jewelle now turned her attention back to her reality. She pulled a few trade magazines out of her bag to catch up on market intelligence. First up, *Variety*, what they used to call the Show Business Bible. She turned quickly to the back to read reviews of just released movies. Most of them were, this time around, favourable. She moved on to *Video Age* and searched the editor's column, "My Two Cents." Jewelle loved the cartoons featured in these editorials because they depicted many of the crazy realities of a world built largely on make-believe. She also admired the editor's courage in shining a light on the underbelly of the industry. Jewelle ended with *Reel Screen*, a trade magazine focused on documentaries. She savoured real stories that show the good, the bad and the downright ugly aspects of humanity and the animal world.

Feeling a little tired, Jewelle closed her eyes. TV3 loomed large in her mind's eye. She could feel the anxiety rising in her as she thought about her job application and the interview that would follow. She reminded herself that with proper preparation, she would ace the interview. She also knew that preparation and qualifications didn't always mean that one would land the job as there were always other variables at play—organizational culture, biases, and many other things that she couldn't name at this moment. Jewelle reminded herself that she's a fighter and that she was prepared to fight for the VP of Sales and Distribution position.

When the train pulled into Union Station, Jewelle quickly packed her tote bag and checked the time and the area around her seat before rushing to the exit. Once inside the station, Jewelle took the escalator down to the subway level, dropped a token in the box then jumped on the northbound train toward TV3. The visit to Montreal had refreshed Jewelle. She was now in fighting form for the next round with Chantal. Rocky had nothing on her. She was committed to upping her A-game to best Cruella De Mercier.

When she arrived at her stop, she exited the subway, took the escalator to street level, and withdrew some money from a bank machine before walking to the TV3 building where she took the elevator to the sixth floor. On exiting the elevator, she stopped to look at the job board where the new VP of Sales and Distribution position was posted. She'd have to follow through on what she had told Chantal by getting her application in as soon as possible. Jewelle pondered how to do so without the entire department, if not the organization, knowing about it. As she walked down the long corridor to her office, her cover letter writing itself in her head, she was distracted by frustrating thoughts about how she could distinguish herself from Chantal, considering that they both did more or less the same job, and if that wasn't enough, sales were combined for a department total, and each territory was averaged so that those who fell short of their sales targets benefitted from those who exceeded theirs. Chantal was benefitting from her hard work. That would all change when she took on the role of VP of Sales and Distribution!

It was two in the afternoon when Jewelle arrived at TV3. Arriving in the sales department, she saw Chantal standing at the water cooler. As she passed by, Chantal sniped, "It must be nice to keep executive hours so regularly!" Without breaking her stride, Jewelle turned her head slightly, and countered, "It is indeed! By the way, I've already surpassed my sales targets, have you?"

"Oh, I guess you haven't heard the news," said Chantal, smiling smugly. Jewelle stopped outside her door and waited for Chantal to share the "news." But when she turned around, she had disappeared. Rather than pursue Chantal, Jewelle went in search of her assistant Heather and found her in the supplies room.

"Hi Heather. What's going on?" asked Jewelle anxiously.

"It's good to have you back. Why do you ask?"

"I just ran into Chantal."

Heather hesitated before replying, "This morning, Marg held an impromptu staff meeting to let us know that there have been more budget cuts so the sales department will have to generate more revenues. Sales targets have been increased."

Jewelle dropped her tote bag where she stood and exclaimed, "So, I misspoke when I told Chantal that I had surpassed my sales target! What are the new sales targets?"

"Each rep. has to bring in an additional $500,000, Canadian," replied Heather quietly.

"What! That's ridiculous given that we don't have a lot of new titles to offer. This feels like Pharaoh ordering the Jews to make bricks without straw," fumed Jewelle.

"I know, I know," griped Heather. "We will have to all put on our creative thinking caps and come up with some new packages to offer our clients."

"Easier said than done but I love a challenge."

Jewelle exited the stationery room and headed back to her office. She slammed the door behind her and shouted, "Half a million dollars more!"

There was a knock on her door, and Chantal poked her head through it. "I guess you heard the news!" she stated cheerily. "But you have only heard some of the news. What I'm sure you haven't heard yet is that my application is in for the new VP position. Enjoy the rest of the afternoon!"

With the last sentence barely out of her mouth, Chantal vanished again.

Jewelle made her way around her desk and plopped herself down in her chair. Feeling frustrated and angry, she fumed. The phone rang and she was forced to gather herself and steadied her voice before picking it up.

"Good afternoon, Jewelle Joseph."

"Hello Jewelle. Just checking that you made it safely back to Toronto," said her mother, Adele.

"Hello Mother, yes, I got back okay. But ..."

"But what?" asked Adele.

"But ..." Jewelle fell silent.

"What's going on Jewelle? Is that woman Chantal bothering you again? She'd better not let me have to come down there and deal with her. Better still I should just set your aunt Constance on her."

The image of Aunt Constance confronting Chantal made Jewelle roar with laughter. She laughed so hard, tears streamed down her face. She envisioned Constance's opening lines: "You are di one dem call Chantal. Well, mek I tell you something ..." This would have been Chantal's cue to make tracks because Constance was about to drop something heavy on her. She would be no match for Constance, a formidable warrior woman.

"Well, I'm glad I made you laugh."

"Thanks, Mother. I will be laughing every time I think about Auntie making Chantal run for the hills."

"So, back to Chantal. How are you going to put this woman in her place!"

"For starters, I have to get my application in for the VP of Sales and Distribution job. I also must generate more sales. Well, I had better get busy and stop feeling sorry for myself."

"Sometimes, we all need a pity party. Just remember that you come from a long line of warrior women. We don't play!" said Adele in a strong and convincing voice.

"Thanks for the pep talk, Mother, I am going to work on the application and then start brainstorming some new sales strategy."

"That's my Jewelle, my phenomenal woman!" said Adele, her voice brimming with pride.

They said their goodbyes, Jewelle hung up the phone and paused to savour her mother's last words, "my phenomenal woman." She could feel the spirit of Maya Angelou nudging her forward, and she swiveled her chair away from her window to face her computer. She booted it and set about composing her cover letter. Over the next couple of hours, she wrote, re-wrote, edited and re-edited. Finally, satisfied that she had crafted a winning cover letter, she printed it along with her resume, placed them in a brown envelope and made her way to the HR Department. Jewelle's thoughts were racing with a myriad of different scenarios as she walked down the hall. She was brought back to reality when she absentmindedly bumped into Gregory George, the chair of TV3's board.

"So sorry, please accept my apology. I really didn't see you."

"I must be invisible," he said dryly.

"I was lost in thought," said a startled Jewelle.

"Well, I'm delighted that our chance encounter has been of benefit," said Mr. George, his words dripping with sarcasm. "TV3 needs workers not daydreamers," he spat out as he resumed his march.

Jewelle turned to watch him for a minute and saw him walk into the Sales Department. She wondered what urgent matter brought him there.

Before entering the HR Department, Jewelle looked around to confirm that there were no Mrs. Kravitz types in the vicinity. The coast was clear. She quickly slipped into the department and let the receptionist know that she was dropping off her resume and cover letter in response to the VP of Sales and Distribution job posting. The receptionist had a peculiar look on her face.

"Is anything wrong?"

"Nooo," the receptionist answered haltingly. "Why do you ask?"

"You just seemed uncomfortable when I told you the position I was applying for," answered Jewelle.

"Well, to be very honest, there are a lot of very qualified people applying for this position ..."

Jewelle cut her off. "I happen to be one of them," she snapped. "Please be sure that my resume and cover letter make it to the desk of the person who will be conducting the interview."

Driving down the east end of Toronto's eccentric and vibrant Queen Street, Jewelle took notice of the shabby buildings and the equally drab people walking on the sidewalk. Thankfully, she was ahead of the streetcar and wouldn't be stuck inching along as it stopped to pick up passengers. There were a few familiar panhandlers. Whenever she was on foot, she'd sometimes stop to give them some money and have a quick chat. She always felt comforted when they'd say, "God bless you," just before she left their company. Despite their hardships some could still offer a blessing. Whenever she told Anthony about these encounters, he would always remind her to be careful as some of these men and women are mentally unstable.

Anticipating that she would get an interview for the VP of Sales and Distribution position, Jewelle began to research and prepare for the interview. When she reached out to her former boss and invited her out for dinner, Barb was happy to hear from her and agreed to meet at the Real Jerk on Queen Street East.

Jewelle parked her car on Broadview, out front of one of the rundown little houses in desperate need. She walked briskly to the restaurant, which Jewelle knew well as her girls-night-out meeting place for the last three years. With its Jamaican roots culture inspired decor, and its relaxed warmth, it reminded her of some of the places where she ate during family holidays to the island. Jewelle walked in and looked around at the bright red, green and yellow plastic tablecloths, the posters of Bob Marley and sheets of corrugated zinc splashed with painted folk-art images of Jamaica—palm trees, Rasta men, Red Stripe beer, and dancehall queens.

When Barbara arrived at seven, Jewelle was already seated at a table on the lower lever. She was enjoying her usual glass of Wolf Blass Australian Shiraz while the sound of Bob Marley's "Natural Mystic" played in the background. Jewelle got up from her seat and greeted Barbara with a warm embrace. Barbara sat down and unloaded her sturdy Roots bag.

"Barbara, so good to see you. How have you been?" Jewelle asked, trying to keep her voice from sounding too concerned.

Barbara looked haggard. The rose-coloured blush on her high cheekbones only served to highlight the pallor of her face and the concealer attempting to cover the dark circles under her eyes. Her normally well-coiffed hair looked a little unkempt.

"Good to see you too, JJ. I'm okay," said Barbara. Her worried-looking eyes darted around the room in search of the waitress.

"Just okay?" Jewelle asked, probing a bit deeper.

"Well, I better order a glass of wine before I get into it," she sighed. "What are you drinking?"

"An Australian Shiraz."

"I'll have the same." Barbara called over the waitress and ordered a glass of wine.

"When she comes back, I think we should place our order," said Jewelle. They both scanned the menu but had already decided on what they were going to eat—Jewelle, ackee and saltfish with fried plantain and a fried dumpling and Barbara, a boneless chicken roti.

"Thanks," said Barbara to the waitress as she set down the glass of wine. "We are ready to place our order now."

As soon as the waitress left, Barbara raised her glass.

"Friendship and TV3," they said in unison followed by momentary silence.

Jewelle looked inquiringly at Barbara, whose sad smile told her that she was burdened by something serious.

Barbara took a deep breath and said with tears in her voice, "Well, I might as well get it out. I left TV3 to dedicate my time and energy to helping my son Grant. He's battling crack addiction."

Jewelle gasped, put her hand over her mouth and quietly said, "I'm so sorry to hear that."

An uneasy silence settled between them before Barbara spoke again.

"I suspected that Grant was abusing drugs, but I thought it was just a little marijuana. When his behaviour became erratic, I knew that it wasn't. But I didn't for a minute think it was crack," said Barbara, pausing to take another sip of her wine.

Jewelle was stunned by the news but put on her poker face for the sake of her friend. Inside, her head was spinning. She was deeply saddened for Barbara. It would be so hard to lose a child to something so destructive she thought.

"Barbara, I really don't know what to say except, I am here for you. If I can help in any way, just ask," said Jewelle.

"Jewelle, I'm really angry with myself for not having intervened sooner. Had the police not caught him breaking into someone's home, I'd probably still be burying my head in the sand," sobbed Barbara.

Jewelle got up from her seat, walked around the table to her friend and embraced her for what seemed like an eternity. "It's going to be alright Barbara, it's going to be alright," Jewelle whispered into her ear.

Once Barbara's tears stopped, Jewelle released her embrace and returned to her seat.

"Now, what do you plan to do?" Jewelle asked, hoping that conversation would lighten Barbara's emotional burden.

"Rehab is a condition of Grant's release. We'll be going to Cuba in a few weeks where he will go through a rehab program with an excellent success rate. He'll need my undivided attention and support. Now, you know why I left so suddenly." Barbara toyed with the stem of her glass before she took another uneasy sip.

"Barbara," Jewelle leaned forward and patted Barbara's hand, "rest assured that this will go no further. Are you sure there's nothing I can do to help?"

"A sympathetic ear is plenty," she said smiling. "That's enough about me. What's going on with you?"

Jewelle understood that her normally private friend was feeling the need to divert attention away from her tragedy. She respected that and was about to reply when the waitress arrived with their meal and set about arranging the plates on the table.

"Thank you," they both said before the waitress turned and walked away.

"It sure looks good and smells even better," said Jewelle, savouring the mouth-watering aromas.

"I'd have to agree," said Barbara, smiling.

Jewelle reached across the table and took Barbara's hands into her own and held them. These two women were genuinely fond of each other and had managed to forge a bond of friendship over time. Jewelle was grateful that Barbara had taken her under her wing and mentored her. It was rare to find people in the industry who were willing to share what they knew and rarer still to find those willing to share their contacts, particularly those with power and influence. They both dug into their meals with enthusiasm.

"So, what's happening in Sales?" asked Barbara lightly.

"Same old, same old," Jewelle said between bites of the tasty ackee and saltfish. "Everyone has been preoccupied with your resignation and the severance packages. I've just been trying to stay focused."

"As you always do," Barbara nodded.

"I try. Being the only Black person in the department is lonely enough. But with you gone, I will truly feel like the Maytag Repair Man. There's no one there who I can really talk to. Frankly, I find much of the gossiping and pettiness tiresome." For a moment, Jewelle felt a wave of sadness and fatigue wash over her.

"I hear you. But as I have always told you Jewelle, use TV3 as a stepping stone to move on to bigger opportunities. You're educated, intelligent and charming. You have a bright future ahead of you," Barbara said with a warm smile on her face.

Jewelle shifted uncomfortably in her chair at Barbara's compliment and could feel her face grow warm. If she was of a lighter hue, her face would certainly have reddened. She humbly thanked Barbara and asked how she was enjoying the roti.

"It's excellent. Not too spicy and there's a lot more chicken than potatoes. You know how it can be the other way around sometimes."

Jewelle smiled and nodded knowingly.

"So, how was MIP?" inquired Barbara.

"It was crazy as always. Chantal was her prima donna self and did nothing to help get the shipping out or set up the stand but I got through it, and there are prospective deals that could close quickly. So, that's the up side. Chantal told me that she applied for the new position that will replace your old job."

Barbara reached into her bag and pulled out a white letter size envelope and handed it to Jewelle. "Here's the reference letter you asked me to write. It basically says you'll make an excellent VP of Sales and Distribution. If there is anything else you need, just ask!"

"Thanks for the letter and all your encouragement, Barbara," said Jewelle. "I'm certainly going to give it my best shot. But ..."

"But what?" asked Barbara.

"Well, I heard through the grapevine that Chantal is dating the head of the Board. It's all supposed to be very hush-hush. But as you know there are no secrets at TV3."

"That woman's behaviour is just scandalous! She has no scruples," Barbara said.

"Now you can better appreciate my concerns about Chantal's application," Jewelle confided.

Barbara nodded knowingly.

Jewelle and Barbara managed to enjoy a few laughs as they ate their meals, reliving some of their experiences at TV3. When the waitress returned to entice them with desserts, they both declined, but ordered coffee, which they sipped slowly, enjoying the ambience of the restaurant.

Two hours on from the time they sat down to their meal, they parted company with a hug and promised to stay in touch. Just as Jewelle turned to walk away, Barbara called out to her: "Jewelle, Jewelle. I almost forgot to give this to you," she said with a mysterious smile on her face.

When Jewelle turned around, she saw Barbara was holding a large brown envelope in her hand.

"Here are a few documents that may be useful later on. Just hang on to them. You'll know when to make use of them," said Barbara.

Jewelle squeezed the large envelope and then shook it. "This sounds very mysterious. Girl Guide's honour," said Jewelle placing her right hand over her heart, "that I will not open this envelope until my guardian angel gives me a sign to do so." Jewelle smiled broadly. She gave Barbara another big hug, thanked her, crossed the street, and walked to her car. Without knowing the contents of the brown envelope, she somehow felt lighter and brighter.

Soon after arriving home, Jewelle showered and, wiping off the condensation from the bathroom mirror, she stood staring at her reflection. The woman looking back at her was the daughter of a Garveyite and a homemaker who had sacrificed so that she could have better opportunities in the world. Now, she was also the woman trying to make her way in a world that didn't think she belonged. However, she was determined to be seen and heard.

Jewelle changed into comfortable, fuchsia-colored velour pants and a matching top before filling the kettle in the kitchen and plugging it in. While the water boiled, she took her favourite bone china mug with its delicate cherry blossom pattern from the cupboard, dropped a green tea bag in and waited. A few minutes later she walked slowly into her living room, mug in hand. There, she settled on the comfortable royal blue suede sofa, curled her legs beneath her, stretched, exhaled, and reached for her mug. She carefully sipped the hot tea and fished Barbara's reference letter out of her handbag. When

Jewelle got to the end of it, a broad smile broke across her face and she shouted, "Yes! Excellent reference. Thank you, thank you, Barbara!" She put the letter back in the envelope before depositing it in her handbag. She'd drop it off at HR first thing in the morning. Just as Jewelle got up from the sofa, there was a rhythmic knock on her front door, rat-a-tat-tat, rat-a-tat-tat. It was her boyfriend's secret knock.

"Who's knocking on my chamber door at this hour?" asked Jewelle playfully.

"It's the big bad wolf. Let me in or I'll ..." replied Anthony in his best baritone.

"Let's just see how bad you really are. Huff and puff and blow the door in."

Anthony made noisy blowing sounds that Jewelle let go on for a minute or two before throwing open the door as Anthony huffed and puffed to the max. Jewelle burst into laughter, and Anthony joined her.

"Look at what I have to do to get your attention," he said, pulling her close to him as he walked into her hallway. Jewelle kicked the door shut behind him. They stood grinning at each other, intoxicated by the moment and their passion for each other. Anthony tipped up her chin, leaned down, and kissed her. Jewelle responded wholeheartedly, her hands running down his body.

"Good to see you, JJ. Better still to feel you in my arms," murmured Anthony.

"You look and feel pretty good yourself," she said gazing deeply into his eyes. "As a matter of fact, you really are easy on my eyes," she said, smiling as Anthony leaned down and kissed her again. Suddenly, he cooled off.

"Anything wrong, JJ?"

"No. Why do you ask?"

"Well, I have been calling you all evening to let you know that I was going to drop by, but you didn't return *any* of my calls."

"Sorry. My phone was on vibrate. I had a business dinner with my old boss Barbara. We went to The Real Jerk for a catch up. Now, I know why she left TV3 so suddenly," she said, softening her voice.

"I don't mean to sound selfish but here we go again. TV3 takes priority over everything and everyone, especially me."

The moment was gone. His anger was rising.

"Yes Anthony, here we go again. When we met, I didn't hide the fact that my career was and still is important to me. I am working hard now to build a solid foundation for us," said Jewelle heatedly. "Would you like something to eat?" she asked to get out of the room and on to another subject.

"Sure, what do you have?" said Anthony, following her into the kitchen.

Jewelle hurried into the kitchen and tore open the fridge knowing full well that it was near empty as it usually was. She spun around and saw the disappointed look on Anthony's face.

"I should have checked before I made the offer. I'll call out for a Mama's pizza."

"It's okay. I don't want pizza, *again*. Why can't you make time to buy groceries?"

"Because I'm busy. My job is very demanding. Haven't you noticed?"

Jewelle walked out of the kitchen to the living room and plopped herself on the sofa. Anthony remained standing near the arm of the sofa close to where she was sitting. He looked down at her.

"JJ, you are working hard now because it's like an addiction and because you are trying to prove something to yourself, Chantal, and the whole of TV3, as far as I can see," said Anthony, working himself into a rant.

"Right you are Anthony Brown! I've got something to prove to myself and all TV3. What's wrong with that?"

"Nothing, JJ, as long as you are not sacrificing your relationships with the people who love and care about you."

"Is that what you think that I'm doing, sacrificing my relationships?"

"Yes! I'm calling it like I see it."

"Clearly you need to have your eyes and your head checked."

"I came here to spend some time with you, not engage in a war of words. I don't appreciate you calling me stupid, either."

"Now you are hearing things!"

"Oh, so now I'm blind, dumb and deaf?"

"Anthony, you really need to calm right down!"

"Me calm down! JJ, you really need to take a good look in the mirror."

"So, now you want to pluck out my hairs and ridicule me because I want to climb the ladder. I was raised to be all that I can be and that's the road that I'm on! If you can't handle this, then we really need to think carefully about *us* and if there is any kind of a future together."

"JJ, I have supported you and your drive for success since we met. However, you are being consumed by your quest. You've made work the end all and be all. What if they fire you one day! What would you do then?"

"Fire me? My hard work is supposed to insulate me from being fired. This is what *you* don't get."

"I get it alright! You are hell bent on working yourself into an early grave. Do you think these long hours, seven days a week are sustainable?"

"I'm relatively young, and fit. From where I stand, I can manage it."

"JJ, I don't think you are in a headspace to hear anything that I have said or that I still have to say. Sorry, I barged in on you. Why don't you get back to your work? I'm gone!"

"As a matter of fact, I had just finished reading a reference letter when you knocked on my door."

"Reference letter?"

"Yes, I have applied for the new VP of Sales position. I am going to be the first VP of the new stand-alone sales company that TV3 is creating!"

"What? If you are putting in so many hours now, what is going to happen when you become the VP? Your day will expand to twenty-five hours per day, eight days per week?

"If twenty-five hours per day is what it takes, then that's what it takes!"

"I've heard enough. I'm tired. Goodnight, JJ. I'm gone." He let himself out and slammed the door behind him.

As he walked down the hall to the elevators, he wondered what more he could do or say to make Jewelle see things from his point of view. He was heartsick. From their first meeting, he knew that he loved her, and this was the woman he wanted to share the rest of his life with.

After Anthony left, she locked the front door, leaned against it for a spell before walking over to the hall mirror. There she stood and uttered, "Mirror, mirror on the wall, am I truly blinded by the brass ring?"

She stood still listening for an answer. She didn't get one. Disappointed, she went to bed and eventually fell asleep reading a *Broadcast and Cable* magazine.

Six

The Interview

Jewelle fretted over her fight with Anthony and waited for him to call. He didn't. The third day came and went. Getting worried, she swallowed her pride and called him on his cell. The phone rang a few times before Anthony picked up.

"Hey Jewelle," he said coolly.

"Hi Anthony, how have you been?" she asked softly.

"How do you think I've been?"

"Well, our last visit did not go well ..."

"I'm glad you noticed."

"We need to talk, Anthony. Why don't you drop by for dinner this evening? I'll make your favourite, Cornish hen and wild rice."

There was an awkward silence before Anthony said, "I've made plans to go out with a few friends who I haven't seen for a while. It's boys' night out. I will take a rain check."

"So, your boys are more important than us," she said, keeping a lid on her anger.

"No. No, they are not. But I *value* their friendship."

Anthony's emphasis on value stung Jewelle. He was right that she was taking him for granted, but she just couldn't allow herself to admit it. Not now. Not at this moment.

"Alright then, you let me know when you'd like to get together. I have no plans except to prep for my upcoming interview."

"When is it?"

"I'm not sure. Just waiting for them to confirm the date and time."

"I'm confident the job is yours for the taking," he said. "You put a whole lot of time and energy into your work."

Jewelle considered letting the barely veiled dig slide. But she couldn't: "Well, I will certainly put in the time to make sure I land on top," she said enthusiastically.

"You always do," said Anthony dispassionately.

"Thanks for your encouragement," said Jewelle brusquely.

"I've got to go. Will call you soon." He hung up.

Jewelle put down the phone. She felt hurt and angry and could feel the blood pounding in her ears. Why did Anthony want her to feel guilty for being ambitious? Well, she didn't, and he would have to live with this or not.

Jewelle had dared to go where no other TV3 sales executive of colour had gone before—the boardrooms of major TV stations, business class travel, and dining at five-star restaurants. She had worked hard, very hard, to get to this place. Now, it was time to climb to a higher rung on the career ladder.

Over the next couple of weeks, Jewelle worked hard to come up with creative program packages that would allow her to meet her new sales targets. While she worked, the nail-biting wait for confirmation of an interview was getting to her. On the outside, she appeared calm, cool, and collected. But inside, she was anxious and nervous about the job interview and the possibility of Chantal becoming her new boss. Each time this thought entered her mind, she swatted it aside and comforted herself with her stellar sales record. Since she started, she had consistently improved TV3's bottom line. Finally, after weeks of turmoil, she received confirmation of her interview date and time.

Since submitting her application, Jewelle had begun the process of preparing for her interview. She researched interview questions and prepared answers for them. Every evening, she carved out a few hours to stage a mock interview in front of the hall mirror while dressed in the suit that she planned to wear. She role played the part of the interviewer and interviewee:

"So, tell us about yourself."

"I'm very curious about our world and its inhabitants. The more I travel, the more I have observed that we humans are more alike than not, no matter where we find ourselves on the planet. At work, I am a highly driven professional who takes great pride in solving programming problems for my clients and prospective clients. On a one-to-one, human level, they sense my genuine interest in them, and that makes transactions go smoothly."

"What are your short- to mid-term career goals?"

"My current position as an international sales executive has satisfied my short-term career goals. It has allowed me to travel, meet interesting people, and use my language, interpersonal, and sales skills. Now, my mid-term career goal is to advance to a management position, which will allow me to take on bigger responsibilities including budgeting, staffing, etcetera."

"What do you consider to be your most significant sales achievement to date?"

"When I started in sales four years ago, TV3 was selling very little in South America. I requested this territory. After making several trips to Brazil, Mexico, and Argentina, I established and managed new relationships with broadcasters and video distributors. Within eighteen months, I tripled sales by expanding the client base and selling larger program packages. Since then, South America has become a key revenue-generating territory for TV3."

"Why are you the best candidate for the job?"

"I am the best person for this job because I have the right combination of skills and experience that sets me apart. Since I started in sales, I have consistently surpassed my targets. I am an organized, flexible, resilient, and resourceful person who has excellent people and communications skills that can be used to motivate and inspire a sales team to do better and to do more. I love television sales and I can deliver exceptional results for TV3. Over the last two years, I have taken a few management courses. My passion for this industry and TV3's programs drives me to excel every day."

"Tell us about a time that you did not get along with one of your colleagues."

"The sales business is very competitive not only between companies but within companies. Every salesperson is trying to hit their targets and is focused on this goal. So, there are periods of jostling to get and hold on to information that may give you an edge. My fellow international sales colleague and I have very different communication styles. I am very to the point whereas my colleague has a very round-about way of expressing herself. Initially this really got on my nerves. I then took her out to lunch to have a frank discussion about our differences. We agreed to be civil to each other and work together for the good of the company."

Jewelle wanted to be truthful but realized that if she spoke honestly about her relationship with Chantal, she'd ruin her chance of getting the job. She thought long and hard about the "right" answer to this question.

Every day prior to her interview, Jewelle rehearsed her answers to the interview questions. She repeated them so many times that she knew them by heart. However, she realized that the point was not to regurgitate the answers but to deliver them as a flawless performance.

At the office, things carried on as usual. Jewelle continued to put in long hours as she pushed to generate more sales. Heather, as usual, was creative and had a can-do approach to all challenges. During one brainstorming session with Jewelle, she came up with the idea to re-edit a children's series to create two new series of shorts. Jewelle ran with this idea and suggested that one of the new series could be opened and closed by a bubbly young host and the other by an animated character. Over the next couple of days, Jewelle and Heather secretly worked on developing the pitch package that she wanted to present to Marg, the head of the department. Jewelle asked Heather to set up a meeting with Marg, which slated in at 10:00 the following morning. Jewelle was thrilled. It was going to be a memorable day—her winning pitch in the morning and her winning interview in the afternoon. She asked Heather to meet her at 7:00 a.m., so that they could make copies of the pitch packages without Chantal being around.

In the morning, Jewelle arrived ahead of Heather and signed them in at the security desk. While she waited, she took off her spring coat and folded it over her right arm. A few minutes later, Heather arrived.

"Morning Jewelle," she said in her lilting Newfoundland accent, walking over to the security desk to show her ID and then over to the elevator where Jewelle had already pressed the up button. As the elevator climbed, Heather said, "You look great! This is your big day. I am sooooo excited about this new company and your interview," she continued.

"I'm even more excited because I have figured out where and how much revenue I can generate from these new packages. Now, I *know* that I will generate the additional half a million. This will get the new company off to a great start. And, I'm soooo ready for the interview. I have been prepping for the last couple of weeks."

"I'm sure you have been."

"Heather, I can't thank you enough for giving your idea to me. Your generosity will not be forgotten. Let's do lunch tomorrow, my treat!"

"Jewelle, you have been good to me, chile. Some of the others in the department just look past and through me. I'm glad I could be of some help."

When the elevator stopped on their floor, they exited and walked the long corridor chit-chatting about life at TV3. As soon as they entered the sales department, they heard the hum of the photocopier.

Intrigued, Jewelle asked, "Who could be here already?"

"We'll find out soon enough," answered Heather.

They walked together, in silence, to the photocopy room. Chantal was busily working a machine.

"Hello ladies! How are you on this glorious morning?" Musical notes trailed behind each word that floated from her mouth.

Jewelle and Heather raised their eyebrows and looked at each other quizzically. Chantal's cheerfulness unnerved them.

"You're some cheery, Chantal," said Heather loudly.

"Aren't I always?" chirped Chantal.

"No!" said Heather and Jewelle in unison.

"That's just your opinion. Anyhow, I am done here. The photocopier is all yours." She swept past them and floated down the hall.

"I wonder what she's up to," said Jewelle, gritting her teeth.

"Whatever it is, we'll know soon enough," said Heather. "There are no secrets at TV3!"

Jewelle took the master copy of the pitch package from her tote bag and handed it to Heather. "Please make four copies. I'll be in my office." Walking, Jewelle had a bounce in her step. She was confident that her pitch would be well-received, and it would better position her for the VP job. When she got back to her office, she hung her spring coat on the hook behind the door, put her tote bag in her bottom drawer, booted up her computer and sat behind her desk. The red message light on her phone was blinking. She punched in the voicemail code and put the phone on speaker. The first couple of messages were from clients inquiring about the status of the delivery of their masters, next was from the posse: "JJ, we are all here," said Bernie, then the others chimed in: "Hey JJ!"

Bernie continued, "Good luck with the interview."

Camilla added, "You've got this! Call us as soon as you get the good news!"

And Maxine chimed in, "Looking forward to dinner soon."

The last message was from her mother. "Jewelle, I know we spoke yesterday, but I just wanted to let you know that I said a special prayer for you. And remember that what is fi yu cyan be un fi yu."

Jewelle smiled at this last bit of Jamaica folk wisdom. "What is yours must be yours." A gentle knock on the door brought her back from her reflection. It was Heather.

"Here are the copies, JJ. I will knock on your door at 9:55."

"Thanks Heather. Thanks for everything."

"Happy to be of service."

When Heather left, closing the door behind her, Jewelle quietly thanked God for the blessing of TV3, her mother, her family, Anthony, and Heather. She was truly blessed that she loved and was loved by family, friends, and colleagues. Over the next couple of hours, she replied to emails and started developing a prospecting list for the new shows to pre-sell to clients. The time slipped by quickly and soon Heather knocked on the door again.

Poking in her head a smiling Heather said, "It's showtime! Knock her dead."

"I just want to dazzle and amaze. We need her alive to greenlight the productions," quipped Jewelle with a wink. They both laughed.

Jewelle left her office to walk down the hall to Marg's. As she neared Chantal's office, she tensed up but kept her head straight. Arriving at Marg's office, she knocked firmly on the door.

"Come in Jewelle," said her boss.

"Thanks for seeing me on such short notice," Jewelle answered, walking over to the meeting area in the office, which had a very warm and homey feel. The walls were covered with various mounted posters of various TV3 programs, and the bookshelf was home to tchotchkes—small brass, glass and wooden sculptures, a few seashells, and framed photographs of family members.

"No trouble at all. From what little Heather shared, it sounds as though you two have come up with an exciting program proposal."

Marg sat at the head of the table with Jewelle to the right of her. She handed Marg a copy of the proposal.

"Well to be totally honest, it was Heather who led the charge on this project. I simply fine-tuned it."

"I'm glad you recognized Heather's contribution. She really is a gem. We are lucky to have her."

"I totally agree," stated Jewelle amiably.

"Well, what have you got?"

"As a response to the increase in our revenue targets, it's evident that we need fresh titles to offer our clients and prospects. A quick way of getting some new content that is saleable is to re-edit some existing shows. I have identified two children's series with live action segments that could be lifted and used to create a new stand-alone series. In one series, the live action segments are centered on animals and the other on flowers and trees."

Marg interrupted her, "Jewelle, please allow me a few minutes to go through the proposal before you go on." As Marg leafed through the proposal, Jewelle watched the expression on her face transfer from light and pleasant to dark and stormy. Her body stiffened.

"Jewelle, your proposal is almost identical to the one that Chantal presented to me an hour ago. Did you collaborate with her?"

"No! The only person who knew about this proposal was Heather. She worked with me," said Jewelle irritably.

"I don't know how this situation has come about. But what I do know is that I got approval from the chair, Mr. Levy, to move forward with re-editing the shows. This initiative has been recognized as Chantal's. I'm so sorry."

Jewelle was speechless.

"She stole our idea! Now, I know why she was in so early and why she was so cheery."

"Jewelle, I understand that you are upset but what proof do you have that Chantal stole your idea? You can't just accuse her ..."

Jewelle momentarily forgot all protocol when she jumped out of her seat and raised her voice. "Really? Proof? Why do I have to be the one to prove anything? You don't have to answer that. Sorry, I wasted your time," said Jewelle, seething with rage.

"You didn't waste my time. I know you are upset but try to shake it off and focus on your interview later today."

Jewelle took up her proposal, and hurried out of Marg's office slamming the door behind her. I should have smelled a rat this morning when Heather and I met her in the photocopy room, thought Jewelle. How did she get her nasty little hands on a copy of my proposal, wondered Jewelle as she made her way to Heather's desk?

"Heather, come into my office," Jewelle barked.

Once inside with the door closed behind them, Jewelle told Heather the whole sorry tale of what Chantal had done.

"What an extraordinary bitch!" hissed Heather. "How did she get her hands on a copy of the proposal? I was on my desk for most of the day except for the short time I went down to the copyright department. But I was careful to put away everything before I left my desk. What are you going to do?"

"At this point, there's nothing that I can do. I have *no* proof!"

"We can't just take this lying down," said Heather.

"I agree but I can't take it on right now. My interview is at two o'clock. I must get myself together. I am going out for a walk."

"Anything that I can do to help?" asked Heather quietly.

"Yes, keep that woman away from me or this may be the day that I take her out," seethed Jewelle. She grabbed her handbag from her bottom drawer and stormed out the door.

Out on the street, Jewelle's anger was tinged with sadness. She felt impotent and disconnected from the outcome of the meeting with Marg. What should have been an extraordinary day in her life, in her career, was turned upside down. Her head felt heavy, weighed down by a million competing and clashing thoughts. Jewelle was disappointed that Marg had not attempted to launch an investigation into the true origins of the program proposal. She reminded herself that she still had another opportunity to put Chantal in her place by securing the VP of Sales and Distribution job in the new company.

Jewelle decided to go to a nearby parkette to relax and try to shake off her cares. As she walked along, she scanned the crowds of people jostling for space on the sidewalk, mothers sandwiched by young children on either side of them, a hot dog vendor, young men and women displaying a wide range of styles and attitudes—the preppies, buttoned-down and buttoned-up; the rebels, tattooed and pierced; the fashionistas, glammed and gamed; the seniors, slowed but moving with the help of a cane or walker; the business types, suited and hurried.

At the end of the second block, she turned right on a side street and made her way to the parkette. There, she sat on a bench, turned her face up to the sun, feeling it caress her face. She tried to shake loose the disappointing meeting with Marg, but it would not budge. It was anchored in her thoughts. Attempting to distract herself, she watched the pigeons as they cooed while scrounging for food. Seemingly, they didn't have a care in the world. But on second thought, Jewelle recognized that they too had to overcome daily challenges as they navigated tall glass towers and managed their encounters with curious dogs and not-so-well-meaning people.

Jewelle allowed her thoughts to drift for a while. No sooner had she taken out her interview notes than an old woman being hauled by a large willful dog entered the parkette. "Slow down Jackson! Slow down! Sit, Jackson, sit! There now, be a good dog, Jackson," the woman begged her pet. Her entreaties fell on deaf ears. The more she begged, the harder Jackson pulled, and the louder Jackson barked. Jewelle was grateful that Jackson pulled his owner straight out of the parkette.

Over the next couple of hours, she reviewed her notes, periodically distracted by the activities in the park. At quarter past one, she headed back to TV3. As she marched up the street, she could feel her heart picking up speed with each step that brought her closer to the building. Just as she was about to enter the building, she noticed a man who looked like Anthony walking down the street with a pretty, young woman by his side. She stopped and waited for them to get closer. Her heart began to race. The young woman hugged Anthony. He lifted her off the ground and twirled her around. Jewelle rushed out of the building, gasping for air as she confronted her boyfriend.

"Who is this?" Jewelle asked, pointing at the young woman, who froze, her eyes popping.

"Hello to you too, JJ", answered Anthony calmly. "If you must know, this is Cheryl ..."

Jewelle held up a finger, interrupting him mid-sentence. Caught between rage and her work pressures, she glanced at her watch. She spun around and rushed back towards the building, leaving Anthony and Cheryl gobsmacked.

Inside the building, she started to breathe deeply to calm herself as thoughts of Anthony and his side-chick invaded her thoughts. Her guilt of taking Anthony for granted was shattered by humiliating jealousy and terror of abandonment. Walking through the lobby, Jewelle noticed a few of her colleagues milling about. She avoided them, beelining for the elevator. As it climbed, she became increasingly agitated wondering how long

Anthony has been stepping out on her and if his boys' night out was just a cover for his rendezvous with the barely twenty *young girl.*

She chided herself for obsessing about the encounter and told herself to shake it off and focus on the interview ahead. Jewelle made a quick stop at the washroom to check her make-up. In the washroom, she took her Mac compact from her cosmetic bag, powdered her face to remove the shine and reapplied Oh Baby, her barely there, Mac lip gloss. Her locks were pulled back and twisted into a neat and tidy bun that she secured with a few more hair pins. Pleased that she looked interview ready, Jewelle tucked in her off white and red abstract print silk blouse, pulled down her black high-waisted pencil skirt and buttoned the form-fitting jacket that completed the perfect suit by Sandra Angelozzi, one of her favourite Canadian designers. It was one forty-five. "I've got this!" she told herself over and over. It was showtime!

Jewelle walked confidently into the HR Department. The receptionist recognized her and invited her to sit in the waiting area. She seated herself on the sofa and quietly said a prayer asking for peace, focus, and total recall. Looking around she noticed a stack of trade magazines and selected *Playback,* Canada's national TV and film daily. Jewelle was mindlessly leafing through it when the door opened. A draft swept into the room. She looked up. It was Chantal sweeping past her to the receptionist's desk where she handed over an envelope. "These are the references that were requested," she said loud enough for Jewelle to hear.

"Hey Jewelle, fancy seeing *you* here," Chantal smirked.

Jewelle was speechless. Having accomplished her mission, Chantal spun around, took the full measure of her rival, and walked out of HR without uttering another word. She didn't need to. Jewelle held her tongue and asked herself, what would Oprah do? The answer came swiftly. "Keep her eyes on the prize." Even so, she was rattled.

A few minutes before two o'clock, the HR manager came out to greet Jewelle and walk her into the interview room. Marg was already seated. She told Jewelle where to sit on the far side of the highly polished, rectangular rosewood boardroom table. The HR manager and Marg each had a brown, letter-size folder, and a notepad in front of them. The room was dull, utilitarian. Marg welcomed her, and they exchanged a few pleasantries before starting the interview.

"So, tell us about yourself," the HR Manager said.

Jewelle paused, then answered the question flawlessly. Marg and the HR manager both smiled and took notes. Their facial expressions gave away nothing. On and on the interview went, questions alternating between Marg and the HR manager as if they were a tennis team. Jewelle's preparation was paying off. She had delivered a thorough answer as to why she was the best person for the job. She talked about her people skills, her excellent sales record and her passion for TV3's programs. She started to relax and feel comfortable. Then, they dropped the bomb.

"Tell us about the time that you did not get along with one of your colleagues."

Jewelle choked. She sputtered, winding up tightly. She heard herself spinning around the question while Marg and the HR Manager wrote furiously on their notepads. No matter how hard she tried to recall the answer she had prepared for this very question, she couldn't put it together. Her mind was crowded with negative thoughts of Chantal and all the nasty tricks she had pulled since her arrival at TV3. Like Humpty Dumpty, Jewelle felt she just had a great fall.

"I hope I have answered the question satisfactorily," Jewelle said, trying to sound more confident than she felt.

They nodded sympathetically. Looking across the table at the two of them, she felt that she had ruined her chances. However, she reminded herself that she had successfully answered all the other questions, and surely one weak response couldn't outweigh all the others. They completed the last of their notes, put down their pens and looked directly at Jewelle.

"Do you have any questions for us?" asked the HR Manager.

"Yes. Will there be second interviews and if so, how soon?"

"We have a strong field of candidates and are confident that we will be able to make a selection from this group."

"How soon will you make a decision?" asked Jewelle.

"Within the next couple of days," replied the HR Manager.

"That's great!"

"If you don't have any other questions, I'd like to thank you for coming in," said Marg. She stood up and the HR Manager followed. They walked around the table to where Jewelle was standing and shook her hand. She thanked them, and they walked her to the boardroom door, and turned around closing the door behind them.

How dare Chantal taint her opportunity! Jewelle fumed as she marched back to her office. She felt like an Olympic athlete who had trained for years and missed out on competing because of an injury or some other mishap. Wearily, she flung herself into her chair and picked up the phone to call her mother. Just as she punched in a few of the numbers, there was a knock on her door. She returned the phone to the cradle.

"Come in," she said glumly. Heather opened the door and entered quickly, closing it behind her.

"So, how did it go?" she asked excitedly.

"It went well but I really messed up on the last interview question. They asked me how I would deal with a colleague I had problems with. Try as I might, I just couldn't answer the question even though I prepared for it. And I was in too much of a tailspin to try to fix things by asking a few solid questions about the scope of the new job and the opportunities to shape and grow a successful company. Not happy about this. But I can't change it now."

"Don't worry about it. One bad answer means that you got at least ninety percent right," said Heather smiling.

Jewelle was unconvinced. "Well, in a few days, we will know who came out on top. By the way, just a few minutes before my interview, Chantal waltzed into HR to drop off her references. I heard her tell the receptionist what was in the envelope."

"You've got to be kidding me!" said Heather angrily.

"I wish I was," replied Jewelle wearily.

"That woman needs to be taught a lesson or two. If she keeps this up, it won't be long. Trust me," said a highly aggravated Heather.

"Well Heather, thanks for all your support. As soon as I hear anything, you'll be the first to know. I have to make a few calls."

That was Heather's cue to make her exit. Before doing so, she gave Jewelle a hug and told her that everything would work out just fine.

After Heather left, Jewelle called her mother. Adele picked up on the first ring.

"Jewelle, I've been sitting here waiting to hear from you. How did it go?"

Jewelle hesitated before answering.

"Are you there?" Adele asked anxiously.

"Yes Mother, I'm here. It went well. But," she faltered. "But I didn't answer one of the questions well. It was an important one," said Jewelle despairingly.

"You only had a problem with one question, so why do you sound so?"

"Mother, you don't understand. It was an important question!" said Jewelle, getting more and more exasperated.

"I know, I am no PhD, but I have lots of common sense which some say is not so common. So, you are telling me that you answered most of the questions well but had problems with just one, and you sound so defeated. What is really going on?"

Reluctantly, Jewelle told Adele about her HR encounter with Chantal.

"I have already told you not to let this *mawga* wretch of a woman get on top of your head. Clearly that's where she wants to climb," said Adele pausing to catch her breath. "Well, I am confident that it is not as bad as you think it is. Don't be so hard on yourself. If things don't work out this time, I am sure there will be other opportunities."

Jewelle was silent. She just didn't have the emotional strength nor desire to engage in a battle with her mother.

"Mother, there is someone knocking at my door. I will give you a call tomorrow."

"Alright then, Jewelle. Thanks for calling. Shoulders up, head up. Bye for now."

The office grapevine was on the verge of collapse under the weight of speculation about who won the VP of Sales and Distribution competition. Jewelle kept her head down and carried on with her routine—frantic back-to-back meetings, phone calls, faxes and emails. As she rushed about, she tried not to think about her recent interview and the possible outcome.

One afternoon, when she got back from a late lunch, Heather told her that HR had called and asked that she come to the office at three. She checked her watch. It was 2:00 p.m. To calm her nerves, she decided to screen the rough cut of a new one-off documentary about the Great Lakes. Images of water always calmed Jewelle. The hour went by quickly. At two fifty-five, she walked down the hall to HR.

The receptionist instructed her to go directly to the board-room where Marg and the HR Manager were awaiting her arrival. The door was closed, and she knocked before entering.

"Hello Jewelle," said Marg in a neutral tone.

Marg and the HR Manager were both sitting in the same place they sat during the interview.

"Well, Jewelle," said Marg, "I'm sure you know why you are here. So, I will just get right to it. You did very well during your interview. Your answers to most of the questions were comprehensive and clear. However, you really struggled with the question about working with a difficult colleague."

Now it was the HR Manager's turn. "As you are aware, the role of a Vice President of a company, particularly a new enterprise is to lead by example and this requires working with all kinds of people, including the difficult and not so pleasant. From your answer, we concluded that it would be challenging for you to work with a colleague with whom you had different approaches and points of view," said the HR Manager.

"One candidate scored higher than you did, and we have offered her the position. We have already notified her," said Marg.

"As the successful candidate has already been notified, may I ask who he or she is?" Jewelle asked.

Marg and the HR Manager looked at each other, unsure of which one should deliver the bitter pill. The HR Manager did the deed. "The position was offered to Chantal Mercier," she said without emotion.

Jewelle could feel her blood pressure rising, but she remained calm.

"What is her start date?" she asked quietly.

"Chantal will assume her new duties in two weeks," said Marg.

"For what it's worth, you did very well during the interview," the HR Manager reiterated.

"But not well enough," said Jewelle coolly. "Thank you for your time." She got up and headed for the door. "I will see myself out."

As she walked past the receptionist's desk, she avoided eye contact and bolted out. Not wanting to face Heather and others immediately, she took the elevator down to the ground floor where she walked around for a while. She wanted to call Anthony, but her cellphone was in her handbag in her office.

Reluctantly, she climbed back on the elevator and went back to the sales department. Heather was sitting in her office waiting for her.

"Hi Jewelle. I've heard the news. Are you okay," she asked anxiously?

"I've felt better," said Jewelle bitterly. "I screwed up, and they gave the job to that conniving, lying and underfed woman."

"What are we going to do?" grumbled Heather.

"Well, that's just what I'm going to have to figure out because I know that I can't work with that woman, least of all with her as my boss!" said Jewelle.

"If you plan to leave, please give me a heads-up before you do," asked Heather.

"Heather, I wouldn't leave without giving you ample warning."

After Heather left, Jewelle felt like having a good cry, but the tears wouldn't come. After all, what was she really crying about? This situation was just another disappointment to overcome. Didn't her late grandmother used to say that "every disappointment is meant for an appointment!" She didn't yet know what that appointment could be, but time would certainly tell. For now, she would show Marg, the HR Manager, and the rest of the staff that she was a bigger person than they allowed. With that thought, she walked over to Chantal's office, knocked on the door and let herself in before any invitation. "Hello Chantal, I guess the best woman won. Congratulations!"

"Why, thank you Jewelle. I didn't think you'd be so gracious about it," said Chantal gaily.

"I learned a long time ago that I have to pick battles. I may have lost this one, but I fully intend to win the war," Jewelle said coolly and left Chantal to think about what she said.

By the end of the day, her mood was at an all-time low—fueled by anger, resentment that her idea for the new series was stolen, Anthony's side chick, the daily pressures of dealing

with Chantal—so on her way home, she stopped at the neighbourhood LCBO to treat herself to a bottle her favourite French
wine, Sancerre red.

When Jewelle got home that evening, the red light was
flashing on her phone. She was certain that all her friends had
called to hear the good news. Since the news was not good,
and she was feeling tired, she decided it was best to keep her
own company. Besides, she was getting together with her posse
tomorrow evening, and she'd fill them in then. She was certain
that her mother had already spread the news amongst family
members. The news eventually would be delivered to Anthony,
Johann and Thérèse. The truth was, she needed time and space
to process the day's trials. Self-care beckoned.

She dropped her bags and marched into the bathroom to set
a bubble bath with two Lush brand Blue Skies and White Fluffy
Clouds bath bombs. While the bath was filling, she put on an
Aretha Franklin record, picked up the bottle of wine, went to
the kitchen, opened it, and poured some into a beautiful wine-
glass with an ornate stem. She took a generous sip and walked
back to the dining room where she lit a sweet grass scented
candle. Wine and candle in hand, Jewelle made her way back
to the bathroom. There, she placed the candle in one corner,
the glass of wine in the other, then turned off the tap. She got
undressed, folded her clothes, and lay them on top of the toilet
tank before stepping into the inviting warm water. Jewelle lay
back, stretched out her legs, and slowly drank the wine, washing
away the day and its disappointments.

Seven

Girls' Night Out

Jewelle's girlfriends, a.k.a. the posse, epitomize Toronto's much lauded multicultural population: Bernie Turner, Jamaican born and British raised, posh British accent obscuring the other twang, Jamaican patois. Successful as a software sales rep, her hard won position allowed for no time or empathy for the questionable "artistes" who pursue indie production, and she was not shy about letting them know. Bernie was single and still seeking. Melanie Ho Sang, single and desperate, Canadian born to a well-to-do Chinese Jamaican family, was a perennial scholar who dreamt of meeting "Mr. Right" in one of her classes. Maxine Martin, a bitter left-leaning Nova Scotia-born independent documentary filmmaker, was fed up with broadcasters speculating on the likes and dislikes of Canadian audiences. Although frustrated by the system, she was committed to fighting on. She was over men. Camilla Kupova, a broadcast executive, of Slovakian heritage, working for a large commercial channel, hunted for a man of serious means to support her lifestyle of brands, brands, and more brands. Joy Singh, a nurse, Canadian born to Trinidadian parents, had a father of South Asian origins and a Black mother. Like Jewelle, Joy was in a stable long-term relationship.

Over the years members of the posse learned to get over and accept their differences to make the friendships work. Bernie, the alpha female of the group, worked all their nerves, but they were all thankful for her straightforwardness and her loyalty to members of the posse. Besides, if you were ever in a crisis, you could rest assured, she'd keep her head and sort things out. Yes, nerves and feelings were sometimes bruised, but they always found a way to navigate their clashes.

Jewelle and the posse had been regulars at The Real Jerk since the restaurant opened. The large sunglass-wearing sun logo outside the restaurant welcomed patrons out of the Canadian cold. The ladies loved the reggae music that throbbed in the background as well as the fact that the restaurant was owned and operated by a Jamaican couple, Ed and Lily Pottinger, who had built this successful business from scratch. Miss Lily's warm smile added to the ambience of the restaurant.

The posse arrived on time to avoid JJ's dressing-down— "Didn't we agree to meet at 7:00? It's now 7:10! I swear you are all going to be late for your own funerals," she'd rail. They had all become accustomed to her quirkiness about being on time. Jewelle was, of course, already there waiting for them. Each one of the women was fashionably turned out in some shade of black, perfectly arched eyebrows on faces beautifully made up and nails brightly lacquered. Camilla's fashion choices routinely turned heads and raised eyebrows, sometimes because they were questionable. She had yet to learn that expensive labels didn't always get it right.

The waitress walked Jewelle's posse over to the table where Jewelle was sitting with menus ready to check out.

"Surprise, surprise, look who's already here," said a smiling Bernie, leading the group, in single file, like the Pied Piper.

Bernie Turner and Jewelle met during one of the many film festivals in Toronto. It was not love at first sight. Bernie had tried to jump the queue, and Jewelle called her out. Bernie's reaction was to heatedly ask, "Who the hell do you think you are?" arms akimbo.

"They call me Miss Joseph!" spat back Jewelle, channeling Sydney Poitier's character from *In the Heat of the Night*. Bernie picked up on Jewelle's reference, they both burst out laughing, and that was the start of a long and rocky friendship.

"Well don't just sit there JJ, get up and let's get a good look at you," ordered Bernie. "Lord knows it may be another six months before we see you again," she continued.

Before Bernie made any more demands, Jewelle was on her feet. She pasted on a smile, turned around slowly then walked past the receiving line. When she hugged Bernie, her friend stepped back and exclaimed, "What's going on, JJ? I noticed you looked slimmer when you stood up but now, I'm sure. I felt every one of your ribs."

Jewelle wondered why Bernie was creating all this excitement about her weight when Bernie herself was a tall rangy woman who reminded Jewelle of Popeye's other half, Olive Oyl, with her baguette-sized arms and legs.

"I'd better just stop now so that everybody can get their hug," said Bernie jauntily while casting her eagle eye over the outfits of her friends as they hugged Jewelle.

Next in line was Melanie, followed by Camilla, then Maxine and lastly, Joy who held onto Jewelle a little longer as though to comfort her. Hugs exchanged; the ladies sat down in the booth that had been set up for them.

"Ladies before we get talking, I think we should place our orders," suggested Jewelle. She continued, "If everyone likes Wolf Blass, how about a bottle of red and a bottle of white?"

Bernie, as always, was the first to speak up.

"That sounds great! What do you guys think?" asked Bernie as a courtesy because they all knew that her endorsement of the Wolf Blass red and white meant that this was *the* selection.

"We are fine with Jewelle's suggestion," answered Melanie pointedly.

"Well, that settles that. Now, does everyone know what they'd like to eat?" asked Jewelle trying her best to maintain order and keep things moving. "We should order now because it's going to get busier and then we'll have to wait a long time for our food. Agreed?"

They all nodded and scanned the menus quickly. Jewelle signaled for the black uniformed waitress, who indicated that she'd attend to them as soon as she had finished with the gentleman who was dining alone.

"Ladies, I haven't seen most of you for a long time," the waitress said jovially when she returned. "Welcome back! How can I help you?"

They ordered the wine, fried plantain as a starter, and their meals—JJ, red pea soup; Bernie, oxtail with rice and peas; Melanie, es fish and festival; Maxine, curry goat with plain rice; Camilla, shrimp roti; Joy, ackee and saltfish with yam, green bananas, and boiled dumpling.

"One more bit of housekeeping, ladies, all cellphones off. All emergencies will have to be dealt with at the end of our chinwag," said Bernie vehemently.

They fished their phones from their handbags, turned them off and returned them to their respective homes.

When the waitress arrived with the two bottles of wine and the fried plantain, Bernie took over from JJ. "Show of hands for red?" she asked and counted quickly. "Show of hands for white?" It was an even split, three reds and three whites. When their glasses were fully charged, Bernie proposed a toast, "To JJ's promotion and friendship!"

As Bernie was about to clink Jewelle's glass, Jewelle lowered her glass and set it down on the table. She looked uncomfortable.

"Ladies," she sputtered. "I ... did ... not ... get ... the ... job," she continued pausing, for emphasis, between each word. "And this is why I didn't return your calls last night."

Posse members, shocked into silence, looked from one to another searching each other's faces for answers. Bernie broke the silence.

"We figured you and Anthony were celebrating and that's why we didn't hear from you and since we were seeing you soon, we didn't call again. JJ, what happened?" asked Bernie with concern.

"I will spare you all the gruesome details. Short version, I really messed up on an important interview question. My nemesis Chantal showed up in HR while I was waiting for my interview," she added. A sour look registered on her face. "And before the interview, Anthony appeared out of nowhere with a pretty young woman who I assumed was a side chick. I got rattled. Chantal got the job. I have no idea what to do next."

"Next?" asked Bernie. "What about Anthony? Who is the young woman?"

"Ladies, I made a mess. Turns out she is one of Anthony's cousins visiting from Trinidad. He tried to introduce her to me, but I blew up and rushed off. When I got back to my office after the interview, Anthony left me a very angry, detailed message reminding me that he had told me about his cousin's visit."

Silence fell over the group. Bernie was the first to speak.

"JJ, Anthony isn't even my boyfriend, and I can tell you that he's not that kind of guy. But I couldn't fault him if he did step out. You don't make time for him."

"Bernie, I don't want to get into this right now. I feel awful about making assumptions about Anthony. And the interview turned into a nightmare."

"Well, JJ, you may not want 'to get into this right now,'" said Bernie, forming quotation marks with her fingers, "but I do. You may not be feeling high on yourself right now, but I just need to let you know how I feel, and I think I speak for the group. You put us on pause. A long pause and it doesn't feel good. We are always here for you no matter what we have going on. And, we all have stuff going on, whether or not there's a man around."

The women remained silent but nodded their agreement.

"As usual, Bernie has said what we were all thinking and feeling. Now you know, and now we can move on," said Joy as the others nodded in agreement.

"Ladies, I'm really, really sorry. Please forgive me is all I can say. And I will do better," said a contrite Jewelle.

She got up from her seat and walked around the table giving each of her friends a warm and lingering hug. Apology accepted, the women got back to the interview. Are you telling us dat de *mawga* woman got the job because you messed up on one interview question?" asked Maxine in disbelief.

"Yes. That's what I was told in the post-interview meeting. It's a hard pill to swallow!"

Jewelle's news fired up Maxine. "Even when you work damned hard, you still can't win! You've worked all kinds of crazy hours before this woman turned up at TV3 and continued after they hired her, and you got passed over because you flubbed one answer! Black folk have had to fight for everything since landing in the so-called new world, and we are still fighting! That's why we need to have our own things—TV stations, radio stations, production companies, et cetera. No offence, Camilla," said Maxine angrily.

"None taken!" said Camilla who was tempted to add, "We've all heard this before." She held her tongue for fear of throwing more fuel on Maxine's flaming fire.

"JJ, I'm really, really sorry things didn't work out this time around. I'm sure there'll be other opportunities in the future," said Joy sympathetically.

"Maybe. But I don't think I can work for or with Chantal. Since she started, she has been actively sabotaging me. Recently, she stole one of my ideas and presented it as her own, and it was greenlit," said Jewelle.

"What!" shouted Joy, usually the quietest of the group. "Didn't you report the theft?"

"I did but I had no proof because she presented the idea before I had a chance to, and I couldn't prove that I had the idea first."

"So, in addition to selling their shows, you need to start gathering clues like Columbo!" said Maxine sarcastically.

"For your information, Maxine, no one was murdered."

Attempting to inject some levity into the conversation, Bernie said, "Anyhow, since no one died and we are all still here, of sound mind and body, why don't we toast to health and friendship?" Bernie raised her glass and said, "Ladies, let's toast to health, friendship and an opportunity for JJ to dropkick, metaphorically speaking of course, the *mawga* woman and mek she know *we run tings, tings nuh run we.*"

The posse raised their glasses and cheered.

The fried plantain had grown cold as Jewelle and her friends chatted and commiserated about her misfortunes. They ate it just the same to soak up the wine that flowed freely. By the time their meals arrived, the wine had loosened their tongues and their appetites.

"Okay, before we dig in, who wants a piece of what from whom?" demanded Bernie.

Melanie was the first to answer. "Camilla, can I have a bit of your roti? Would you like some of my fish and a piece of festival?" asked Melanie.

"You know, I'm not going to refuse," answered Camilla smiling.

And so, the ladies continued to share their food with one another until each was satisfied. Since Jewelle had ordered soup, she was not in on the swap. She wished she had made a different choice because she enjoyed how they would create their own buffet by having a little bit of this and a little bit of that off of each other's plates. They ate ravenously. Between mouthfuls, they talked boyfriends—past and present—work, and fashion. Camilla gushed about a few new local designers she had recently discovered.

"Is that outfit you are wearing by one of your new discoveries?" asked Bernie with a little smile.

"Yes," beamed Camilla. "Do you like it?" she asked eagerly.

Melanie, Maxine, Joy and Jewelle held their breath because Camilla knew better than to ask Bernie's opinion about her fashion choices.

"Honestly Camilla, I understand the whole 'fashion forward' thing," Bernie said, using her fingers to place fashion forward between quotation marks, "but the naked truth is, there's not much here to like. I get that it's deconstructed but it just looks like a hot mess."

"Clearly we have different tastes," snapped Camilla regretting that she had entertained Bernie's opinion.

"It may not be our taste, Camilla, but *you* can definitely carry it off," said Melanie, softening the blow that Bernie had leveled.

Camilla smiled and thanked Melanie.

The group was distracted by the loud chatter coming from a group of twenty-somethings who were seated nearby. The posse had tried to tune them out when a fragment of a boyfriend drama reached their sensitive ears.

"Can you imagine him trying to tell me that lipstick on his fly was tomato sauce," bellowed the blond-wig-wearing dark brown diva.

Bernie couldn't believe what she had just heard and asked, "Ladies, did you hear?"

Members of the posse nodded in unison turning in the direction where the words came from. The posse bristled.

"Why do these young women feel they have to broadcast all of their business in public? They are about to be schooled in *mahnazs*!" said Bernie, bolting up from her seat and marching over to the table where the young women were seated. She was greeted with bewildered stares as she inserted herself between two of them, leaned in and whispered, "Which one ah yu discova di tomato sauce?"

"None of your business!" spat Blondie aggressively.

"Right you are. So, I'd like to remind you that children should be seen and *not* heard," she said softly before turning to walk back to her table.

When Bernie's words connected with Blondie's ears, she jumped up and shouted, "Who the hell do you think you are?"

The two women now had the full attention of everyone in the restaurant. Bernie spun around quickly, planted her feet, and hissed.

"They call me Bernie Turner!" Bernie threw her head back and howled with laughter, the other members of the posse joining in. They all intimately knew the story of Jewelle's and Bernie's first encounter. The "children," looking bewildered, continued spewing vitriolic remarks in the direction of the posse.

When the waitress came running, to find out what was going on, Bernie assured her that the matter was settled and ordered more wine for good measure.

"My treat, ladies," Bernie said with a mischievous wink and chuckled. "Now back to our affairs, so to speak."

Melanie bit the bait. "Bernie, I wish there was something new to report in the male department. I have been keeping a close eye on my fellow students and some of the professors, but the ones who have got some personality and panache have little or no strength of cash and nothing else to offer for that matter. The ones who have got some educational and career strength, are dull, dull, dull."

"What do you expect them to offer?" asked Bernie. Before Melanie could answer, Bernie began to impersonate her, "At this point, I am looking for a man who is bringing something to the table: love, career and cash, in that order."

Melanie snickered. "Since you already know, why did you ask?"

"I was hoping there were some new things you wanted brought to the table," said Bernie with a devilish smile.

"Nothing wrong with being clear about what you want, Melanie," added Jewelle. "It's not like when we were in our 20s trying to figure out who we are and what we want. And while we were figuring things out, we were frustrating the hell out of all the men who dared to ask us out."

"I certainly remember those days," said Bernie glowing. "Ladies, we were hot, hot, hot, and we knew it."

There was a lull in the conversation as each member enjoyed their own private reminiscences. They sipped on their wine, looked around the restaurant and commented on some of the patrons. The waitress came by to ask if anyone was interested in dessert. They all declined.

"JJ, you told us about this Johann fellow that you had dinner with in France and how he liked your dress, but you haven't said a peep about Anthony except that you thought he was stepping out. What's going on?" demanded Melanie.

All eyes focused on Jewelle. She squirmed and sputtered.

"Let me just interject here, ladies," said Bernie, "the situation as I see it is JJ has the hots for Johann but isn't sure about him, and she's got some reservations about Anthony, too. Must be nice to occupy the minds and possibly other parts of two eligible men!"

"Don't go there Bernie," said Jewelle crossly. "But if you all must know, Anthony and I had a serious quarrel, and he has been very cool and distant. I have never seen him like this before."

"JJ, if Anthony sees you as little as we see you, he can't be very happy," said Melanie.

Camilla jumped in quickly to defend her friend. "JJ and I work in a very competitive industry. If we don't put in the hours, someone else will. That is just the sad truth."

"And you forgot to note that Jewelle has the added burden of being a Black woman working in a space that is still pretty monochromatic," Maxine snapped.

"I knew you'd fill in the blank," said Camilla starchily.

"Aren't we supposed to be talking about Anthony?" Bernie focused her attention on Jewelle as quickly as she had refocused the conversation, "JJ, does Anthony know that you didn't get the job?"

"No. I have been putting off calling him."

"Since I'm the only other person here with a steady partner, I think I have something to contribute," said Joy quietly.

Bernie rolled her eyes and drummed her fingers on the table before replying, "Let's have it, Joy. All of us who are unattached may actually learn something."

"Bernie, I'm not throwing shade at you or anyone here, I'm just saying that I better understand JJ's situation because I've been there. When I started at the hospital, I was working around the clock. I took every shift I could get because I was trying to save to buy a house. Before I knew it, this became my norm. Then I met Curtis."

Bernie interrupted Joy's flow. "Is this where the violins come in?" Her voice was syrupy but there was nothing sweet about it.

"Bernie, I'm not picking up what you're putting down, so I'm just going to keep it moving," said Joy calmly and firmly. "As I was saying before I was interrupted, during the first year that I started dating Curtis, I continued to work like a lunatic until Curtis told me that if I kept going at that rate, I'd have a breakdown. At first, I was just angry that he couldn't appreciate why I was working so hard. Then, one day my workaholic dad collapsed with a heart attack. I was forced to re-evaluate everything," said Joy quietly. "I still work hard but my life is more balanced. I make time to play and for family and friends."

"I remember visiting your dad in the hospital. I'm glad he made a full recovery," said Jewelle. "My aunt Constance is forever warning me that *'nerves nuh sell ah shop.'* Nerves are not replaceable when they break down," she explained for the benefit of Camilla.

"Alright, alright, I hear what everyone has had to say," Bernie cut in. "Joy, you are right. Balance is the way to go, the yin and the yang. Easier said than done. Anyhow JJ, I hope you are not just listening but hearing."

"Now, I have officially had enough of all this serious talk. I need a good laugh. Jewelle, tell us again about your aunt Constance and the vertically challenged salesman."

As the evening wore on, Jewelle and her friends chatted for hours over many glasses of red and white wine. They lost track of time and did not notice that the restaurant had emptied. When their weary waitress brought the bill and placed it on the table, Bernie grabbed it.

"Ladies, I'm feeling mighty generous tonight. This is on me," she announced, smiling broadly. "I know I'm a handful ..."

"A handful!" Camilla interjected. "I think two handfuls is a more accurate description."

They all laughed. While the waitress was processing the credit card, they hugged each other and promised to make time to see each other more often.

PART II

Eight

Boss Lady

Chantal had quickly settled into her new role. She flaunted her ascension with a makeover of her office: a giant desk with a throne-like chair, framed abstract prints on the walls, a new bookcase littered with paraphernalia gathered from trade shows over the years, and a new planter for her wheatgrass. Not contented with only an *office* makeover, she extended it to include herself. She was no longer to be addressed as Chantal but as Miss Mercier. This elevated title was supported by a completely new wardrobe consisting of barely-there skirts, sausage-casing-like jackets, garish chandelier earrings and robust perfumes that announced her arrival long before she came into view. The *look* was completed with six-inch stiletto heels.

From day one Chantal wielded her authority. She struck the first blow when she demanded daily phone logs from all staff under her supervision; office and sales territory re-assignments followed. Daily, she announced new initiatives, all flash, no substance—costly dinners to attract buyers of programs that TV3 did not sell, skids of glossy coffee table books too costly to ship that were gathering dust in TV3's storage, a glitzy promotional campaign for a series that couldn't be sold internationally. Periodically, Marg would abort one of these initiatives. The rest of the time, Chantal ran amok. She terrorized Jewelle, Heather and other department personnel with late night phone calls and never-ending tasks of a personal nature—arranging furniture delivery for her home, appliance repairs, finding plumbers and carpenters, not to mention post office runs to send and pick up personal packages. They had all begun to feel as if they had two full-time jobs: one with TV3 and another as Chantal's personal concierge.

Early one morning, Chantal summoned Jewelle to her office. As she walked in, Jewelle prayed for patience and discipline to hold her tongue. Queen Chantal was leaning back on her throne with an amused and self-satisfied look on her heavily made-up face. A brown letter-size folder sat in the middle of her desk.

"Jewelle, sit down," she commanded, motioning with her hand to the chair that she had placed in front of her desk. "I am really pleased to see how well you are adjusting to the change in leadership," said Chantal, leaning forward to open the folder.

Jewelle remained silent.

"I have been reviewing your sales record. You have done well. But as you know TV3 continues to experience a slump in ad revenues and we, TV3 Sales and Distribution Inc., are expected to make up the shortfall. Marg had increased our targets by $500,000 Canadian. However, we now need to generate more than $500,000 in additional revenues. As of today, your sales target has been increased by an additional $200,000. Based on your track record, I'm sure that you can do it. Just let me know if there's anything I can do to help you," she said with an air of finality.

Jewelle listened passively as Chantal chirped on and on. She was trying to process news of yet another increase in her sales target. "When will the new series be completed?" asked Jewelle stoically.

"They should be delivered early next month."

"Great! I have a few prospects," said Jewelle, maintaining a poker face. "If there isn't anything else, I had better get back to my desk, so that I can sell, sell, sell."

She got up, and just as she was about to close the door behind her, Chantal said, "Oh, I almost forgot. I am taking over Scandinavia which, as you know, includes Sweden. Please prepare a report of any pending deals in Sweden. The report is due by noon tomorrow."

Jewelle's head recoiled as if she had been slapped.

That's all!" said Chantal with a smug expression and an undercurrent of sadistic pleasure crossing her face.

Jewelle's blood boiled. She was livid. It was bad enough that she had lost Germany. Now Scandinavia, particularly Sweden, was being grabbed too. Jewelle was not going to let Chantal have the satisfaction of seeing her upset. She had to restrain herself from administering a slap followed by *a rahtid lick*. It was a good thing the Mandinka wasn't carrying a staff.

"You mentioned the territories that I am losing. What will they be replaced with?" asked Jewelle.

"To be honest, I hadn't thought about giving you any additional territories. Did you have something in mind?" asked Chantal.

"Yes. I'd like to take on the English-speaking Caribbean and Nigeria. I'm sure no one else wants them," Jewelle said.

"You are right about that. They don't have any money. You can have them," said Chantal gleefully.

"May I have that in writing please?" asked Jewelle. Without waiting for a reply, she walked out slamming the door behind her.

When she sat down at her desk, she thought about the loss of her territories and Chantal's perception of the Caribbean and African countries as places that no one wanted because they have no money. Yes, their license fees were low, but they did have some dollars. Chantal's dismissal of these countries, coupled with the stress of the last couple of weeks, opened the floodgates. Tears streamed down Jewelle's face and she sobbed uncontrollably, wondering how much more of this she could and would take. Difficult though it was, she would never let Chantal win. If she did leave TV3, it would be on her own terms.

When the feelings of being wronged faded, Jewelle took a copy of the MIP-TV guide and began to research Caribbean and Nigerian TV stations. There were a few Nigerian stations listed, but nothing for English-speaking Caribbean countries. She'd have to find the information elsewhere. It occurred to her that her father and a few of her girlfriends could provide her with some leads. She opened a new file on her desktop and created an Excel sheet to build her prospective Caribbean and Nigerian client list. A firm believer in working with what you have, Jewelle used the information in the MIP-TV guide to start the African prospecting list. When she got home, she would call Radcliffe, Joy, and Maxine to get leads for Jamaica, Trinidad, and Grenada. As she was completing the last entry on the spreadsheet, there was a tap on the door.

Heather poked in her head.

"Are you busy?" Heather asked, glancing over her shoulder to the hallway behind her.

"Never too busy for you. Come in," replied Jewelle brightly. She was feeling good that she had started to build a new client base and revenue stream.

"Heather, you look like you've got some juicy news."

"Well, there are a couple of things. Chantal has been giving me cash to purchase money orders to send to her parents. Who knows what exactly is going on?"

"What's your second discovery?" asked Jewelle.

"I was reviewing the company's Amex card and noted a whole bunch of personal items, mainly clothes, jewelry, and perfume. I think they are Chantal's purchases. There were also four expensive dinners with the chair of the board. Anyhow, I am giving you a copy of the statement for *your* files. For now, just put them away. I'm sure they will come in handy down the road," said Heather with a wink.

"Mum's the word. I'll put them in my handbag right away," whispered a smiling Jewelle. She reached for her bag in the bottom drawer of her desk and carefully placed the Amex statements in the inside, zippered pocket and returned the bag to the drawer.

"When I come across any other interesting documents, I will try to rain them down on you," said Heather. She chuckled before lowering her voice, "Chantal doesn't seem to realize that there are many ways to skin a rat. Ooops! I said rat."

She and Jewelle burst into laughter.

"Thanks Heather."

Pleased that Heather wanted to bring a torturous end to Miss Chantal's dictatorship, Jewelle went home and quickly made dinner—penne with tomato sauce and freshly grated Parmigianino balanced with a spinach and beet salad. Surprisingly, she did not rush through her dinner. She took the time to enjoy her meal rather than treat it simply as fuel to keep her going.

After dinner, she loaded the dishwasher, but did not turn it on because it wasn't full. Aunt Constance would be pleased that she wasn't wasting water, soap, and electricity. This thought made her smile.

It was time to get down to work. She called her father, and told him about her meeting with Chantal and the new territories that she had chosen. He assured her that he could connect her with the right people in Jamaica and Barbados. She repeated the same call to Maxine and Joy, leaving detailed messages and asking that they call her when their time permitted. Next, the matter of Chantal's report on the Scandinavian countries that she was taking over. She wasn't much in the mood to work on it but forced herself to since she had brought home the files. As she sat down to work on the report, her cell started to vibrate. It was Chantal. Jewelle let it go to voicemail. Her cell vibrated again. It was Chantal. Once again, Jewelle let it go to voicemail. It vibrated again. And again. Jewelle turned off the phone.

Over the next two hours, Jewelle diligently worked on the report. She double-checked her writing for spelling errors and the sales projections for accuracy. Satisfied, she set the documents aside and made a mental note to return to them in the morning before leaving for the office. After shutting down her computer, she remembered the Amex statements that Heather had given her earlier. She had not had a chance to look at them closely and now was as good a time as any. As she reviewed the statements, her eyes grew wider and wider as she registered the audaciousness of Chantal's spending. Why would she think that she could get away with it? Heather had told her about only a handful of her many extravagant purchases. The Amex statement was proof, at last, of Chantal's unscrupulous behaviour. Jewelle decided to put the statement in the same hanging file folder with the envelope Barb gave her. She had not yet opened the envelope but sensed that it may soon be time to do so. Just as she crawled into bed, the house phone rang. She ran to get it.

"Hello."

"Hi Jewelle, it's Maxine and Joy," said Maxine. "Sorry for calling so late but we figured you'd still be up. We saw each other this evening and found out you left us more or less the same message."

"We do have a few contacts," added Joy, "but we'll need a week or so to pull the information together. Is that okay?"

"Of course!" exclaimed Jewelle. "Ladies, thank you, thank you."

"Well, you go back to whatever you were doing. It's time to get some shut-eye. Good night," said Maxine, followed by Joy.

Jewelle slipped back into bed and quickly surrendered to sleep.

The next morning, a brilliant sunbeam nudged her awake. When she turned to the clock on her night table, it was eight thirty.

"Oh no," she cried jumping out of bed. She had forgotten to set the alarm. Jewelle called Heather. It went straight to voicemail. "Heather, it's me. I slept in. Forgot to set the alarm. Please let Chantal know that I'll be in a little late. Thanks!"

Jewelle hung up, rushed to the bathroom, and climbed into the shower. She forgot to put on her shower cap, and the gush from the showerhead-soaked part of her locks before she could turn it off. She twisted her hair into a knot and drew down the shower cap. The soap bar kept slipping from her hand; she'd no sooner retrieve it than it would slip from her hands again. Frustrated, she parked the soap in the dish, grabbed the bottle of liquid soap and quickly completed her shower. In the middle of brushing her teeth, her phone rang. She ran to grab it. It was Heather.

"Hi Jewelle. Try to get here as soon as you can. She's on the warpath," Heather said with concern.

"Of course, *this* would be the morning," said Jewelle. "I am moving as quickly as I can. See you soon."

As she had not selected her clothes the night before, she grabbed her faithful black pants suit and paired it with a white crew neck T-shirt. She called for a taxi and quickly applied her make-up while she waited. Jewelle was frantic. Her anxiety soared. She called for the taxi again, grabbed her tote and handbag, turned off the lights and rushed out the door, praying that nothing important was left behind.

By the time the elevator deposited her on the ground floor, the taxi had arrived. Jewelle climbed in and gave the driver TV3's address. "Please hurry," she pleaded.

"Miss, traffic is heavy this morning," replied the driver.

"Great, just great!"

Just her luck that the one morning that she's late everything seemed to be working against her. Despairing, she called Heather again and left a message to let her know she was stuck in traffic. As the taxi inched along, she could feel the perspiration gathering on her forehead and under her arms. She felt trapped.

"Sir, as soon as you get to the nearest subway station, I'm going to jump out," said Jewelle.

"Ok, Miss."

Twenty minutes later, they had barely moved a block.

"How much do I owe you," Jewelle asked frantically looking at her watch. It was nine fifteen.

"It'll be $10.80, Miss."

"Here's $15.00. Keep the change. I'm getting out here."

"Be careful, Miss."

Jewelle was out of the car in a flash in the centre lane. She held up her right hand as she bobbed and weaved between the cars, trucks, and motorcycles until she made it to the sidewalk. Then, she began to run. What wouldn't she do right now for Wonder Woman's cape and invisible airplane? She ignored the questioning stares directed at her. By the time Jewelle reached the subway, sweat was dripping into her eyes, and her mascara was running. She checked her watch again. It was nine thirty. Jewelle called Heather again. She picked up.

"It's me. I'm about to get on the subway. I should be there in ten minutes if there are no delays," said Jewelle between laboured breaths.

"Are you ok?" asked Heather.

"Let's just say that I've seen better days." She hung up and ran down the subway stairs. Thankfully, there were no train delays. By the time she arrived at the TV3, Jewelle was exhausted.

Chantal's demands and expectations were draining her. There never seemed to be enough time for all the tasks assigned to her. Ever. In that moment, she questioned why she was putting herself through this torture. Should she just resign? At the same time, she felt guilty that she was late because she forgot to set the alarm. She also worried about neglecting her friends, her boyfriend and family members. There wasn't really any justification for her negligence.

By the time Jewelle limped into the sales department, it was ten. Her feet hurt. She felt as though she had run a marathon and smelled like it too.

Jewelle had barely settled in her chair when Heather slipped a note under her door. *Chantal wants to see you in her office immediately,* Heather wrote. *Please bring the report for the Scandinavian clients with you. Brace yourself. We'll talk later.*

Jewelle mopped up her brow, powdered her face then printed two copies of the report. It was time to face Chantal. She wished the monster dead then immediately felt a pang of guilt. This was not good Christian behaviour. Wasn't she supposed to love her enemy as herself? But wasn't it also human for her to be angry and upset? Jewelle didn't bother to knock on Chantal's door before letting herself in.

"Did you forget to knock?" snapped Chantal.

"No. I knew you were expecting me, so I let myself in," said Jewelle. The hot seat had once again been placed in front of the large desk.

"Why are you still standing there? Sit down," said Chantal irritably.

"I'd prefer to stand," answered Jewelle coolly even though her feet were tired and sore.

"Suit yourself." Chantal's face wore a sneer. "I called you last night but got no answer. Did you lose your phone?"

"No. I turned it off so that I could concentrate on completing the report that's due by noon. Here it is," said Jewelle walking forward to place it on the desk. Chantal quickly took up the report and scanned it.

"Are you sure these projections are in the ballpark?" she sniffed.

"Yes. They are, in part, based on the relationships that *I* have with these clients."

Ignoring Jewelle's dig, Chantal continued, "By now, you must realize that TV sales is not a nine to five job. So, when I call you, whenever that may be, I expect you to answer!" Chantal screeched.

"Was there something urgent that you needed to speak to me about?" asked Jewelle.

"Yes. I reviewed your phone log and noticed some personal calls. This ends as of today! I also noticed that you are not making enough cold calls. That changes as of today. I expect you to make at least twenty-five cold calls per day," said Chantal imperiously.

A battle raged in Jewelle as she stared at this scarecrow of a woman who was making her life hell. She determined passive resistance would be the order of the day until she figured out her next move.

"I am a little confused so please clarify. I am to make *no* personal phone calls at the office, but I am to accept *all* work-related calls at home at any hour seven days per week. Correct?"

"Glad to see we have an understanding," said Chantal icily.

"Please put our *understanding* in writing," Jewelle said firmly.

"That won't be necessary. Just do what is expected of you and what you are told. You may go now!" said Chantal, waving her hand dismissively.

Jewelle was filled with fury.

"You may think you have had the final word, Miss Mercier, but your day of reckoning is fast approaching," said Jewelle in as controlled a voice as she could manage.

Chantal glared at her. Jewelle had hit a nerve.

"Get out."

She didn't have to say it twice. Jewelle vanished.

Back in her office Jewelle sat quietly reflecting. It was now clear to her that she would have to move on from TV3 but not before putting a hurt on Chantal. The Amex statement was just the start. She now had a hunch that Barbara's envelope contained some proof that could bring Chantal to her knees. Jewelle was eager to get home, but she'd have to be patient as it was only three o'clock.

With her newly acquired powers, Chantal made Heather one of her ladies in waiting. Every morning Heather was now required to make Chantal's green juices to specification, pick up dry cleaning, schedule nail and hair appointments, and make restaurant reservations. Heather's daily encounters with Chantal were opportunities for the Boss Lady to recommend yet another diet and/or exercise regime. Some days, she would deliver a micro sermon: "The key to losing weight is a complete re-thinking of what goes in your mouth. No sugar, no carbs. These are the culprits that generate all that fat. Yuck, yuck!" she pontificated.

Heather looked on in complete bewilderment as her corpulence was not a problem to her. Discouraged that her suggestions were being met with outright resistance, Chantal took matters in her own hands. It was all out war against Heather's sinful, calorie-rich, peppermint knobs. She launched a covert operation to seek and destroy Heather's beloved candy. At first Heather thought her colleagues had grown to love the knobs and were helping themselves. This would explain why the jar emptied so quickly. The mystery of the missing peppermint knobs was solved late in the afternoon when Chantal tripped and took off like a rocket that didn't make it to its lofty destination but instead had a crash landing. She landed flat on her bottom, legs splayed, and the contents of the plastic bag she was carrying rained down into a carpet of pink peppermint knobs. Chantal's yelps pulled everyone from behind their desks like metal to a magnet. Heather was the first on the scene, followed by Marg and the others. Chantal was on her knees struggling to stand up, but her stilt-like heels made this difficult.

Heather zeroed in on the peppermint knobs scattered everywhere. "Busted!" she exclaimed triumphantly. "No need for explanations, Chantal. Now I know you are the peppermint knob thief."

Chantal was helped to her feet by the mailroom clerk who was doing his rounds. She neglected to thank him because she was too preoccupied brushing off her legs and her embarrassment.

Marg invited Chantal back to her office. Once inside, she closed the door behind them and asked Chantal to sit.

"Heather may not need an explanation, but I do," said a visibly upset Marg.

"Well, I have spoken to her repeatedly about the benefits of avoiding sugar but she's still eating these awful candies. So, I decided to take temptation out of her way," replied Chantal dispassionately. "The way I see it," she continued, "I am doing her a huge favour."

"Chantal, for the record, your job description does not include dietary advice. You owe Heather an apology. This incident will be noted in your personnel file," said an angry Marg. "I'd suggest that you spend some time thinking about what you did."

"That won't be necessary. I thought about it before I did it! Go ahead and put your note in my personnel folder if you must. I think we are done here," said Chantal before bolting from Marg's office.

Marg was stunned by Chantal's boldness and made a mental note to dig deeper. What made her so confident that she could speak to her the way she did? Marg sat down at her desk and tried to get back to work but found it difficult to concentrate as Chantal's words kept playing over and over in her head. She needed to pay closer attention. She'd start by meeting with the staff to get their feedback on Chantal's behaviour since becoming the VP of Sales and Distribution.

That evening, when Jewelle arrived home, she dropped her bags by the door and rushed to her filing cabinet to retrieve the envelope that Barbara had passed on to her. Though tempted to rip it open, she searched for the letter opener and used it. Jewelle dumped the contents of the envelope on her dining table then sat down to sift through each item. There were photographs, many of Chantal with the chair of TV3's board—shots of them dining together, walking hand in hand, kissing and shopping. And there were copies of emails detailing arrangements made for clandestine meetings. Jewelle could not believe her eyes. Proof! Proof of the rumoured affair between Chantal and the chair of TV3's board was staring her in the face. She sat still absorbing what was before her and began to think about next steps. Jewelle wondered if she should simply take the package to Marg, or was it too soon? Her instincts told her to remain silent about the new weapons in her arsenal. Just as she was gathering the documents to drop them back in the envelope, the house phone rang.

"Jewelle, it's your mother. Remember me?"

Jewelle's heart started to race. She had been avoiding her mother, and it could no longer be put off.

"Yes Mother, I remember you. Work has been even more hectic with the new boss."

Adele cut in, "You know that's not what I'm talking about, Miss Jewelle! I haven't heard a peep out of you since you spoke with your father. What stories did he tell you?"

"Mother, this is not a good time to talk about this. I'm coming home next weekend and I will fill you in then," said Jewelle calmly.

"So, I am right that he, your father, has been filling your head with nonsense!" Adele shouted.

"Mother, I assure you that he did not fill my head with nonsense. And I don't want to speak about this anymore. At least not right now," said Jewelle firmly.

"Miss Jewelle, do you think you are talking to one of your little girlfriends? I'm your mother and I demand respect!"

"Mother, respect is a two-way street. I told you that I would speak about the matter next week, but you are pushing me to get your own way. Is that respectful?" asked Jewelle pointedly.

"Well then, I guess I will just have to wait," said Adele, disregarding Jewelle's question. It was another standoff between Jewelle and Adele. Adele was aware that Jewelle would only allow her to push her so far and no more. She changed the subject. "So, how are things going at work?"

"Rough. I got in late this morning because I forgot to set my alarm clock. Traffic was horrible and I had to jump out of a taxi and run to the subway. When I got to the office, the boss was on the warpath," said Jewelle.

"Well, that's how it is sometimes. You have to take the bitter with the better," said Adele.

"Of late, it's all bitter and better is MIA. I am seriously thinking about resigning," said Jewelle wearily.

There was an awkward pause.

"You are going to quit a job that pays you well and allows you to travel all over the world?" asked Adele incredulously.

"Mother, it's not just about the money. Every day, I am on edge wondering what other ways this woman is going to disrespect and sabotage me. I am sure that I can find another job," said Jewelle uneasily.

Adele took a deep breath before she pounced. "Miss Jewelle, do you know what our people had to put up with when they came to this country? Hard work, covert and blatant racism and low wages on top of all that! Your boss may be getting on your nerves but it's not the end of the world. You try to hang on to that job. She's not going to be there forever."

Jewelle felt hurt that Adele wasn't hearing anything that she was saying and had little appreciation of the stress that had taken over her life like a malignant cancer. Like her domineering sister Constance, she felt that if you were being paid reasonably well, you simply put up and shut up. However, Jewelle didn't see it that way. She was born and raised in this country and had a right to be treated like she belonged. Her boss was not doing her a favour.

She had earned her position through hard work and dedication. She thought about thanking her mother for the history and sociology lesson but held her tongue to keep the conversation from escalating into a blown-out quarrel.

"Mother, since I am the person living through this daily hell, I think it is my decision to make," said Jewelle.

"What's gotten into you! I was just ..."

"Mother, as I told you, I had a hellish day, and my nerves are on edge. I'd better go. I will call you when I am in a better mood. Bye for now." She hung up.

Adele was stunned.

Almost immediately, Jewelle regretted how she ended the conversation with her mother and knew that the entire family would soon learn how rude and bold she had been.

Half an hour later Jewelle was still thinking about her conversation with her mother and the compromising photos of Chantal and Mr. Big. Agitated, she paced back and forth trying to calm down. It didn't help ... perhaps a glass of wine would.

While Jewelle poured a glass, her cellphone started to vibrate. She ignored it and took the first sip. A few minutes later, the cellphone buzzed again and continued to do so every couple of minutes for the next half hour.

When Jewelle finished the glass of wine, she checked the phone and dialed Chantal.

"Hello Chantal," said Jewelle flatly.

"I'm glad you called back. I was starting to think that our conversation earlier today fell on deaf ears," said Chantal haughtily.

"How can I be of service, Miss Mercier," asked Jewelle, tongue firmly in cheek.

"Glad you asked. I reviewed your report on the Scandinavian countries this evening. The numbers don't add up. I'm glad I checked or you would have made me look bad with Marg and the Board. This is basic arithmetic, you know, two plus two equals ..." Chantal paused, waiting for an answer.

Jewelle remained silent, her blood pressure climbing.

"Are you there? I want an answer," Chantal demanded.

Jewelle remained silent.

"It's bad enough that you can't add," shouted Chantal, "you are also being insubordinate! Tomorrow another letter will go into your personnel file.

"Correct the report and bring it to me by eight tomorrow morning. Are you still there? Jewelle Joseph, you had better answer me!"

Jewelle remained silent.

Chantal finally hung up.

Chantal's call gave Jewelle the push she needed. It was time to start planning her exit from TV3. She poured herself another glass of wine before pulling her copy of the Scandinavian report out of her tote bag. Jewelle carefully went over the numbers adding everything twice to ensure that the totals were consistently the same. They were. As she suspected, it was Miss Mercier who needed to figure out the answer to two plus two.

The next morning, Jewelle got up at six fifteen to make a few phone calls before heading to the office. She called Bernie to tell her about the latest drama with Cruella and of her plans to resign on her terms. Bernie was supportive and agreed to let the other members of the posse know what was going on. Next, she called Anthony, but he didn't pick up. Her final call was to Johann.

"Hello," Johann mumbled into the phone.

"Hey Johann, it's me Jewelle. How are you?"

"What time is it?" he asked while trying to suppress a yawn.

"It's about six forty. What time is it over there?" asked Jewelle.

"Six forty. I'm in New York on a production. I'll be here for a couple of weeks."

"Sorry, I woke you up," said Jewelle regretfully.

"No apology needed. It's always nice to hear from you. Anyhow, to what do I owe this call?"

Jewelle spewed out her most recent frustrations and challenges with Chantal. Johann listened attentively, offering words of comfort intermittently.

"Hey Jewelle, since I am just next door, so to speak, why don't I drop by Toronto on my way home? We can spend some time brainstorming your next steps."

Jewelle was reluctant at first. It then occurred to her that this would be an excellent opportunity to introduce Johann to *Miss* Mercier who had taken over Sweden. The thought made Jewelle smile.

Her final call was to Heather. When she didn't pick up, she texted: *Miss Mercier called late. It may be time to deploy.*

Nine

Love Him or Leave Him

The relationship between Jewelle and Anthony was in free fall. Since their last quarrel, Anthony had cut Jewelle a wide berth, giving her the space she claimed she needed for work. Though she had made it clear that her career was a priority, she felt abandoned by him. Many of her calls to him went unanswered, and when they did speak, it was awkward, even uncomfortable. To cut conversations short, Jewelle would claim she had another call to deal with. And this was usually the truth. Work consumed her waking hours and even her sleep as her many tasks swirled around in her dreams. Her work and unbridled ambition had come between them.

She found herself reminiscing about the early days. On their first date, she greeted him nervously at the door and invited him in. She wore a bias-cut, jade green silk peau de soie shift, accessorized with silver chandelier earrings and a silver cuff. Anthony complimented her on her dress as he handed her a single yellow rose. She thanked him, found a bud vase in the kitchen, and walked toward him admiring his navy blue wool sports jacket, crisp white shirt, and khaki slacks. He looked *fine*. She brushed her lips against his flirtatiously. He smiled seductively.

Anthony had made a reservation at Centro's, an upscale Italian restaurant in midtown Toronto that was one of Jewelle's favourites. It was known as much for its ultra-modern décor, as for its food and the beautiful people it attracted.

At their table, they were both a little nervous at first but soon settled into pleasant conversation. Jewelle learned that Anthony lived within walking distance of the restaurant and had grown up in that part of town with his Trinidadian parents, both high school teachers. They had hoped their son would follow in their footsteps, but he was not academically inclined. Instead, he pursued an IT (Internet Technology) diploma at one of the local community colleges. Now, he worked with a large company that provided technical support for corporations around the city.

"So, I know that we both like to swim and enjoy good food. Do you like to read?" asked Jewelle.

"The sports page and car magazines," replied Anthony. At least he's honest, Jewelle thought to herself. Still, this was a first strike against him.

"Where do you see yourself five years from now?" she probed, immediately regretting the question. This wasn't a job interview.

Anthony picked up on that. "Well, I like to take things one day at a time. I don't know what tomorrow's going to bring, let alone where I'll be five years down the road."

Strike two. Jewelle suddenly lost her appetite. How could he not have any plans for his career? She had been raised to "be all that you can be." By any measure, Anthony had a secure well-paying job and by all accounts he was exceptionally good at his job. His company valued him. The fact that he did not aspire to advance up the ladder shouldn't be a strike against him. But it was. She wished his ambition matched her own. Ambition was drilled into her by her father.

Radcliffe had worked very hard as an accountant to ensure that she and her siblings were comfortable. He had been fortunate to receive a scholarship to Concordia University in Montreal, from which he graduated with honors. He was the first in his family to attend university, and he had trained his own children to set their sights high—even before they were born. Family lore had it that Radcliffe read *Pilgrim's Progress* to Jewelle and her siblings when they were still in the womb!

Jewelle was determined to climb to the top of the heap in television sales and earn a healthy six-figure salary by managing a team of committed sales professionals who were prepared to go above and beyond their job description. She was prepared to put in eighty-hour workweeks for as long as it took and do anything that didn't involve sacrificing her integrity—morally, sexually, or any other fundamental—to make that happen. As her father put it, "Work for what you want!" That was what she knew how to do, *work*!

Anthony made it through dinner without striking out completely, so Jewelle agreed to a second date. They went to the Art Gallery of Ontario to see the Chagall exhibit, which Anthony found "interesting" but he certainly wasn't over the moon. He was just happy to be there with a fine sister who seemed to have her head on straight. She was happy to be there with a brother who was charming and knew how to romance her.

They walked through the museum, arms around each other, sometimes stopping for a kiss. Anthony was a welcome change from the Bay Street lawyers she had dated, all of them in love with themselves and their law degrees.

A few months went by before Jewelle and Anthony became an official couple. The months quickly turned to years of affection and compromise. Anthony turned a blind eye to Jewelle's need for obsessive order and her workaholic tendencies; she tolerated his obsession with sports and lack of interest in the arts. Still, he made her feel special, and she glowed, loving that way his deep reassuring voice told her that he loved her.

Anthony routinely slipped love notes under her door, sent roses to the office, and arranged surprise weekend getaways to help her unwind. His steadiness comforted her, and so did his love. She loved gazing into his eyes when they made love, especially in the morning. But sometimes Jewelle felt as though she were "settling" and had lingering doubts as to whether Anthony would be the right husband for her, not that he had asked.

After Jewelle's interview for the VP of Sales and Distribution position, she had called Anthony to tell him that she had lost out to her rival. Anthony was sympathetic. In trying to comfort her, he said that it wasn't the end of the world because she still had a great job. This did not go over well with Jewelle.

She blasted him.

"What did you just say Anthony Brown?" she screamed as he held the phone away from his ear. "I know it's not Armageddon or anything close, but I have worked my arse off for this promotion!" And she was just warming up. "But you wouldn't understand what I'm talking about with you doing 9-to-5, would you?"

Her words stung.

"JJ, you had better calm down before you say something that you will regret," said Anthony, trying hard to keep his cool.

"So now you're going to tell me how I should feel and behave! I'm just sick and tired of tiptoeing around you not trying to get ahead. Just because you don't have any ambition ..." As soon as the words left her mouth, she knew she had gone too far.

The next sound she heard was the dial tone.

Immediately, she began calling him, each of her voicemails a plea for forgiveness and understanding. In the final message, she attributed her nasty outburst to work-related stress, sleep deprivation and frustration.

Anthony had turned off his phone.

She felt sick. Jewelle called Bernie in a panic. Bernie didn't pick up.

"Hey Bernie. Urgent, please call me now." Her anxiety grew worse with each passing minute. She continued calling posse members until she reached Joy.

"Hey Joy," said Jewelle quietly.

"Hey JJ. Surprised to be hearing from you so soon. What's going on?"

"Joy, I just did something awful. I had another fight with Anthony, and I went too far. I accused him of having no ambition."

Joy was speechless.

"Joy, are you still there?" asked Jewelle nervously.

"Yes JJ, I am still here. Shocked into silence. Anthony has *chosen* not to give all his time to his career. That doesn't mean he is without ambition. You know better! Have you lost your mind?"

"Joy, I am sick to my stomach. Anthony hung up on me and is not taking my calls. What should I do?" Jewelle started to cry.

"Well," Joy said, "you really do need to do something to fix this. I don't have an immediate answer. Have you tried Bernie?"

"Yes, I have been calling everyone, but you are the first to pick up," said Jewelle, tears spilling from her eyes.

"Look, I'd suggest that you go for a walk to clear your head and calm your nerves. I will call around to the other ladies and give you a call back."

Jewelle took Joy's advice and walked aimlessly through the neighbourhood observing people with their dogs, joggers, skateboarders, and yummy mummies with babies and energetic young children. To be that age again she mused. Not a care in the world, just worlds to discover, worlds to explore. When one mother strolled by, she peered in the pram at a sleeping baby boy dressed in a blue romper. He was beautiful. A smile broke out on Jewelle's face as she looked down at him. She asked his age. He was a month old. As she continued walking her stress began to fade.

When Jewelle got back to her condo, she immediately checked her messages. Bernie had called. She called back and Bernie picked up on the first ring. "Hey, JJ, Joy told us you're in hot water with Anthony. Is that right?" demanded Bernie.

"Yes. I was wrong," Jewelle said in a quivering voice as her shoulders drooped like a wilting flower.

"Well, at least you got that right," said Bernie curtly. "I'm sure you feel bad enough about what you did, so I'm not going to heap more hot coals on your head. The ladies and I talked things over, and we think you should send Anthony a hand-written letter by regular mail. Beg, and I mean beg for forgiveness and then explain what you have been living through. After you send off the letter, wait for him to make contact. Let me repeat, do not call, or text him. Give him space!" Bernie was vehement.

"Bernie, I can't thank you guys enough for being here for me."

"That's what girlfriends are for," said Bernie sympathetically. "Go write the letter." She hung up.

Over the next couple of hours Jewelle attempted to compose what she wanted to say to Anthony. It proved to be more difficult than she thought, and after writing a few lines, she'd get stuck. Sheet after crumpled sheet landed in the wastepaper basket. This went on for a while. Finally, she found the words that struck the right tone.

Dear Anthony,

I am truly, truly sorry for what I said to you. It is inexcusable. I know that my words hurt you deeply. More so because what I said is untrue. Please forgive me. It will never happen again.

I tried calling you but understandably you wouldn't pick up. So, I am writing in the hope that you will read these words knowing that they come from my heart.

"Le verbe 'aimer' est difficile à conjuguer, son passé n'est pas simple, son présent n'est qu'indicatif et son futur toujours conditionnel"

~ Jean Cocteau

I hope you will find it in your heart to forgive me. Please give me a second chance to make things right.

Love,

JJ

When Jewelle completed the letter, she sprayed it with his favourite perfume, Chanel No. 5, folded it, placed it in the envelope, sealed it, and carefully added the stamp. She was too restless to wait until the morning to post the letter, so she walked out to the red mailbox on the corner and dropped it in.

The next couple of weeks flew by in a blur as Jewelle dashed about frantically trying to meet Chantal's unreasonable demands. Daily, she reminded herself to keep her eyes on the prize, her exit from TV3.

During lunch with Heather, she told her about her planned departure. Heather was upset, and begged Jewelle to reconsider, suggesting that she take a leave of absence or a holiday. Jewelle promised to think about it. After the dessert was served, Jewelle divulged the contents of the envelope Barb had given her.

Heather squealed with delight. "Now you have proof of what everyone has been gossiping about forever. This is just what we need to take her down. But we'll have to think it through. Timing is everything."

"I agree. For now, I am just going to sit back and wait for the right opportunity to leverage the dossier," said Jewelle. "When I met with Barbara for dinner, she remarked that I would know when the time is right."

"We'll be patient. But in the meantime, let's toast to Operation Miss Mercier," cackled Heather.

They touched their water glasses and continued chit-chatting about work and personal matters. They brainstormed sales opportunities for the new children's series that would soon be delivered. Heather also asked about Anthony. Jewelle told her they had had a quarrel but left out the details about the hand-written letter. Heather reminded her that Anthony loved her and that in time, things would work out. Jewelle took comfort in her words.

◇

Jewelle arrived home earlier than usual. During a doctor's appointment that afternoon, she said that she was feeling a little run down, sleep deprived and stressed. He recommended a holiday or a leave of absence. After she left the doctor's office, Jewelle called Heather to let her know that she would not be coming back to the office after her 4.00 p.m. appointment with a client and could be reached on her landline or cellphone from 6.00 p.m. onward.

The commute home was as exhausting as ever. People packed in like sardines, backpacks and bicycles, and the usual grumblings from irate passengers.

Jewelle had scarcely walked through the front door when the home phone rang. Anthony's name and number showed up on the call display. She hurried to grab the phone quickly. "Hello," she answered happily. "So, good to hear from you," she gushed.

Anthony was silent for a moment.

"I got your letter, JJ. Thank you. Are you available for dinner at eight tomorrow evening?" he asked quietly.

"Yes, I am," she answered, keeping her excitement in check.

"Great. I will pick you up at seven thirty."

"Where are we going?"

"It's a surprise. Wear something nice. See you tomorrow at seven thirty."

She held onto the phone for a few seconds more after Anthony hung up. Then she spun round and round in circles like a child let loose on a playground.

"Thank you, God, for answering my prayer. Thank you, thank you!" Jewelle exclaimed.

"I have to let the posse know."

She called Bernie first. Bernie picked up on the second ring, and before her friend could say a word, Jewelle squealed into the phone, "Bernie, Bernie, he called!"

"He who?" asked Bernie, teasing her.

"Anthony! The letter worked. He's taking me out to dinner tomorrow night."

"Where's he taking you?" asked Bernie.

"I don't know. He just asked me to wear something pretty," Jewelle gushed. "What am I going to wear?"

"Don't start that, JJ. You have a walk-in closet full of clothes. Anyway, since you asked, I would suggest that khaki coloured dress by that German designer. Can't remember her name. It's got a great neckline and the cut is very flattering."

"I think you mean Annette Görtz," said Jewell brightly.

"Yes, that's her. What do you think?" asked Bernie.

"Great suggestion! It fits well and isn't too flashy."

"Bernie, please tell the posse my good news. Let's get together soon to celebrate."

"Ok. Try not to mess this up. He's a good guy and I think he'll give you a second chance."

"That's what I'm hoping, Bernie," said Jewelle softly.

Jewelle was unaware that the posse had met with Anthony. He told them his side of the story and his many frustrations. They sympathized and comforted him. Then, they pleaded Jewelle's case. Anthony told them he needed more time to think things over. Bernie wrapped up the meeting with, "Take all the time you need, she's not going anywhere."

The following evening, Anthony picked up Jewelle at 7:30 sharp. When Jewelle opened the door, he presented her with a single yellow rose accented by baby's breath. He hugged her gently and kissed her softly. She could feel his well-toned body against her own and shimmied against it. The thought of doing the deed right there flashed through her mind, but of course Miss Big Woman Propriety would never give into that impulse. It all felt good after being separated these many weeks by her busy work schedule. Anthony looked good. He smelled even better. He was a handsome Black man. More importantly, he was a good man.

"Jewelle, you look great."

She sparkled. Her locks were piled high on her head in a loose bun with a few cascading strands. Hairpins decorated with cowrie shells held it all in place. Her make-up was minimal except for the Saturday night red lipstick that brightened her lips. Dangling silver earrings adorned her ears.

"Thank you. You look great yourself! Let me put this in a bud vase and then we can get going."

Anthony admired her as she walked quickly into the kitchen. There, she took a vase from the cupboard, filled it with water, deposited the plant food, freed the rose and baby's breath from a plastic wrap, and placed them in the vase. When she returned to the hallway, she set the vase in the center of the table below the hall mirror, grabbed her clutch and announced, "Okay, I'm ready."

During the drive to the restaurant, conversation was spotty. They talked about current affairs and family. Jewelle told him about her father's recent visit, and her brother's promotion into management. When they turned south on Yonge Street, Jewelle knew where he was taking her, Grano, the restaurant where they went on their second date. This was a good sign.

Grano, a charming Italian restaurant nestled between a cluster of retail stores, was a popular eatery that served delicious unpretentious food. Its signature black and white awning served not only as a decorative detail but also as a shield against the intense sunrays that streamed through the tall windows at the front. Cobalt blue–and–red walls were dotted with an eclectic mix of vintage black and white photographs, advertising posters, framed prints, and ceramic plates from the old country.

When they arrived, the restaurant was already busy. The waiter walked them to their table and filled their water glasses as soon as they were seated.

"I'll be back to take your order in a few minutes," the waiter said and walked away. Jewelle and Anthony looked over the menu.

"Do you know what you are going to have?" asked Anthony, smiling.

"Yes. And do you know?"

They both laughed.

When the waiter returned, Anthony ordered two glasses of Citra red, eggplant parmigiana as a starter, two spinach salads and two raviolis, their favourites.

They looked around the restaurant and commented about some of the patrons as they drank their wine and ate their starter. Conversation was difficult at the start. They'd lapse back into silence, each lost in their own thoughts about what had been said between them and what had yet to be said. Jewelle took the plunge.

"As you know, I have been so full tilt at work. I pride myself on being thorough and competent. But lately things have been going sideways."

Pride cometh before the fall, thought Anthony.

"Anthony, I have had time to think about losing out to Chantal, and it's not just about the increase in pay and the authority that the position would give me. For me it would also be about making a difference in people's lives by implementing policies that are more humane and that don't discard people at the drop of a hat. This is worth fighting for, don't you think?" she asked him quietly.

Anthony nodded, looking right at her with a look of complete honesty and understanding. Jewelle wondered why she just couldn't accept what Anthony had to offer without throwing up barriers. Perhaps, it had to do with her parents' divorce. She shrugged this off, chiding herself for playing pseudo-psychologist.

As the evening wore on, the ice broke. They relaxed and began to enjoy each other's company. The meal ended with a shared tiramisu and the exchange of warm affectionate smiles.

After Anthony paid the bill, he stood up, walked over, pulled out her chair, and offered her his hand to help her up. When she stood up, he grasped her hand, and they walked slowly out of the restaurant in silence. Anyone looking at them, Jewelle thought, must think they are a beautiful couple. This thought made Jewelle feel warm inside.

Out on the street, the cool night air made her shiver. He gave her his jacket and hugged her protectively. She wasn't sure what to think, what should she be thinking. All she knew was that she was feeling joy and contentment.

When they arrived back at her condo, Jewelle invited Anthony in for a drink. While she went for the wine and the glasses, he looked through her record collection, selected a James Ingram album, placed the record on the player and dropped the needle at the start of "Just Once."

Jewelle returned with two glasses of red wine. Anthony asked her to set them on the coffee table.

"JJ, dance with me."

She allowed him to pull her close, and she lay her head against his chest as she sang along to the lyrics. *Can we find a way, to finally make it right?*

At the end of the song, Anthony told her he had an early start, so he was leaving. Jewelle felt another wave of desire and was disappointed, but on second thought figured this was best, slow and steady wins the race. She walked him to the door.

"Anthony, it was really a nice evening. Thank you."

Anthony nodded in agreement. "I really enjoyed it too."

He gave Jewelle a hug, they kissed passionately, and he turned to go, but stopped. "JJ, I feel that there is a chance for us. Let's hit the reset button." And with that he left.

Ten

Daddy's Home

At sixty-eight, Radcliffe Joseph still turned heads. Tall, dark, and handsome was a precise description of the dandy who took to shaving his head when it became clear that his hairline had decided to disappear—for good. His dark brown face was smooth and wrinkle-free, his teeth his own, a source of pride. Radcliffe's vanity led him routinely to the gym and the pool where he did laps to elude any hint of a paunch. He was prepared to fight the fat fight until his body was returned to the soil.

Like many Jamaicans of his vintage, he was proud, self-assured, and intolerant of anything that he considered nonsense. Most evenings when he watched the news, there was a long string of "Nonsense!" pronounced with such force, that Jewelle got the impression that he thought his opinion mattered to the folks reading the news.

Radcliffe was a staunch Garveyite, wedded to the philosophy that Black people were their own rescue, and education and self-confidence were the main weapons in their arsenals. Garvey, with limited resources, started an international movement that survived him. To Radcliffe's way of thinking, if Garvey could achieve that at a time when there were such immense political and economic barriers, what was holding back his people was a lack of courage and determination. Although he was not an avid reader, he loved biographies or articles about some of the people he admired and who inspired him: Paul Bogle, Martin

Luther King, Malcolm X, Frantz Fanon, and Michael Manley. When Jewelle wondered why there weren't more women who he found admirable, she reminded herself that he loved the music of Sarah Vaughn, Ella Fitzgerald, Billie Holiday, Mahalia Jackson, and Nina Simone, whose "Young Gifted and Black" was required listening for his children. Every Sunday, his family—and the neighbours—were obliged to listen to hours and hours of Mahalia Jackson's powerful gospel recordings.

Although Radcliffe was not a cultured man, he had great taste in clothes, furniture, and cars. He knew quality when he saw it, and his dream car was an Aston Martin.

Recognizing his culture deficit, his wife Adele set out to correct the unacceptable imbalance. At first, Radcliffe played along. He accompanied her to the theatre, the museum, and a few art galleries. These excursions bored him, but he was trying to keep his wife happy—happy wife, happy life. Radcliffe reached the end of the culture rope during a contemporary art exhibition at the Musée des beaux-arts de Montréal where for him each piece was "styled nonsense," and for good measure he added, "I am no artist, but I am sure I can do better!" Adele finally gave up and gave in, freeing Radcliffe to pursue his great passion, dominoes.

The truth was, Radcliffe preferred to spend time with his Jamaican buddies who sported nicknames such as "Sir Lancelot," "The Don" and "Cowboy." Radcliffe was known as "The Count." These men met during their early years in Montreal when they had their first jobs at the Royal Victoria Hospital as orderlies while going to night school preparatory courses so that they could re-sit exams and work in their chosen fields—electrician, insurance broker, actuary. The game of dominoes, with its patois-laced trash talk fueled by J. Wray and Nephew overproof white rum, was the ritual that held these friendships together. They played often. They played hard into the wee hours of the morning. Each player attempted to assert dominance and claim mastery of the game. From the shuffling and distribution of the domino pieces to the thunderous table-top crash landings that caused the drinking glasses and the domino tiles to jump as though startled, they loved it all. If the tabletops and the dominoes could speak, these men would be doing hard time for battery and the revelation of their secrets would land them in the doghouse, or the courthouse.

Radcliffe and his buddies reveled in Jamaican trash talk—*"Tek dat! Now me ah go mek you bow! Oh, so yu tink yu can ramp wid big man! Mek mi see wha yu ah go do now! Yu ah go get a beating tinight!"* Between moves, they caught up on each other's news, talked about women, politics, the economy and gossiped about the happenings at work and in the neighbourhood.

These men had a profound and unwavering love for each other. They had stood by each other during the years of scarcity when funds were low, bills and worries high. When the years of plenty arrived, they never forgot the journey that brought them to this place.

For most of her childhood, Jewelle had been a daddy's girl. He had taught her to swim and played softball with her. From her earliest memories, she could remember him motivating her to succeed. Throughout the teen years, Radcliffe taught his children how to "value a dollar" and to "watch the pennies so that the dollars will follow." He taught them the difference between interest and compound interest. "If you don't *need* to spend a penny, then don't!" These lessons were re-enforced by her aunt Constance, who was known to stretch a dollar until the Queen hollered, "No more!" Although there was no love lost between Radcliffe and Constance, when it came to money and its management, they were two peas in a pod.

Radcliffe was not demonstrably affectionate. However, he showed his love by providing for them and occasionally surprising them with gifts. When Jewelle graduated from university, Radcliffe was very emotional. He cried during the ceremony. Later he hugged her, told her how proud he was of her, and then presented her with a beautiful Mont Blanc fountain pen. Jewelle was surprised that he had spent so much on a pen. He told her that if she used it well and often, it would pay for itself over time.

Radcliffe considered every interaction a teachable moment. He made it clear to Jewelle and her siblings that success was coded in their DNA, often reminding her that he fought his way out of poverty to create the life he envisioned for himself, a successful accountant with an educated wife and ambitious children. For Radcliffe, no work was demeaning if you earned an honest wage, and it was a means to a bigger end. He'd often tell his children to keep their eyes on the prize, that a solid education would lead to a good job and respectability. To Jewelle, her father could do no wrong. He was her hero as much as her mother was.

Then suddenly, everything changed when she overheard her mother telling her aunt Constance about the "discovery" of yet another of Radcliffe's affairs with a much younger woman and possibly a second family. She was devastated. This couldn't possibly be the father she knew. What made it even more painful, was how much she loved, admired, and trusted him.

Late one Saturday evening while Jewelle was folding her laundry, the phone rang. It was Radcliffe.

"Hello Jewelle. How are you doing?"

"Do you want the truth or the stock answer?" asked Jewelle wearily.

"I can handle the truth, Jewelle," replied Radcliffe, now ready to spar with his daughter.

"Well, I applied for the VP of Sales and Distribution job, and I lost out to a half-starved woman who has been making my life hell for the last two years. I don't know how much longer I can stomach her," spewed out Jewelle.

"Why do you think she was successful?" probed Radcliffe.

"To be completely honest, I gave a poor answer to a very important question. However, I assumed that because I did well on all the others, I was still well-positioned to succeed."

"Jewelle Joseph, yu know dat *we* av to be ten times betta. Since you was a child, I bin drummin dat into yu head," he said heavily. "The fact is, we have made progress, but there's still a long, long way to go."

"Daddy, I really feel awful that I lost my focus. I spent weeks practicing and preparing for the interview. I should have sailed through." She sighed.

Radcliffe paused. He could sense Jewelle's disappointment and wanted to comfort her. "Jewelle, yu av many more opportunities ahead a yu. Don't waste nuh more time beating up yuself. You are going to get to where you want to go. Yu just ah tek a likkle detour," he added tenderly.

"Thanks, Daddy. I'll try to shake it off and keep moving forward. Were you calling about anything in particular?"

"Yes. I was calling to remind you that I will be leaving for Jamaica in a couple of days and plan to visit with you on the way back."

"How long will you be in Toronto?"

"Just a few days."

"Okay Daddy. Just call me the morning of your flight to confirm that it's on time. Would you like me to pick you up?"

"I know you are very busy. I'll take an airport taxi to your place."

"It was really good to talk to you. Have a good flight. I'll see you in nine days."

When Jewelle hung up the phone, her mood improved. She had forgotten to ask Radcliffe what he would be doing in Jamaica.

Over the next week, each day felt more frantic than the day before. She was still stewing over the loss of the promotion to Chantal, but she kept moving forward. She enrolled in another leadership course and took up meditation, something she had sworn off as yet another fad to take up time and money. Although a new convert, she could already feel the difference meditation was making in her life. Her anxiety had plummeted, and she was better able to cope with Chantal and all the folly that swirled around her.

By the time Jewelle escaped the office, it was 9:00 p.m. She stopped to pick up groceries, so her father would have some food to eat. When Jewelle arrived home, she fumbled with the key and pushed open the door. She was loaded with bags of groceries and a bouquet of white daisies encircled by an assortment of green leaves. Like Mother Hubbard her cupboards were bare, and so was her fridge. She rested her handbag and tote bag near the front door, then lumbered to the kitchen with the bags, placed them near the fridge and filled the kettle so that she could make herself a cup of tea. While the water boiled, she put away the groceries. She started thinking about cooking and how much she enjoyed it. Unfortunately, her job did not leave her with much time to prepare meals. She had become accustomed to bolting in and out of restaurants and coffee shops or wolfing down meals at her desk so she could go back to her work. She made a mental note to herself that this was a situation that she would like to change sooner rather than later.

With the groceries stocked away, Jewelle arranged the flowers in a tall, cylindrical turquoise blue vase and placed it on the small table below the hall mirror. She stepped back to get a better look and to decide if this was the best place. Not being one hundred percent certain, she put the vase in a few different spots before returning it to the hall table. She gave the living room and dining area a light dusting and fluffed the cushions on the living room sofa. The rooms looked manicured, and this made Jewelle smile.

It was now teatime. She made herself a cup of lemon ginger tea, sat in the living room and listened to her messages using the cordless. One message was from her father. He had called a day early to confirm that his flight would arrive at one in the afternoon. She was looking forward to her time with Radcliffe.

Happy that everything in her apartment was in order, Jewelle jumped into the shower wearing a floral shower cap. She wasn't up to washing her locks tonight; it was quite an undertaking, and they took almost a full day to dry. She soaped herself from head to toe with a bar of oatmeal honey soap and allowed herself to luxuriate in the warm water cascading over her body. In this moment Jewelle felt truly blessed. She stepped out of the shower and as she toweled herself dry she began to hum Nina Simone's "Feeling Good." Yes, Jewelle was feeling good.

The next morning, on her way out, Jewelle stopped at the concierge's desk to inquire if he would be on duty all day. He was, so she handed him a small bubble wrap envelope that contained the spare key. She told him that her father, Radcliffe Joseph, was due to arrive between two and four and would pick up the envelope. With that settled, Jewelle headed off to the bus stop where she had a long wait. She climbed on and elbowed her way to the back, ignoring the angry looks as she pushed through. For some reason, this morning she was not bothered by the bodies packed shoulder to shoulder on the bus. She was simply grateful that everyone smelled clean. The traffic was heavy, but it was moving steadily, and the bus arrived at the subway in good time. As the horde rushed towards the trains, Jewelle allowed herself to be swept along until she reached the escalator and took hold of the rubber rail, standing still until it was time to step off. She got on the train and exited two stops later.

The department was empty when she arrived. Jewelle quickly got busy so that she could get as much done before the phone started ringing, and demands were made on her time. She dreaded having to remind Chantal that she would be leaving early. As luck would have it, Boss Lady had called in sick. Jewelle went to see Marg and explained that she had requested an early leave because her father was visiting for a few days. Marg granted her request.

Without the oppressive presence of Chantal, the day flew by quickly. Jewelle, with the assistance of Heather, completed all her urgent tasks and set up a few meetings for the following week. She was grateful to have Heather watching her back, always there to encourage and always willing to go above and beyond.

As Jewelle tidied up her desk, she checked her watch. It was almost 3.00 p.m. By now her father should be settling in. She had left him a welcome note, taped to the vase on the hall table, and told him to make himself comfortable and help himself to anything in the house. Jewelle took her handbag and tote from her bottom drawer and looked around one last time before heading out the door. Then the phone rang. She turned back. It was her mother. For a moment she was torn between taking the call and letting it go. She took the call.

"Hello Mother. How are you?"

"Better now that I got you on the phone. How are things with you?" she asked warily.

"Everything's good. Daddy is …"

"I heard!" she said coldly. "So, you didn't think you should tell me that your father was visiting with you."

"Mother, I wasn't hiding it from you. There's just a lot going on right now and it slipped me," said an exasperated Jewelle as she wondered if her mother had any intentions of ever treating her as an adult.

"So, it slipped you. I hope his bad behaviour hasn't slipped you as well."

"Mother, let's not go there," said Jewelle wearily. "I was just leaving the office. I will call you later."

"I'll expect your call," Adele said imperiously and hung up.

Jewelle held the phone to her ear for a few seconds longer and let out a heavy sigh before hanging up. The truth was Adele had put up with a lot of unhappiness and emotional abuse before finding the courage to ask for a divorce when she finally admitted to herself that Radcliffe had no desire to abandon his reckless philandering. She had lost all concerns about finger-pointing, tongue-wagging friends and family members. She had done her duty. Her kids were "past the worst" and could now fend for themselves. She no longer had to accept other people's idea of married life. Her sense of self was no longer tethered to the beliefs of others. Adele had come to this understanding a long time ago and could now live the life she desired. Yes, she was fearful of what lay ahead, but the fear did not get in her way. She hoped someday she'd be able to forgive him and that he'd get to a place where he could honestly examine his life and his motivations. The truth was Adele loved Radcliffe despite his unfaithfulness.

A swift commute and Jewelle was back at her condo. She knocked on the front door as a warning signal and slowly opened it. There was Radcliffe, in all his charming glory, awaiting her. Jewelle rushed over and hugged him. He stiffened, delicately embracing her as though she might break if he held her firmer, and then released her.

"What time did you get here?" she asked cheerily.

"Around two thirty. We hit patches of heavy traffic, but it didn't last for long."

For some reason the "we" registered. Suddenly Jewelle became aware that the shower was on.

"Is someone else here?" she asked carefully.

"Yes. My friend Jenna travelled with me. I thought I mentioned that she'd be with me," said Radcliffe casually.

"Daddy, that's something that I would remember. You did *not* mention any such thing to me," she spat out harshly.

"Is this a problem?"

"Don't you think it should be?"

"Not really. I really thought I had told you. Sorry that I forgot."

"Sorry? You are sorry?!" said Jewelle raising her voice. She was growing increasingly upset. What was unfolding before her was a very different scene than the one she had imagined. Not only wasn't she going to be able to spend some one-on-one time with her father, but a stranger, his girlfriend, was in her bathroom.

"Tell you what!" Jewelle continued. "Why don't you ..." her voice trailed off.

"Radcliffe, who are you talking to," shouted Jenna before she came into view. She was wearing Jewelle's bathrobe, her hair wrapped in a towel.

"I am talking to my daughter. Jewelle meet Jenna, Jenna meet Jewelle," said Radcliffe awkwardly.

Jewelle stood speechless as she studied Jenna—tall, light-skinned, curvy (more meat than potatoes), pretty, and probably the same age as Jewelle.

"Hello Jewelle," said Jenna, stepping forward with her outstretched hand. It remained suspended in mid-air.

"Hello Jenna, glad to see you have made yourself right at home," Jewelle barked through clenched teeth.

Jenna let Jewelle's remark wash over her. "Oh this," said Jenna, holding the collar of the bathrobe. "I forgot mine, so I borrowed one. Hope you don't mind."

"And if I do!"

"And you do! So, I'm going to give it right back to you." She sneered before sauntering off to the guest room.

When Jenna was out of earshot, Jewelle lit into her father. "You intentionally didn't tell me about Jenna because you knew I wouldn't want her here."

"Jewelle, I have always respected your choices and I wish you'd do the same," said Radcliffe in a measured and weary voice.

"It's not as simple as you'd like to pretend!"

"Pretend! No pretending here. I am an adult, and I am not seeking your approval of my choices."

Jewelle felt as though she had been slapped. The words stung because he was right.

"You know, this is a bigger conversation that I was hoping to avoid, but now that you have created this situation, I just need to get everything off my chest," shouted Jewelle. "Since you have company, and I'd like to talk to you privately, I would suggest that we go to the garden at the back of the building."

Looking at him with a steady gaze, Jewelle felt unnerved but also energized. She had carried around Adele's and Radcliffe's secret long enough. It was time to unload this burden. This was the moment to show what she was made of.

Radcliffe went to the guest bedroom to let Jenna know that he was going out with Jewelle. He returned with his girlfriend in tow. Standing beside Radcliffe, she shoved the used bathrobe towards Jewelle.

"Yu can tek yu robe back! Yes, I'm bilingual—patois and the Queen's English."

"Jenna, was that really necessary?"

"Your daughter has all kinds of attitude. She's your problem, not mine," snapped Jenna.

The air in the apartment was charged. Jewelle had given up any idea that her time with her father was going to be a happy occasion. Now, she just had an overwhelming desire to spill her guts and let the chips fall where they may.

Out in the garden, the trees were budding, and the grass was a vibrant shade of green. Jewelle and Radcliffe sat on one of the benches under the gazebo, she at one end and he at the other. For a few minutes, they sat in silence. Radcliffe was the first to speak.

"So, Jewelle, what's on your mind?" he asked quietly.

She wanted to speak, but her throat was suddenly dry, and she felt as though her tongue clung to the roof of her mouth. She swallowed hard before she spoke.

"Here goes. Just before moving to Toronto, I overheard mother telling Aunt Constance that she discovered that you not only had a new girlfriend, but that you had a second family."

Radcliffe looked genuinely surprised.

Jewelle continued, "When she got off the phone, I questioned her. She told me that she had lived with years of your philandering and that was what led to the divorce and that you tried to hide all your money during the divorce so that she wouldn't get a good settlement. She made me swear never to speak about this to my siblings or to you."

Jewelle felt emotionally and physically drained. She started to cry. It soon escalated to sobbing and wailing. Radcliffe grew anxious. He slid over to her end of the bench, wrapped his arms around her tenderly and tried to comfort her. They sat together like this until Jewelle's tears dried.

"Jewelle, your mother is correct that I was not faithful to her throughout our marriage. I can't offer you any kind of explanation that would make sense except that I was selfish and self-indulgent," said Radcliffe softly. "On the matter of the divorce settlement, I tried to be fair to your mother, but her demands were unreasonable because she was angry. In the end, she did get a fair settlement. Lastly, there is no second family on the side. One of the women I had an affair with had two young children. Her husband, a lawyer, left her with very little. I felt responsible, so I gave her a monthly allowance to help with the kids until they were eighteen. I assure you that you do not have any half brothers and sisters out in the world. I made sure of that," said Radcliffe.

"Daddy, this is a lot to process. Thanks for being straight with me. I really need to be alone right now. It would be best if you and Jenna find accommodations elsewhere. The concierge can recommend a few hotels in the neighbourhood. I'm going to stay here while you go back and pack."

"Jewelle, I regret that things turned out this way. Please keep an open heart and mind," he said somberly.

"I'll try."

Radcliffe stood up and walked away. Jewelle called out, "Daddy, I hope you find what you are looking for."

He turned, gave her a thumbs-up, and kept on walking.

Jewelle remained in the gazebo for a long time. She listened to the cacophony of birdsong to keep from thinking about all that her father had shared with her. Although it saddened her to hear her hero tell her that he was not much more than a flawed human being, she also felt at peace that he now knew what she had kept hidden these many years. She was also thankful to get his side of the story. Difficult as it was, Jewelle had to acknowledge that her mother Adele was a demanding and exacting woman. Although this did not excuse her father's behaviour in any way, she felt some sympathy for him.

When Jewelle went back to her condo, they were gone. On her way to the kitchen, she noticed a post-it note with a small gift box beside it sitting on the coffee table. *I had hoped to give this to you, but it didn't work out that way. Hope you like it. Love, Dad.*

Jewelle opened the box and took out a gold charm bracelet with three charms, her initials, a Jamaican flag and, she gasped when she fingered the third charm, a baby tooth capped in gold. She was touched that her father had kept this memento and now shared it with her. Her emotions ran amok. She walked to the kitchen and poured herself a glass of wine and decided that she couldn't face Adele tonight. It would have to keep until tomorrow.

Eleven

The Gathering

Chantal's edict banning personal calls from the office had a dramatic impact on Jewelle's daytime communication with Adele. When her mother grew increasingly upset that Jewelle was not returning her calls in a timely manner, she turned to her sister Constance for help. And so, they both peppered her with voicemails, expressing their displeasure. In one message, Adele fumed, "Miss Jewelle, guess you have outgrown your mother!" In another, she declared, "Oh, you left me off the guest list for your marriage to your job."

Her aunt Constance's messages were even more biting, "Miss Jewelle, mi sista, yu madda, tell me dat she no hear from yu because yu work roun di clock. Mek a remind yu dat if yu drop down, di job caan mek yu a cup a tea or tek care a yu. Fi di umpteenth time, *nerves nuh sell ah shop*. When yu bruk down, dem will fine somebody fi replace yu and not yu nerves. Rememba dat!"

The verbal battering hastened Jewelle's return visit to Montreal.

Jewelle suffered through the rush hour crush on the TTC, the Toronto Transit Commission, because it was the most efficient way to make it to Union Station to catch the 6.00 p.m. Montreal train. Jewelle was thankful that she had picked up her ticket the day before so there was no need to join the queue at the ticket counter. She went directly to the platform where boarding had already begun. Jewelle settled into an economy seat and called her mother. Adele picked up after the second ring.

"Hello Mother," said Jewelle cautiously.

"Oh, you finally found my number," said Adele acerbically. Jewelle didn't bite.

"Mother, I'm on the train. If there are no delays, I will get in around eleven. No need to wait up for me. Please ask Cass, Deeana, and Ryan to drop by tomorrow around six," said Jewelle.

"So, now I'm your secretary," said Adele crossly.

"No Mother. I'm simply asking you to round up the troops," said Jewelle, fighting hard to conceal her annoyance. Jewelle loved Adele, as did her brother and sisters. However, as they matured, they discovered that their mother was very demanding and insisted on having the final word even in matters that were not her business. Jewelle's siblings played along to avoid the arguments. But with each passing year, Jewelle began to push back and assert her independence.

"Ok, Miss Jewelle, I will call your brother and sisters who you haven't been calling either," kvetched Adele.

"Well, they'll soon see and hear me."

"Miss Jewelle, I don't like the sound of that! I hope you are not coming home to stir up trouble because you met with your father!"

"Mother, I have said all that I am going to say. Bye for now."

When Jewelle hung up, Adele was stunned and angry. She felt that Jewelle had been rude and disrespectful. Adele smoldered for a while before finally hanging up the phone.

Jewelle covered her mouth to hide a wide yawn that threatened to indecently expose the back of her throat. She was tired, so very tired. The long days and evenings were taking a toll on her. There seemed to be no time for anything but work with her early morning departures and late returns home from the office. She wondered if this is what success really looked and felt like.

Jewelle sipped the piping hot coffee she had picked up at a Second Cup and prayed that the family gathering would not descend into finger pointing and accusations of one sort or another. She sighed, reflecting on how she didn't really want to be part of this family gathering but felt that it was necessary. The last thing she needed at this point in her life was more family drama to add to the daily drama that was unfolding at TV3. Her mother and aunt Constance routinely reminded her that *"nerves nuh sell a shop,"* yet they were both stress manufacturers and distributors who were oblivious to the turmoil they routinely stirred up.

By the time Jewelle arrived in Montreal, she had learned the life story of the not-so-gay divorcee who was now preparing to walk down the aisle for a fourth time. She looked at her watch. It was eleven fifteen when the train pulled into the Gare Centrale. She swiftly exited the train and headed to the nearest taxi stand where she slipped into the first one in line.

Skyscrapers lit up like Christmas trees loomed overhead as the taxi cruised through the streets. Jewelle looked out the window at the buildings. She thought about the men and women whose visions, blood, sweat and tears had grown small businesses into large companies that now occupied some of these edifices. She comforted herself with the thought that these individuals had worked incredibly hard to achieve success. However, she reminded herself that they were putting time into their own businesses that could be passed down from generation to generation.

By the time the taxi stopped in front of her mother's house, Jewelle could feel the anxiety building in the pit of her stomach and radiating upwards to other parts of her body. Jewelle checked her watch. It was almost midnight. She knew that Adele would be up waiting for her even though she had asked her not to. As soon as she turned the key in the lock, it was pulled open from the inside.

There stood Adele in all her commanding glory. Jewelle removed her key and closed the door behind her.

"Hello Mother. I thought you'd be in bed," said Jewelle evenly as she walked over to give Adele a hug. Her mother stood frozen like a sculpture, arms glued to her sides.

"Miss Jewelle, I'd like to talk to you because I really don't appreciate the way that ..." Jewelle disrupted her flow.

"Mother, it is after midnight. I just had a long train ride. This will have to wait until the morning. I need to get some rest," she said as she stifled a yawn and began walking towards the guest bedroom.

Adele trailed her, stopping in the doorway after Jewelle entered. There was a pause, filled by the silence of the night.

"Well, I would like to talk now!" shrieked Adele, her face registering rage.

"Mother, again, I'm tired. I'm going to have a shower and go to bed. That's all that I'm prepared to do right now," said Jewelle firmly.

Adele stood there glaring at her. When she realized that Jewelle was not going to give in to her, she marched down the hall to her room where she slammed the door hard enough to take it off its hinges.

The confrontation with her mother plagued Jewelle's mind, and her sleep was restless. By 7 a.m., Jewelle quietly crept out of the house to avoid her mother and headed downtown for her usual walkabout. The metro spat passengers out quickly at each stop along the route. The largest exodus was at the stops in the downtown core—Atwater, Guy and Berri-UQAM. The unique design of each metro station always pleased Jewelle. The stained-glass mural at McGill, which depicted the history of Montreal was a favourite. Other stops with more contemporary designs reflected the evolution of the city. From her seat on the metro, Jewelle observed her fellow passengers, a wide cross-section of Montrealers. Although she had ridden the

Montreal subway many times, and knew the stops inside out, today she looked at her fellow Montrealers with fresh eyes and was pleased with what she saw, men and women of all races, religions, nationalities—short, tall, thin, fat and everything in between. *Vive la différence,* she thought warmly.

Jewelle switched metro lines at Berri-UQAM and exited the Metro at Champs-de-Mars. She walked up the street to Old Montreal, a vibrant historic neighbourhood sandwiched between the St. Lawrence River and downtown. European in character with its seventeenth- and eighteenth-century buildings, cobblestone streets, horse-drawn carriages, quaint and charming restaurants, cafés and museums, Old Montreal drew tourists from all over the world. Jewelle stopped at one of the cafés on Place Jacques-Cartier and sat outside under the red awning, waiting for her order to be taken.

"*Bonjour Madame,*" greeted the pleasant waiter.

"Bonjour," replied Jewelle.

"*Êtes-vous prête à commander?*" asked the waiter, notepad at the ready.

"Oui. Je voudrais un chocolat chaud et une *crêpe nature,*" ordered Jewelle.

"C'est tout Madame?" asked the waiter in his distinct Québécois accent.

"Oui, monsieur, c'est tout," replied Jewelle.

"Bon. Merci," he said before walking to the kitchen to place the order.

While she waited for her food, Jewelle watched the square come to life as the sun crept out from behind the clouds— stores opened, awnings unfurled, sandwich board signs were strategically placed out front of various restaurants. Artists set up their easels and their work for sale, and buskers staked out their performance spaces.

Jewelle soaked up the ambience of Old Montreal while she ate her breakfast. She allowed her imagination to take her back to the days when horse-drawn carriages ruled the cobblestone streets, and women of means dressed in beautiful clothing made from rich brocades, velvet, and lace. The scene reminded her of the Musée du costume et du textile du Québec on rue de La Commune, and the many delightful exhibits she had seen there.

Her daydream was disrupted by the buzz of her Nokia cellphone. She let it go to voicemail. Adele kept re-dialing, but Jewelle ignored the interruption. A few minutes after Adele's last call, the phone buzzed again. It was Chantal.

"Good morning, Miss Mercier."

"Jewelle, what time can I expect you at the office?" asked Chantal with greeting-like courtesy.

You can't," replied Jewelle crisply, "I'm in Montreal visiting my family. Is there something urgent?"

"As a matter of fact, there is. You still have *not* formally introduced me to Johann Eriksson. I want to jump on this file today. Why wasn't this done last week?" Chantal asked angrily without waiting for an answer. "I want the introduction done this afternoon!"

"Please double-check the report. I noted that Johann is in New York and plans to visit Toronto shortly, and that I recommended a face-to-face introduction. Since you made no objections, I thought this was fine with you."

"Jewelle, I don't recall reading anything of the kind in your report. Either way, I would like an email introduction today! When will it be done?"

"Within the hour, Miss Mercier."

"Okay. There'll be a sales meeting at 8:00 on Monday. I'll see you then."

"Yes, Miss Mercier," hissed Jewelle through clenched teeth.

Emotions now ablaze, Jewelle needed to douse the flames. She signaled for the waiter, paid the bill, and headed for Notre-Dame Basilica, a masterpiece of Gothic revival architecture with deep blue vaults decorated with golden stars, intricate wood carvings and beautiful stained-glass windows depicting religious history including encounters between the First Nations and the clergy. Jewelle knew that the serenity of Notre-Dame's sanctuary would soothe her. There, she dropped a twoonie in the box beside the rows of candles in red containers, lit one and prayed for inner peace and ongoing blessings for her friends and family and wisdom for leaders at home and abroad.

When Jewelle left Notre-Dame, she checked her watch. It was ten thirty. She found a quiet corner near the Basilica to compose and send the introductory email to Johann and Chantal.

> *Hello Johann,*
>
> *By way of this email, I'm introducing you to Miss Chantal Mercier, the new VP of Sales and Distribution. Miss Mercier is now responsible for all of Scandinavia and will be working with you directly. Chantal, meet Johann Eriksson. Please let us know when you'll be in Toronto so that we can arrange a lunch or dinner meeting.*
>
> *Warm regards,*
>
> *Jewelle*

She hit the send button.

With Chantal off her back for the moment, Jewelle turned her thoughts to the family gathering coming up at six. She knew there would be fireworks but was prepared to deal with them. Jewelle had long been fed up with the secrecy and the one-sided information she and her siblings had been subjected to by their mother.

Jewelle gave her father a quick call to remind him to drop by Adele's home at seven thirty. The rest of the day was dedicated to walking around in downtown Montreal with visits to a newly discovered gallery, museum, or boutique. She also stopped to admire window displays in some of the new buildings that had been constructed while she was away. Fashionable people were everywhere.

Jewelle's final stop was the Promenades Cathédrale, a high-end mall located beneath the Anglican Christ Church Cathedral. Here, she went directly to Femme de Carrière to check new arrivals and items on sale. She picked up two beautiful silk blouses, same design, one in black and the other in an emerald green. They were half price. Delighted with her purchases, Jewelle boarded the metro at 4.00 p.m. to head back home.

It was 5.15 p.m. when Jewelle turned the key in the front door. This would give her enough time to smooth things out with her mother before the others arrived.

"Hello Mother, I'm back," she called cheerfully out from the hallway. Her greeting was met with silence. "Mother, are you here?" She tried again. Silence.

Jewelle placed her bags in the guest room and then started searching from room to room. She found Adele reading in the living room.

"Mother, didn't you hear me calling out to you?" asked Jewelle.

Adele shot back, "Didn't you hear me calling you over and over again this morning?"

"Yes, I did but I was in the middle of breakfast, and it was my quiet time."

"Well, it's my quiet time!"

"Mother, I'd like to clear the air before the others get here. I told you that we'd talk about my visit with Daddy, so let's do it now."

"I'm all ears!" said Adele dryly.

"Since the divorce, we have really only heard your side of the story. When Daddy visited me, he admitted that he behaved badly, and he regrets it, and he has tried to make things right. I also asked him about the secret second family. There is no secret second family. He has been providing financial support for the children of one of the women he had an affair ..."

Jewelle was interrupted mid-sentence when Adele bolted upright from the sofa and shouted, "Enough! You mean that worthless man told you all this and you believe him?"

"Yes, he told me and yes, I believe him. At this point in his life, he has no reason to lie. Remember what *you* told us, 'He is still your father and deserves some love and respect.'"

"Jewelle, I can't believe that you are taking his side," moaned Adele.

"Mother, you are *not* listening. I am not taking sides, just balancing what I have been told all these years," said Jewelle quietly. "I know this conversation dredges up some bad memories, but we all need to confront and deal with them. I've already told Cass, Deeana and Ryan what Daddy shared with me."

"You did what!" screeched Adele. "You have no right to be telling my business to everybody!"

"Mother, I didn't tell it to everybody, I told my brother and sisters, your children."

"After all that that man put me through. I live to see my daughter taking his side against me."

"Again, I'm not taking sides. I'm just thankful that I now know the other side of what led to the divorce."

"It's very easy for you to stand there and say all of this. You have no idea what I endured."

"I don't know all of it. But remember we all lived through the bitterness of the divorce! We were all affected by it. You don't have to take my word for it. Ask the others when they get here!"

At that moment, the doorbell rang, and Jewelle and Adele waited for Cass, Deeana, and Ryan to come through the door. They didn't. Instead, the doorbell rang again. Adele went to answer the door. When she opened it there was Radcliffe Joseph in all his splendiferous style. She was speechless.

"Hello Adele," said Radcliffe carefully.

"What are you doing here?" she demanded.

"I knew Jewelle was visiting so I dropped by on the off chance that she and her siblings might be here," replied Radcliffe.

"Jewelle is here, and the other kids should be soon," said Adele without inviting him in.

When Adele did not return to the living room, Jewelle went to see if there was a problem. She saw her father standing on the front porch and checked her watch. It was just six fifteen. He was very early.

"Hi Jewelle, I knew you were in town, so I dropped by to see if you were here," said Radcliffe.

Jewelle played along. "Daddy, why are you still standing out there? Come in."

Calmly, Radcliffe asked Adele if that was okay.

"Since you are already here and *your* daughter is here, you might as well," replied Adele, then she quickly turned and walked away.

As she did, Radcliffe winked at Jewelle and whispered that he'd explain later.

Shortly after Jewelle closed the door, the bell rang, and the key turned in the door. Cass, Deeana, and Ryan walked in. They greeted Jewelle warmly with hugs.

"Hey JJ, how are you holding up under the new management?" Ryan asked sympathetically.

"It's rough but I'm hanging in. Daddy's here!"

"Mother let him in?" asked Cass incredulously.

"Yes, but she wasn't happy. He's in the living room with her. We better go rescue him," smiled Jewelle.

When they entered the living room, Adele was sitting at one end of the sofa, book in hand, pretending to read and Radcliffe was in the wing chair. He got up to greet and warmly embrace each of his children. Adele looked on in anger and disgust.

"Daddy, it has been a long time since we were all together under the same roof. This is great," gushed Deeana.

"So, you too are taking his side?" snapped Adele.

"Mother, I'm just happy that we are all together. That's all!" Deeana replied cheerfully.

Radcliffe looked around the room at his adult children. Warm memories of their childhoods flooded his thoughts— teaching them to swim, making and flying a kite with Ryan, taking the girls to Brownies. Radcliffe was sorry about Jewelle's encounter with his latest girlfriend. He thought long and hard about his behaviour and the women he had hurt, especially Adele. A single tear rolled down his cheek, and Radcliffe stoic- ally said, "I am sorry for any hurt that I have caused all of you. Please forgive me."

A heavy silence fell over the room. Time stood still. The spell broke when Jewelle, followed by her siblings, walked over, and hugged their father. When she looked over his shoulder, Adele was crying softly. Adele had waited many years for his apology.

PART III

Twelve

The Swede Has Landed

Jewelle was sitting at her desk in her office lost in concentration on a report she was writing when she was startled by the ringing of the phone.

"Hello, Jewelle Joseph."

"Hi Jewelle. It's Johann."

"Hey Johann. How are you?"

"Better now that I'm speaking to you," said Johann, his voice softening.

Jewelle ignored his line. "Where are you?"

"Downstairs in your lobby,"

"Seriously?"

"Seriously!" replied Johann, imitating Jewelle. "I'm here to see Miss Mercier. And you, of course."

"I'll send Heather down to bring you up," said Jewelle happily. "We will let Miss Mercier know that you are here."

She walked out to Heather's desk and told her that Mr. Sweden was in the lobby waiting to come up.

"At last, I get to meet this Johann," said Heather mischievously.

"Please seat him in the boardroom when you get back. Thanks! Off to see Miss Mercier, now. Fun, fun," smiled Jewelle.

She knocked on Chantal's door and waited to be invited in.

"Who is there?" Boss Lady growled.

"Miss Mercier, it's Jewelle."

"Come in."

Jewelle opened the door and stood in the doorway. "Johann Eriksson is downstairs. Heather has gone to bring him up. I have asked her to seat him in the boardroom."

"Did he just turn up here?" she asked sharply.

"Yes, he just turned up. Surprise!"

"That's highly irregular. But since he's here, I'll meet with him," Chantal said brusquely.

"When I introduced you to Johann, I noted in the email that *we* would all meet when he's in town. However, you stated that *you* will meet with him. Please clarify," asked Jewelle.

"Not much to clarify. He's now my client. I have your report, and I'll take things from here. I'm sure you have work to do. If you don't, I can easily fix that, Jewelle Joseph!"

It took all Jewelle's strength not to slap Miss Mercier and tell her a few choice words before bolting from her office. Jewelle was livid. She marched down the hall grumbling to herself hurrying past Heather. When she opened her office door, there was Johann looking at the pictures on her bookshelf. She burst into a smile. "What are you doing in my office?"

"Is that how you greet a friend?" he asked, walking over to give her a hug and a kiss on each cheek. "To answer your question, I asked Heather to bring me to your office without telling you. I wanted to see where you spend most of your time and how your office is decorated. Nice family photos. Malcolm X. Pretty radical, Jewelle," said a smiling Johann. "I take it the handsome young man is Anthony Brown," said Johann without waiting for confirmation. "Well, now I know what the competition looks like, and I can now imagine you in your workspace when we speak on the phone."

"There's no competition ..."

Before Jewelle could finish her sentence, Chantal barged into her office. "Hello Johann, nice to see you again," said Chantal rushing forward to shake his hand.

"Hello Chantal. Heather directed me to the boardroom, but I asked her to redirect me to Jewelle's office. So, here I am," explained Johann.

"Well, let's make our way to the boardroom," said Chantal, striding ahead of Johann.

When Jewelle stopped in the doorway of her office, Johann quietly asked if she would be joining them. Jewelle explained that Miss Mercier did not want her to attend. Smiling, Johann asked her to grab her notebook, took her by the hand and walked down the hall with her. As the pair walked into the boardroom, Chantal's face reddened with anger. Johann noticed. "I asked Jewelle to join us because any business that TV3 does with our company, she will have to be involved," said Johann lightly.

"You do understand that I am now responsible for *all* of Scandinavia?"

"I do. However, I'm insisting that Jewelle continues to be involved in all new business with our company. Is that a problem?" asked Johann.

Chantal sputtered. "I don't think it should be," she said unconvincingly.

"Miss Mercier, to be totally transparent, I have already discussed the matter with *your* boss and was assured that Jewelle would continue to work with our company," said Johann in a tone that demanded agreement and a look to match.

"Now that we have cleared up this matter," he continued, "let's get down to business."

Over the next couple of hours, Chantal, Johann and Jewelle discussed a new co-production agreement for a new natural history series. The deal would result in TV3 acquiring worldwide rights excluding Scandinavia, the UK and Italy. When the meeting ended, Johann walked Jewelle back to her office.

"Jewelle, it's clear that Miss Mercier has it in for you. How much longer do you think you can put up with her nonsense?"

"I am weighing my options. I had planned to resign but my parents think I should hang on for a while longer. The long hours are really getting to me now. I'm also thinking about taking a leave of absence or a holiday," declared Jewelle followed by a heavy sigh.

"Well Jewelle, you could make a clean break and move to Sweden. I'm sure you'd do well there. And of course, you have the bonus of a man who adores you. No, a man who loves you."

His last words hung in the air.

"Johann, sounds tempting but it would be very difficult for me to pick up and leave my family, my posse and boyfriend behind," said Jewelle. "I love them."

"Does that mean that you don't love me?" he asked and paused. "On second thought, ignore my question. No answer required."

Jewelle felt badly that she could not give Johann the answer that he wanted to hear. Yes, she was attracted to him, but "love" was another matter altogether. Seeing each other at markets and speaking on the phone, to her way of thinking, was not enough to really know that much about him, his background, and what he was like in daily life. Besides, she didn't wish to open this can of worms. Her life was already challenging.

"Well, a lot has been said," Johann added thoughtfully. "All I'd ask is that you think about my suggestion of moving to Stockholm for a month or two on a trial basis."

"Okay, I promise I'll give it some consideration and let you know. How is that?" she asked, flashing him an optimistic smile.

"Sounds good. Well, Jewelle Joseph, I am going to let you get back to your report. Must keep Miss Mercier happy!"

"Indeed! What are you up to for the rest of the day?" asked Jewelle.

"I have one more meeting before heading to the airport," said Johann. Checking his watch, he added, "I better get going if I'm going to be on time for the meeting and my flight."

"I'll walk you out."

Before Johann left the office, they hugged, and he kissed her on each cheek. They walked down the hall in silence to the elevator where Jewelle waited with him. When the elevator arrived, he stepped on, turned around and blew her a kiss before the doors closed. No question that Jewelle felt a *frisson* in this man's presence. But she didn't want to become Ms. Radcliffe.

Shortly, Jewelle got back to her office. Heather knocked on the door and poked her head in.

"Jewelle, that Johann is some good-looking! Seems like he's really nice too. I hope he visits again soon. Handsome men are always welcome!

"Oh, Miss Mercier would like to see you in her office in half an hour. Just a heads up. She tore a strip off me for bringing Johann to you. Said, she was going to put a note in my personnel file. What else is new?"

"Thanks for the warning, Heather. I'll suit up in my invisible armour and spear!" said Jewelle, smiling.

Jewelle knocked on Chantal's door and waited.

"Come in!" barked Chantal.

When Jewelle walked in, the chair was sitting in front of her desk.

"Sit there," ordered Chantal pointing to *the* chair. Jewelle obliged.

"So, you are going over my head to get special favours," Chantal accused Jewelle.

"What are you talking about?" asked Jewelle calmly.

"Don't play innocent with me!" howled Chantal. "Are you trying to tell me that you didn't ask Johann Eriksson to speak to Marg about you continuing to work with his company?"

"That's exactly what I'm saying, Miss Mercier. I had no knowledge that Johann spoke to Marg or anyone else," said Jewelle irritably, jotting down a few lines in her notebook.

"Well, I don't believe you! I thought you had accepted my authority but clearly you have not, and something needs to be done about this. I fully intend to bring this situation to the chair of the board," she said heatedly.

"Miss Mercier, you do what you need to do. I've told you the truth. Just remember that people who live in glass houses should not throw stones."

"What are you accusing me of?" yelled Chantal.

"Absolutely nothing! Is there anything more that we need to talk about?"

"You have been warned, Jewelle Joseph. Get out of my office!" Chantal commanded, unsuccessfully trying to hide the trembling in her voice.

Jewelle left Chantal's office rattled by her accusation. She had the feeling that she was losing the battle even though she was fighting as hard as she could in the ways that she knew how. On the walk back to her office, she thought about Heather's suggestion that she take a holiday and Johann's that she visit Sweden for a while. In that moment, she made the decision to take some time off. This would allow her to think more clearly about future plans without having to manage tyrannical demands and increasingly paranoid behaviour. It would also allow her to use up some of the many hours of overtime that she had banked. When Jewelle got back to her office, she completed a requisition form for a month's leave of absence and later dropped it in Chantal's mailbox.

Jewelle waited patiently for two weeks to get confirmation on the leave of absence that she requested. None came. So, she sent a follow-up email to Chantal.

Subject: Leave of Absence
Date: 2000-06-23 14:14
From: JJoseph@TV3.com
To: CMercier@TV3.com

Miss Mercier,

Two weeks ago, I submitted a requisition form to request a four-week leave of absence. To date, I have yet to receive a reply. When can I expect to receive confirmation?
Your prompt attention to the matter is appreciated.

Jewelle Joseph

International Sales Executive
TV3

Subject: Re: Leave of Absence
Date: 2000-06-23 15:14
From: CMercier@TV3.com
To: JJoseph@TV3.com

Jewelle,

I guess you have not learned that sometimes, no answer is THE answer. But for the record, your requisition has been denied because your services are critical to the success of TV3, and as such, your absence would negatively impact the company's bottom line.

Chantal Mercier
VP, Sales & Distribution
TV3

When Jewelle received Chantal's email reply, shock morphed into anger and then outrage. Chantal's reason and explanation made no sense to Jewelle. To her way of thinking, her request would be no different than if she had to take a leave of absence due to illness. In fact, the requested leave supported her mental and psychological well-being. The fact that this was not spelled out in the request should make no difference.

Jewelle paced around her office as she tried to figure out her next move when she decided that a second opinion about the situation would be helpful. She forwarded a copy of Chantal's email to Heather, asked her to read it, and then come see her. A few minutes after sending the email, Heather knocked gently on her door and walked in and stood arms akimbo in front of Jewelle.

"Jewelle, I read the email. What Chantal is doing is wrong. She needs a serious correction!"

"I agree but am not sure how best to go about this."

"It's not complicated. Forward a copy of the email to Marg and ask for a meeting. When you meet with Marg, focus on the email and the requested leave of absence. There's plenty of time, later on, to deal with all of Miss Mercier's nasty stunts," Heather huffed.

Heather walked around to the other side of the desk where she could see the computer screen while Jewelle typed the short note that read, *Can we discuss the emails below at your earliest convenience,* before hitting the send button.

"Thanks Heather as always for your support and uncommon sense," said Jewelle.

"No problem. I better get back to my desk. Let me know how things turn out."

Jewelle resumed work on yet another report that Chantal had requested. She was frustrated and could feel tears welling up in her eyes. She wiped them away angrily with the side of her thumb and continued typing for the next hour. Jewelle was interrupted when Marg called and asked her to come to her office. Jewelle took a deep breath and quietly prayed that Marg would be understanding.

"Hello Jewelle," said Marg.

"Hello. Sorry to have to trouble you. I know that you are under a lot of pressure trying to deal with the revenue shortfall, but I didn't know what else to do."

"No need to apologize. I'm glad you brought the matter to my attention. I have already spoken to Chantal and HR and signed off on your requisition form. You have earned the time off you requested. Besides, you need to use up some of your overtime hours," said Marg sympathetically.

"Thank you, thank you. I really need a break," said Jewelle gratefully.

"Are you planning to go anywhere special?" asked Marg.

"Thinking of going to Paris to visit friends and think about my future."

"Well, enjoy Paris and don't make any hasty decisions while you are away. Promise,"

"Promise," replied Jewelle happily.

On the way back to her office, Jewelle stopped at Heather's desk to share her big news.

"I'm so happy for you, Jewelle! Miss Mercier is now going to have to find someone else to harass while you are away."

They both burst out laughing. Back at her desk, Jewelle, breezed through the rest of the report. Before leaving the office, she printed it and dropped it in Chantal's mail slot.

Out on the street, the sun was still shining, and all felt right in Jewelle's world. This was another Nina Simone "Feeling Good" moment—"It's a new life for me, and I'm feeling good ..."

Before getting onto the subway, she called Anthony. He didn't pick up. She left him a voicemail asking him to drop by at eight. Once back in her neighbourhood, she stopped at the grocery store to pick up a roast chicken, a small bag of carrots, a small bag of baby potatoes, and a few pastries for dessert. She planned to surprise Anthony with a nice meal.

When she got back to her condo, she put her bags in her bedroom, washed her hands, and then took the groceries to the kitchen. She placed the chicken in the oven to keep it warm and lay the rest of the groceries on the counter. She washed the carrots and potatoes, sliced them, and placed them in a colander over a pot of boiling water. While they were being steamed, Jewelle prepared a tossed salad of Boston lettuce, cherry tomatoes and walnuts and placed it in the fridge. With the food under control, she went to the dining area to set the table. She covered the table with a French Provençal tablecloth, a beautiful design of sunflowers, wheat, and olives on a yellow, blue, and green background. She added two white candles with melted wax that had converted them into sculptures that reminded her of Gaudi's famous La Sagrada Familia. She added the cutlery, simple white dishes, and plain crystal wine glasses. When the table was set, Jewelle stepped back to admire her handy work. She was pleased. There was still time for her to grab a quick shower and change before Anthony's arrival.

Anthony knocked on the door and let himself in as Jewelle had instructed in the voicemail she left him.

"JJ," he called out.

"I'll be out in a minute," replied Jewelle.

"Something smells great!" said Anthony as he walked to the dining area. He was admiring the table when Jewelle walked into the room wearing the emerald-green top that she bought in Montreal, with slim black slacks and a pair of black ballerina flats.

"Well, you are in for a treat," said Jewelle smiling brightly, walking towards Anthony who was admiring her from head to toe. When she got close, he hugged her, and they fell into a long, lingering kiss. They stood back, looked into each other's eyes, and smiled.

"JJ, you look great. Your hair is down for a change. You should wear it this way more often."

"Thanks, Anthony. Glad you could make it. And, if you are hungry, I'm starved. Forgot to eat lunch again."

"Not a good habit to get into. I'm hungry and ready to eat if you are. Do you need help with anything?"

"If you could grab the salad and the wine from the fridge, that would be great."

Anthony followed Jewelle into the kitchen. After he took out the salad and the bottle of wine, he returned and kissed her again. Jewelle followed him into the dining area with the salad dressing and a small bowl of olives. They sat across from each other, looking happy. Anthony opened the wine and filled each glass.

"Should I say grace or will you?" asked Jewelle.

"I got this. Father God, thank you for your continued mercy, grace, and the food we are about to partake of. May you bless it to our bodies and bless our time together. I ask this in the name of Jesus."

"Amen," said Jewelle and Anthony in unison.

"I'd like to propose a toast," said Anthony. "To love and friendship." They clinked their glasses, and each took a sip.

Throughout the evening, they talked amicably about their respective families, and Jewelle shared the details of her recent trip to Montreal, inviting Anthony to join her on her next visit. After they finished their salads, Jewelle brought in the main course beautifully plated, setting one plate in front of Anthony and the other at her seat.

"JJ, thanks for this lovely meal. I really appreciate you making the time to do this. I know how busy you are. Speaking of busy, how was work today?"

"Well, let's just enjoy our food before I get into that whole mess. Okay?"

"Fine with me," said Anthony. "Let's dig in!"

Jewelle chuckled, and then dug in. Over dessert, they talked about local politics, the economy and Anthony's family. When dinner was over, Anthony selected a Charlie Parker CD, which they listened to as they sat on the sofa together, Anthony in one corner and Jewelle stretched out with her head resting in his lap. He looked down at her tenderly and stroked her hair.

"So, now that our bellies are full and the kitchen is clean, do you want to tell me what's going on at work?" asked Anthony.

"Like all the other days since Miss Mercier has become my boss, she made my day hellish. She's mad at me right now because one of our Swedish clients came in for a meeting, and he told Chantal that his company will only continue to do business with TV3 if I continue to handle their account. Chantal was furious because she has now taken over all of Scandinavia."

Jewelle's momentary thought of telling Anthony about Johann, and his interest in her, vanished as quickly as it appeared. Her instincts told her it would create more problems than it would resolve.

"Well, understandably, she thinks her authority is being undermined," commented Anthony.

Jewelle was annoyed with this thought, but she let it slide for the moment. "Anthony, the only thing I understand is that Miss Mercier would like me to bow down to her and that is not going to happen. Anyhow, I put in a requisition for a leave of absence, so that I can get some perspective about my new situation. Miss Mercier turned me down cold even though I have tons of overtime hours that must be used, or I will lose them."

"Why did she turn you down?"

"She said my services impact the company's bottom line, so I must stay put."

"Sounds like a reasonable explanation."

"It only *sounds* reasonable, Anthony," bristled Jewelle. "Anyhow, I brought the matter to the head of the department's attention, and she overruled Miss Mercier and signed my requisition form. Naturally, Chantal is angry and is threatening revenge of one sort or another."

"So, when does your leave start?"

"Next Friday. I plan to take a month off," said Jewelle gleefully.

"A month! What are you going to do with all that time?"

"I'm thinking of going to Paris to see my friend Thérèse ..."

"Jewelle," Anthony interrupted, "this sounds like you have already made a decision. Am I correct?"

"Yes. I didn't think it would be a big deal for you. My mother, yes. But not you," griped Jewelle.

Anthony stiffened. Jewelle could feel and sense the change in him. She sat up and looked at him.

"Is it a big deal?"

"The fact that you don't think that it would be a big deal to me is a big deal. And the bigger deal is that you didn't even think this is something you should even discuss with me," said Anthony, bowing his head to hide the hurt and disappointment displayed on his face.

"Anthony, to be honest, I just thought about going to Paris today after the confrontation with Chantal. Heather, my assistant, and my father have suggested that I might benefit from time away from the office. So today, I decided to take their suggestion."

"Jewelle, you don't have to sell me on the need for you taking a leave. I know how hard you work. My concern is that I'm trying to get from me to we, but I don't think that's where you are at. If you think Paris will help you sort out your feelings and priorities, then by all means go," said Anthony firmly. "I'll be here when you get back."

Anthony thanked Jewelle for the dinner, politely excused himself and left. Jewelle sat frozen staring at the door, chiding herself for ruining what could have been a perfect evening.

Thirteen

Office Chaos

From the moment Marg authorized Jewelle's leave of absence, Chantal went on the warpath. Marg had become a new target. Chantal plotted and devised schemes to bring down the woman who stood between her and her desire to become head of the TV3 Sales and Distribution Inc. She had to be removed.

Suddenly, important files started to disappear from Marg's office. At first, she thought she was simply misplacing them because of fatigue and the pressure she was under to increase revenues. However, she slowly came to the realization that her files were being deliberately tampered with. She had no proof but was committed to finding a way to prove her suspicions. Marg engaged the support of a member of the technical department and hired a private company to install a small camera in her office.

Early one morning, Jewelle saw Chantal sneaking out of Marg's office. She hid herself so that Chantal was unaware of her presence, made a mental note of what she saw and wrote down the date and time. Later that day, Heather told Jewelle that Marg's laptop was missing and so was the electronic file of the annual report presentation draft. Tech support had been called in to try to retrieve a clone of the file. There was a flurry of activity around the missing device and the file, but it was all kept hush hush. In the end, the electronic file of the annual report was not retrieved in time for Marg's presentation to the board. With Heather's help, she managed to throw something together quickly, planning to wing whatever was missing.

The following day, Marg delivered her presentation to the board, trying her best with what she had available. At the end of the presentation, Gregory George, the Chair, was aggressive in his questioning and commented that he thought the presentation overall was substandard. Marg explained that her laptop with the PowerPoint presentation had been stolen, and that Tech Support couldn't recover the clone of the file. As she looked around the room at the board members, she got the impression that they were not sympathetic. The Chair grudgingly accepted her explanation and requested that a copy of the original PowerPoint be sent to all the board members as soon as it became available.

When Marg returned to her office, she was agitated and disappointed. Nothing like this had ever happened to her before. It made her recall meetings that she had had with Jewelle when she came to see her about missing files and the missing DVDs during MIP-TV. Each time she told Jewelle she needed proof that someone was intentionally trying to sabotage her. Now, she was in the same boat.

Were these random coincidences? Marg decided to pull Jewelle's file to review the notes she had made after each meeting. She slowly went through the files, organized in alphabetical order. Jewelle's was missing. She called Heather to her office.

"Heather, have you seen anyone go into my office recently," asked Marg somberly.

"No. Why do you ask?"

"I was looking for a file in my desk drawer and it is missing. It's Jewelle's personnel file," said Marg with concern.

"Let me look to see if it was just misfiled. A fresh set of eyes picks up these types of mistakes faster," said Heather.

Heather looked slowly and carefully through the files in Marg's drawer. She did not find Jewelle's.

"Sorry Marg. I guess it's really missing," said Heather. I will also check my files to see if somehow, it's there.

Heather left and went directly to her filing cabinet to do a thorough search. When nothing turned up, she went to see Jewelle.

"Hi Heather, what's up?" asked Jewelle, already suspicious that some new crisis was brewing.

"You can't breathe a word to anyone," answered Heather in a hushed voice.

"Zip!" answered Jewelle, pulling an imaginary zipper across her lips.

"Now things are starting to go missing from Marg's office. Her laptop with her presentation for the board was stolen. I had to quickly pull something together for her, but it only had some of the information she needed. Tech Support recovered the file from my desktop, but not in time for Marg's presentation." Heather paused to catch her breath having captured Jewelle's full attention. "Something is definitely going on. Since I've been here, we have never had a theft in the department. And there's more. Your personnel file is missing. Marg and I have searched, and we still haven't found it. I have a hunch that Miss Mercier is behind all of this."

"She's using the same tactics to sabotage Marg because she gave me the leave of absence. Who knows? She is probably also going after her job," said Jewelle worriedly.

"You may be right, but we need proof. What kind of cheese can we set in a trap for the resident rat? You think about it and I'll do the same and see what we come up with."

"Sounds like a plan! You'd better go. Let me know if you hear anything else."

In a flash Heather bolted from Jewelle's office. After Heather's departure, Jewelle remembered seeing Chantal coming out of Marg's office early one morning. Now, she felt sure that there was a connection between the missing items and the Boss

Lady. It struck Jewelle that it may soon be time to share Barb's documents with Marg because she may have a better idea how to use them.

For the rest of the day, Jewelle dealt with pressing emails and phone calls. She also worked on an extensive to-do list of all the tasks that Heather would have to cover while she was away. Although she had every confidence that Heather would do the work well, she was concerned that The Rat would interfere and create real problems. The truth was, Jewelle would have preferred to resign than be fired.

By the time Jewelle returned home from work that evening, she was emotionally and physically exhausted. The day had been one filled with a trail of crises and meetings to deal with each one. As soon as she got through the door, she went to her filing cabinet and pulled out the envelope with Barb's documents. She put it in her tote bag and prayed that it would be of some help to Marg and herself. All she wanted to do was crawl into bed. She did so as soon as she got out of the shower.

The following morning, she was up at six. She rushed through the morning routine—shower, dressing, checking emails and a quick breakfast. After breakfast, she called Thérèse in Paris. The phone rang and rang. Just as she was about to hang up, Thérèse picked up.

"Oui, allô."

"Bonjour, Thérèse."

"Jewelle, ezz zat you,"

"Yes Thérèse. How are you?"

"*Très bien, merci et toi?*"

"Things are really rough at the office. Chantal, my new boss, is making my life hell."

"Oh, zat ezz not good. What are you going to do?"

"I am thinking about quitting, but my assistant, my father, my mother and my boyfriend think I should hang in there. Anyway, I have taken a leave of absence, which is one of the reasons why I am calling. I'm planning to visit Paris for a holiday and to clear my head."

"*Merveilleux!* When will you come?"

"In eight days. I am just making my arrangements now. As soon as everything is finalized, I will let you know."

"Ow are tings wid your Anthony and Johann?"

"It's complicated. Johann visited Toronto recently. I saw him briefly. Anyhow, he thinks I should consider moving to Europe to explore other job opportunities. Of course, he had ulterior motives. But that's a longer story. More details when we see each other."

"Alors, Johann may be right. Something to tink about," said Thérèse.

"It would be a very big and difficult move for me, but I will think about it," said Jewelle. "I have to wrap up now and get to the office. I'll call you as soon as my flight and hotel are booked. Good to talk to you. Bye for now."

"Bon. J'espère te revoir bientôt. *Au revoir.*"

When the call ended, Jewelle checked her watch. It was 7:20 a.m. when she headed out the door, and by the time Jewelle arrived at the office, Marg and Chantal were already there. She quietly knocked on Marg's door and let herself in. Marg looked wild-eyed, worried.

"Morning Marg. Sorry to disturb you. I just wanted to give you this package."

"Morning Jewelle. What is it?"

"Barbara gave it to me after she left and now, I'm passing it on to you."

"It all sounds very mysterious."

"I don't think it is. All I'd ask is that you keep it under lock and key or take it home with you. You'll understand why when you take a look. I'll leave you to review it at your leisure. Bye for now."

"Thanks, Jewelle. I'll follow up if I need to."

Jewelle slipped into her office and turned on her desktop computer. While it booted up, she listened to her voicemail.

There were a couple of messages from her mother, and a few from her aunt Constance. She made a note on her to-do list to call them when she got home. Her phone rang. It was Marg.

"Thanks for the package, Jewelle."

"You are welcome."

Marg continued, "I'm going to work from home the rest of the day. I need some uninterrupted time."

"Ok. I'll see you tomorrow morning," said Jewelle. She hung up.

The morning started off like any other until everyone in the department heard Marg yell, "Chantal, get in here!" She had never done this before. The water cooler gossip erupted. Jewelle sought out Heather. She was confident that she'd know what was going on. She did.

"Where do I begin!" sighed Heather.

"Let's try the beginning," snapped Jewelle.

"Yesterday when Marg left, she met with the chair of the board to review the budget because it was completely out of whack."

"How come?"

"This is the juicy part. Apparently, the swish promotional events and the coffee-table book-cum-doorstop were not under-written by sponsorship as Chantal had claimed."

Jewelle gasped. "What?!"

"There are *no* sponsorship dollars coming in to offset the costs, and she concealed the real cost of decorating her office. She has been on a real spending spree," said Heather, sighing deeply.

"The organization is already experiencing revenue shortfalls, surely this will cost her her job," declared Jewelle.

"It should, but the Board is unfairly trying to pin it on Marg," said Heather.

"What is poor Marg going to do?" asked Jewelle with concern.

"I don't know but she'll figure something out. She's tough. She worked hard for many years to get where she is. I don't think she'll take this sitting down," said Heather.

"FYI—Yesterday, I gave her Barb's package. Timing is everything," said Jewelle.

"You didn't!" shrieked Heather. "What did she say?"

"She thanked me. I left before she looked at the documents," Jewelle explained.

"You didn't mention anything I told you about the stolen laptop?"

"I promised I wouldn't, and I didn't," answered Jewelle, irritated that Heather doubted her.

"Well, now you know as much as I know. Am keeping my ear to the ground. I have to go."

Jewelle sat back in her chair and reflected on the news that Heather just broadcast in her office. Surely this latest stunt of Miss Mercier would end in her being walked out the front door, she thought triumphantly. Maybe things would work out after all. She took a late lunch and went to the parkette to relax and call Thérèse with her flight information. Paris, here I come, she mused.

Fourteen

Gay Paris

On a bright morning, late July, Jewelle landed at Paris's Charles de Gaulle Airport. Thérèse was there to meet her. The two women embraced each other warmly and exited the airport with Jewelle's Goyard trunk, a source of amusement and amazement for Thérèse who admired its beautiful construction but found it nonetheless to be awkward and impractical. Since the trunk could not fit into Thérèse's mini, Jewelle and her belongings were transported by taxi to the small apartment that she had rented around Hameau du Passy in the *16th arrondissement*, close to where Thérèse lived. An area that featured handsome buildings and pretty shops and was close to the metro. Thérèse followed the taxi.

When they arrived at the apartment, Jewelle asked the driver to help her carry the trunk into the building where he squeezed Jewelle and it into the tiny elevator that took her to the second floor. Thérèse followed. Satisfied that the apartment was in order, she left Jewelle to get settled and take a rest. Thérèse would pick her up at 7.00 p.m. for dinner. After Thérèse left, Jewelle began unpacking but was soon overcome with fatigue and surrendered to sleep but not before setting her alarm clock. She woke up at 5.00 p.m., finished unpacking, showered, and waited for Thérèse.

Promptly at 7.00 p.m., Thérèse knocked on her door. Jewelle let her in. They embraced each other and exchanged a kiss on each cheek.

"Jewelle, deed you get some rest?"

"I did. I feel much better now."

"Bon! We are going to Le Dauphin restaurant dans le quartier," said Thérèse smiling broadly. She remembered that Jewelle liked this quaint little family restaurant. "Wee can walk dere. Eet's juste around di corner."

When they arrived at the restaurant, it was busy, and they waited to be seated. The restaurant hummed with chatter of tourists and patrons from the neighbourhood. Waiters in black slacks and crisp white shirts crisscrossed between tightly spaced tables covered in white linen anchored by vases displaying brightly coloured flowers, to deliver mouth-watering meals to eager patrons. Jewelle enjoyed the dance that was being performed while they waited.

Finally, a table was liberated from a couple who looked like honeymooners. Jewelle was thankful that it was in a quiet corner where conversation would be easier. Shortly after being seated, they ordered un *pichet de vin rouge*, deux salades vertes et deux soles meunière.

"Alors Jewelle, tell me all your news," enthused Thérèse.

"There's so much to tell. Well, as you know Chantal got the promotion. Since then, all the people who report to her are required to call her Miss Mercier. I am surprised she didn't also ask us to curtsey as well."

Thérèse chuckled as Jewelle continued, "The worst part of this whole experience is that she has stolen my ideas and has also been sabotaging my work. Every day, she demands another report of one kind or another. It's endless. No matter how many hours I work, I can't seem to get caught up." Jewelle sighed.

"Have you spoken to the head of the department?"

"I have. I think she's sympathetic. However, she said I need to provide proof, and I have not been able to get the proof that I need."

"You cannot continue working around de clock seven days a week. You will av a breakdown, non?"

Before Jewelle could answer, the waiter arrived with their salads, a basket of bread and the wine.

"Mesdames, salades vertes," he said, setting their plate in front of each of them, the breadbasket in the center of the table. Then, he poured the wine before running off to serve the next diner.

"A toast to friendship, health and happiness," said Jewelle gleefully before touching glasses with Thérèse.

Between bites, the two women talked about and talked through Jewelle's situation at TV3. Based on the new developments with Chantal and Marg, Thérèse advised her to wait until she got back to Toronto before making any final decisions. Soon the salad plates were cleared and replaced with the sole meunière. *Tarte tatin* enhanced with a *boule de crème glacée à la vanille* completed the meal. "*L'addition, s'il vous plaît,*" asked Jewelle.

After they left the restaurant, they walked through the neighbourhood admiring the window displays and talked about the latest fashion trends. The walk gave them an opportunity to reconnect and to burn off some of the calories consumed over dinner.

"No need to come up with me," said Jewelle.

"Jewelle! Good to have you back. *Dors tard demain matin. Nous irons chez Angelina pour le brunch,*" said Thérèse warmly.

"Angelina! Are you sure, Thérèse?" asked Jewelle. "They are hideously expensive."

"I know. Eet's a treat!" said Thérèse cheerfully.

They embraced and wished each other "*Bonne nuit.*"

Jewelle had a hard time falling asleep. Her body clock had not yet adjusted, and she tossed and turned most of the night alternating with short periods of watching TV until she finally drifted off.

When the sun rose and streamed in through the airy white cotton lace curtains, Jewelle stirred. She slowly opened her eyes stretched her limbs under the soft white cotton sheets. The sun was insistent. It beckoned her. She yawned, stretched again, threw back the covers and bolted from the bed to her window, and threw it open. The sounds of the street flooded her room. She looked out the window, admiring the beautiful architecture and flower boxes of red geraniums that hung from balconies. Jewelle felt blessed, thankful to be alive and in Paris.

The days prior to her departure had been a steady stream of work with little time for personal matters. However, she did manage to squeeze in drinks with the posse at a bar near her condo, a working lunch with Heather, and a dinner at Grazie with Anthony.

During dinner, she told Anthony about Johann. He was surprisingly calm about the situation and calmly asked if she'd be seeing him while in Paris. She told him yes and assured him that she intended to impress upon Johann that they could be nothing more than friends and colleagues. Anthony also made it clear to Jewelle that this was his last attempt to make "them" work. When she got back, they would either move forward together or apart.

Jewelle had not gotten around to calling her mother or her aunt; she just didn't have the energy to do battle with the two of them. What energy she had was reserved for TV3. That was her sad reality. But in Paris, she had some time and space for her mother. She called Adele.

"Bonjour maman," said Jewelle lightly.

"Oh, the prodigal daughter has returned," said Adele.

Jewelle disregarded her comment. "How are you?"

"How do you expect me to be? I have not heard from you for weeks; I don't know what's going on with your brother's wedding plans, and my sister Constance is talking about getting married again. Madness!"

"If Aunt Constance can find a suitable partner, she has my blessings. From what I have observed, it's hard to grow old alone," said Jewelle quietly.

"You can say whatever you want, Constance can't live with anybody. I don't think if Jesus himself tried, he could manage her," fumed Adele.

"Mother, that's not nice! Yes, Aunt Constance is difficult but she's also charming and wickedly funny. She could very well find a partner who will focus on her good qualities."

"So, where have you been hiding?"

"I haven't been hiding, just working. The last couple of weeks have been torturous. I'm trying to hang on to the job. But it's hard."

"Nothing good comes easy," spouted Adele. Jewelle bristled whenever Adele threw out one of her stock platitudes.

"I have taken a leave of absence. I'm in Paris, France," said Jewelle lightly.

Adele dropped the phone. She picked it up and said, "I know where Paris is located! You just picked up yourself and flew to Paris like that. Is Anthony with you?"

"No Anthony is not with me. He has to work."

"Jewelle, I am warning you that if you are not careful that nice young man is going to get tired of you flying all over the place and walk away. Wait until your aunt Constance hears about this." Adele was on a roll.

"Mother, contrary to what you may believe, Anthony doesn't mind me travelling for work. He does mind the long hours, and I'm going to try to do something about that when I get back. As for Aunt Constance, she has always made her own choices and that's what I am trying to do," said Jewelle firmly.

"Miss Jewelle, are you throwing words at me?"

"No Mother, I'm simply expressing how I feel."

"I really don't know what's gotten into you, but I don't like it," lamented Adele.

"Mother, I didn't call to argue with you. I called to see how you are doing and to let you know that I'm okay," said Jewelle wearily.

Adele was silent.

"Mother, are you still there?"

"Yes, I'm still here. Sorry if I sound cross. Thanks for calling and look after yourself."

"I love you."

"I love you too, Jewelle. Bye for now."

"Bye, Mother."

Jewelle was pleased that her call to her mother ended on a pleasant note. She recognized that Adele was lonely. Visits to galleries, museums and symphony attendance were not enough to fill her life. This was the underlying reason why she held on so tightly to her children and interfered in their lives.

Shortly after Jewelle got off the phone, she took a leisurely shower, singing Nina Simone's "Feeling Good." And she was feeling very good. While she was getting dressed, Thérèse called to let her know she was running late, would be there at twelve thirty, and asked Jewelle to meet her out front of the building. Jewelle took her time to dress carefully and settled on an Audrey Hepburn look of a black linen boat neck top with mother of pearl buttons down the back, slim black silk trousers, a small white silk scarf tied at the neck, and red ballerina shoes. She piled her locks in an unstructured bun and held it together with a scrunchie made from Ankara. Her make-up was minimal except for her eyelash-extending mascara, and her Saturday night red lipstick. A few dabs of Chanel No. 5 behind the ears completed the look. As she passed the hall mirror, she caught sight of her reflection. She was pleased with the image that stared back at her. She checked her watch. It was twelve fifteen. She grabbed her handbag, locked the door, walked down the stairs to the main floor and exited the building. Within minutes of standing outside, Thérèse pulled up to the curb. Jewelle quickly climbed into the car. They exchanged the usual kiss on each cheek.

"You look très chic, Jewelle," remarked Thérèse.

"Merci Madame," replied Jewelle, smiling happily.

It wasn't long before Jewelle was reminded of Thérèse's aggressive approach to fellow drivers. She ducked in and out of lanes and tailgated, not to mention the poor signaling and sudden stops that hurled them towards the windscreen. Yet she complained bitterly about the poor driving skills of her fellow motorists. Her mantra was, "You *av* to be *aggresseeve* to drive in Paris." There was some truth to this. However, by the time they reached Angelina's, Jewelle's nerves were threadbare.

The first time Jewelle visited Paris on business, she was taken to Angelina's, a beautiful old tearoom decorated in *belle époque* style. It was elegant and charming, and the food was delectable, a foodie's paradise, particularly the exquisite *pâtisseries*. In its early years, it was the place where the Parisian aristocracy went to see and be seen. Not much had changed except now anyone who can pay the staggeringly pricey bill, can claim a table there.

Thérèse had made a reservation, so they were quickly ushered to their table, one that gave a great view that allowed them to observe the coming and goings of fellow patrons. When the waiter arrived, they both selected the brunch option which included the restaurant's famous hot chocolate. Jewelle ordered crepes and Thérèse, eggs Benedict.

"Thérèse it's great to be back here. It brings back pleasant memories of the first time," said Jewelle wistfully.

"For me too," murmured Thérèse. "So, what would you like to do while you are here?" asked Thérèse

"I have mapped out some places I'd like to visit that are connected to some of the African American artists who lived in Paris."

"Zat ezz very interesting. I saw Nina Simone perform here many years ago."

"She's one of my favourites," gushed Jewelle. "Just this morning, I was singing "Feeling Good" in the shower," she said, smiling broadly.

"So, you can sing?"

"Yes, I can carry a note or two," Jewelle chuckled

Well, I av learned someting new about you," said Thérèse warmly.

"I know you have to work while I'm here, so we'll get together when your time permits. This week is planned out. And next week, Johann will be here for three to four days."

"I tink you have things organized like always. Alors, what about Johann? Are you serious about im?" asked Thérèse

"I'm attracted to him, but I don't think it is much more than that on my part. He, however, thinks he is madly in love with me."

"Follow your instinct, eet's toujours right."

"He told me that he has found a few positions in Europe he thinks would be perfect for me. So, I will take a look at what he found. But my instinct is to stay in Toronto closer to my family. And of course, Anthony. Already, I don't see enough of them."

"*La famille est très importante.*"

"I am now starting to better appreciate this," said Jewelle quietly.

The waiter appeared with their meals.

"*Le chocolat chaud* et la crêpe pour Mademoiselle et le chocolat chaud et les oeufs Bénédicte pour Madame," said the very fastidious waiter.

Over brunch Jewelle and Thérèse continued to share bits of their personal and professional lives with each other. By the end of brunch, they had each discovered new things about the other.

Jewelle dreaded the ordeal of driving with Thérèse. The trip back mirrored the drive to Angelina. After a crazed daredevil ride, Thérèse dropped Jewelle off at the Monoprix, a French supermarket chain that sold food on the upper level, and clothes, household goods, cosmetics and greeting cards on the lower one. Jewelle loaded up her shopping cart with her favourite fruit, cheeses, teas, crackers, *pâtisseries*, tapenade, and pineapple yogurt. When Thérèse dropped her off, she thanked God for bringing her back to the apartment unharmed.

In the lobby, she eased herself and her grocery bags into the skinny elevator. After stashing the groceries, she changed into her nightie and watched an old episode *Taratata* with Nagui. It wasn't long before the sandman came a calling.

It was eleven before Jewelle stirred the following morning. She had enjoyed a sound sleep. When she slithered out of bed, she threw open the windows and invited the sounds of Paris to take up residence in the corners of her charming apartment. She plugged in the kettle to make herself a cup of tea before calling Anthony. The phone rang a few times before he picked up.

"Good afternoon, Sir Anthony of Brown," quipped Jewelle.

"Good morning, JJ. Good to hear from you. How are you?"

"All is well, I'm settled in my charming little apartment. It's close to the metro and there are lots of nice shops around."

"Sounds great. You also sound relaxed. Have you checked in with the office yet?"

"No. I'll call them on Monday. Trying to enjoy the weekend. I spoke to Mother yesterday. We got off to a rough start. She told me that she's convinced that you are going to leave me because of my travel for work. I told her that it's not my travel that's the problem but the hours that I commit to work and that I plan to make a change when I get back."

Anthony was silent as he gathered the right words for what he was about to say. "Well, you are right. Try to understand your mother. I think she's lonely and that's why she interferes in the way that she does. You know she loves you. I love you too, and I want *us* to work."

"Anthony, I have never doubted your love. I'm the problem in this relationship, and I'll have to sort myself out." When the words left her mouth, they sounded strange to her ear, but they also rang true.

"JJ, I hope your time in Paris allows you to figure out what you really want and what's important to you," said Anthony softly.

Jewelle reflected for a moment. A sad smile crossed her face as she recalled some of the ways she had taken him for granted.

"Anthony, things will change for the better, I promise. I love you too." As soon as the words left her mouth, she also felt them in her heart.

"Well, I have to get going. I'm going to see my parents," said Anthony.

"Give them my regards. We'll pay them a visit when I get back."

"That would be nice. I'm sure they'd appreciate it. Enjoy gay Paris!" said Anthony with a chuckle.

"I will. Thanks for everything, Anthony Brown."

Bright and early Jewelle called the office and spoke with Heather. She learned that things were still upside down and that Marg was trying to raise sponsorship money to offset Chantal's overspending. Heather assured her that she had everything under control.

Jewelle's first week in Paris flew by in a blur. She focused on visiting places and spaces where James Baldwin, Josephine Baker and her beloved Nina Simone and other African American writers and artists, who fled America's corrosive and ugly racism, had found refuge—the Café de Flore where Baldwin worked on his novel *Go Tell It on the Mountain*, Les Folies Bergère where Josephine Baker caused a stir by dancing in a banana skirt and little else, and Théâtre des Champs Elysées where Nina performed and also disciplined audiences. Although Paris wasn't then nor now without its own brand of racism, it allowed these artists to develop themselves, their art and to live as brilliant creative beings in keeping with the country's national motto, *Liberté, égalité, fraternité.*

Jewelle spent several days walking through les Halles, one of the most ethnically diverse neighbourhoods in Paris in the First Arrondissement on the Left Bank, one of the *quartiers difficiles* where the underclass is contained. It reminded her of Ontario Housing in the edgier parts of downtown Toronto.

That weekend, she reached out to Johann, who told her that he'd be in Paris on Tuesday of the following week. He had booked a room at the Hameau de Passy Hotel, just around the corner from her apartment.

Johann arrived late Tuesday afternoon. As soon he unpacked his suitcase and sent a few emails to his office, he called Jewelle.

"Jewelle, the eagle has landed," said a smiling Johann.

"Welcome to Paris, Johann."

"Where are you, Jewelle?"

"I'm wandering about in the huitième arrondissement over on the Right Bank. This place just oozes serious money. You can't throw a rock without hitting a bank or multinational business."

"Are we on for dinner?" he asked hopefully.

"Definitely. I've asked Thérèse to join us."

"Okay," said Johann hiding his disappointment that he would not have Jewelle all to himself on his first night in Paris.

"I'll meet you in your lobby at eight and we'll walk to the restaurant. Thérèse will meet us there. Italian, okay?"

"Sounds great! Looking forward to seeing you later."

"Me too. Bye for now," said Jewelle quickly.

The rest of the afternoon, Jewelle dashed about in Parc Monceau, an unusual garden with buildings of all styles and eras—a Gothic castle, minaret, Dutch mill, Egyptian pyramid, Chinese pagoda encircled by majestic sycamore trees with twisted branches. The beauty and calm of the garden helped Jewelle let go of her cares and the stress that had settled in her spirit. She ended her day on rue du Faubourg Saint Honoré, home to France's most celebrated fashion brands—Chanel,

Saint Laurent, Louis Vuitton, Hermes, Ferragamo, to name a few. She was enthralled by the beautiful window displays and ventured into a few stores. However, she abstained from buying anything. Jewelle simply couldn't justify spending that kind of money on clothes or accessories.

During the train ride back to her apartment, Jewelle admired the fashionably dressed commuters. Parisian chic was on full display. That evening when Jewelle arrived at the Hameau de Passy she was dressed in a sleeveless, long olive-green silk column dress and strappy black sandals with slim heels. She had let down her hair for a change and wore her luxuriant locks over her right shoulder. Johann was standing in the lobby when she got there. They warmly embraced each other.

"Jewelle, you look great as always. That colour suits you."

"Thanks. You don't look too bad yourself," said a smiling Jewelle. "Shall we go?"

"Certainly! Lead the way." During their walk to the restaurant, Jewelle told Johann about her day and plans for the next couple of days that included him. He was delighted. When they arrived at the restaurant, the waiter took them to the table where Thérèse was seated. After the introductions, they ordered their meals. Conversation was engaging and lighthearted as Thérèse observed the chemistry between Jewelle and Johann. They talked about the foibles of the industry and some of the new programs they came across recently. Half-way through the meal, Johann took a few sheets of paper from his pocket and handed them to Jewelle.

"Jewelle, here are the job descriptions that I mentioned to you, one in Sweden, one in the UK and one here in Paris."

"Thanks, Johann. I will look them over in the morning. Thérèse, do you want to take a look?" asked Jewelle, pretending to be interested.

"Oui."

Jewelle handed the three job descriptions to Thérèse who quickly scanned them and stated, "You are certainly qualified for all of these positions. It will be a big decision if you decide to leave Canada."

Johann remained silent but noted Thérèse's comment. As the evening wore on, they shared many laughs and stories about their experience working in the industry. When they parted, Johann and Thérèse promised to stay in touch.

Johann walked Jewelle back to her apartment. She did not invite him up. He was not surprised, but he wished it were otherwise. They agreed to meet at noon to start their Paris adventure.

That evening, Jewelle reviewed each of the job descriptions. They were interesting and challenging positions that she'd enjoy. But in her heart, she knew that she did not want to leave Canada. Toronto had become home, and it was close enough to Montreal for her to see her family regularly. Equally important, she wanted to build a life with Anthony Brown.

The next day, Jewelle and Johann visited Montmartre cemetery. They strolled through it leisurely, stopping to take pictures of the flamboyant mausoleums and gravestones of some of the legends who were buried here and whose work Jewelle admired—Edgar Degas, Alexandre Dumas, Emile Zola. They each lit a candle in La Basilique du Sacré Coeur de Montmartre, admiring the gleaming white dome that can be seen from almost any point in Paris.

The following day, they spent time at the *Marché aux Puces de St-Ouen*, the largest flea market in Europe. You could find everything from expensive antiques to cheap knick-knacks. Johann shopped for family members and friends. Jewelle did the same.

On his last evening in Paris, Johann took Jewelle to an upscale restaurant. The meal was outstanding and there was a warm feeling of comradery. However, there were also awkward moments because of what was unspoken between them. During dessert, Jewelle quietly told Johann that she would not apply for any of the positions because she did not want to leave her family or Anthony.

When she left him, he didn't know what to think, what he should be thinking. The street was very quiet, and the moon was full. He questioned how he really felt about Jewelle. He wanted to be angry with her, but he couldn't really. After all, she had never hidden the fact that she was in a committed relationship, and she was not interested in a "market affair." However, he had persevered because he felt he could win her over. He hadn't won in the way that he wanted. But he knew that they could and would be friends.

The next week flew by—more galleries, museums, and dinners with Thérèse, who she told about her final evening with Johann and her decision to remain in Canada close to her family. Thérèse remarked that she could see the *frisson* between Jewelle and Johann but that this was not necessarily the foundation on which to build a lasting relationship. She again reminded her to follow her instincts.

The last week in Paris was more than less like the others. Now she could fully empathize with Adele. Visits to the galleries and museums were no replacement for meaningful relationships and for sharing experiences with someone you love. Jewelle was homesick. She thought about returning home early but didn't want to throw away money on a reservation change.

One afternoon when she returned to her apartment, she found a note pushed under her door. The message read, *Meet me in the lobby at seven.* She did not recognize the handwriting. It was unsigned. Jewelle was curious as to who was the anonymous author and asked the front desk if they could describe the person who left the note. They said the note must have been handed over to someone on the earlier shift. Jewelle had no choice but to wait for each agonizing minute to pass.

When Jewelle entered the lobby at seven, it was empty. She turned around toward her room thinking that someone was playing a prank on her. Suddenly she heard a familiar voice call, "Jewelle Joseph." She spun around to see Anthony wearing a big grin. Jewelle squealed with delight and ran over to him. They embraced, kissed, and stood holding each other lost in the joy they were both feeling. In that moment, their differences vanished. They were one. A shift had taken place.

The following morning Jewelle woke up beside Anthony and got out of bed to call her mother and the posse to let them know that he was in Paris. The girls played along as though this was "news" to them, but they had been instrumental in helping him plan and execute the trip.

When Anthony woke up, Jewelle announced that she had a jam-packed schedule for them and inquired if there were any of the sights that he wanted to see. The Eiffel Tower and Notre Dame were his choices, and dinner with Thérèse who he had heard so much about.

They dressed quickly, pausing here and there for lingering embraces, and then walked down to the breakfast room that was dotted with small tables covered in vibrant blue and yellow Provençal cotton tablecloths, each with a different pattern— some lavender, others lemons, sunflowers, and olive branches. At the centre of each table was a white vase with red and white flowers. Here Jewelle and Anthony enjoyed a satisfying continental breakfast that included oranges, grapes and *chocolat chaud*. After breakfast, hand in hand, Jewelle and Anthony set out to discover Paris together.

First stop, the Bouquinistes of Paris, sellers of used and antiquarian books who ply their trade along the banks of the Seine—left and right bank. On the Left Bank while Jewelle was leafing through books on the recommendation of an English-speaking vendor, Anthony secretly purchased an old French copy of Sartre's *Huis Clos* for Jewelle. From here, they choreographed an escape from reckless drivers intentionally blind to pedestrian walkways.

The next stop, the Eiffel Tour. Anthony was on cloud nine and often remarked, "I can't believe, I'm here," as the elevator climbed to the top. Jewelle glowed. She felt happy spending "off the clock" time with Anthony. It felt new and different. He had stepped out of his comfort zone and crossed the big pond after so many years of turning down her invitation to join her on one of her European sales trips.

Early that evening, they stopped for dinner at a small café in the quartier of their hotel. Over Kir Royale, they watched well-dressed Parisians going about their daily lives, some pausing to admire beautiful window displays, others speaking animatedly to each other and a pedestrian or two arguing with drivers who had nearly run them over. Jewelle and Anthony enjoyed a light dinner of *salade verte*, baguette, an omelette au fromage, a bottle of chardonnay, and Badoit avec gaz. They wrapped up the meal with *tarte tatin*, carmelized apple on pastry *avec une boule de glace à la vanille,* and île flottante, a dessert of meringue floating on crème anglaise, and *café au lait.*

"Try some of my tarte," said Antony, feeding it to Jewelle from his fork with a bit of ice cream.

"It's sooo good," moaned Jewelle.

"Now, your turn. Try a bit of my île flottante." Jewelle scooped up a spoonful of meringue and crème anglaise, playfully circled the spoon in front of Anthony's mouth before feeding it to him.

"That's really good. Can I have some more?" he asked smiling.

"Another Oliver, the boy who dared to ask for more," said Jewelle fighting to hold back her laughter.

She lovingly fed him another spoonful. Taking her hand in his, looking into her eyes, Anthony said, "I wish *we* could always be like this. I know that's asking a lot, but I'd like us to try."

"I promise," whispered Jewelle.

The next day, they visited Notre Dame, a magnificent cathedral of French Gothic architecture. They were both in awe of its beauty and majesty. Before leaving they lit candles and said a prayer. Jewelle prayed that she would create more balance in her life and time for Anthony. She also thanked God for this moment in her life. Back out on the street, they tried to navigate the crowded sidewalk jointly but became separated.

Jewelle looked around and spotted Anthony attempting to cross the street. As he stepped into the crosswalk, a car careened around the corner and sped into the crosswalk. Anthony jumped out of the way but fell hard on the ground. A crowd quickly gathered around him. A frantic Jewelle forced her way through them to get to him.

"Are you okay? No, let me answer that. Of course, you are not okay. Let's try to get you up."

With the assistance of an onlooker, she helped Anthony get to his feet. He winced when they touched his right arm. Relieved that monsieur was not seriously hurt, the members of the crowd went about their business, with many complaining loudly about motorists who treat the roads like racetracks and seemed to take sadistic pleasure in sweeping pedestrians from walkways and sidewalks alike.

"Stretch your arm back and forth," commanded Jewelle.

"It hurts a lot, but I don't think it's broken," grumbled Anthony.

"I'm going to call Thérèse to see if her brother, Dr. Cartier, can arrange for a doctor to see you at the hotel.

When they got back to the hotel, a friend of Dr. Cartier's was waiting for them. She examined Anthony and diagnosed him with a sprained arm and bruising. He was prescribed Tylenol 3 for the pain. When the doctor left, Jewelle allowed herself to breathe and stop to think "what if" Anthony had been killed. She shook the thought from her head and gave thanks they had both been spared—him his life and her sorrow and grief. Jewelle cancelled their dinner and scheduled breakfast for the following morning.

Breakfast with Thérèse, at a neighbourhood café, was delightful. Their ease of conversation felt like that of close friends. There was much laughter and camaraderie as they broke bread together and shared stories from their lives. When Anthony excused himself to go to the *toilette*, Thérèse bent forward and whispered, "He is the one," and gave her a kiss on the cheek.

After Anthony returned, both thanked Thérèse again for her assistance in getting Anthony a doctor, hugged and said their goodbyes.

Walking back to the hotel to get their sunglasses, Jewelle and Anthony narrowed their eyes against the glare, but still managed to soak up the beauty of the neighbourhood and this moment in their relationship.

With their sunglasses now shading their eyes, they set out for Montmartre, a charming district in the heart of Paris once called home by many of the Impressionist artists. They wandered the cobbled stone streets of Montmartre stopping here and there to visit gardens, vineyards, galleries, bistros and the Sacré Coeur Basilica, a masterpiece of grace and grandeur, perched on the Butte.

When the sunlight switched to moonlight, Jewelle and Anthony took an evening stroll. Their glow brightened their path as they shed their social masks and became vulnerable to one another. Wandering through Montmartre, one café flowed into another, lovers lost in each other's embrace exchanged kisses. Jewelle and Anthony paused to accept the serenade of a sidewalk busker. Caught up in the moment, Anthony drew Jewelle close to him, twirled her around and then slowly danced with her, right there on the sidewalk. The busker seized the moment and asked to take a picture that captured their story of love.

It was time to go home.

PART IV

Fifteen

Back on the Job

Jewelle's Paris trip had a fairy-tale ending because of Anthony's surprise visit. It allowed them to spend time together without the distraction of work and family interference. As they discussed their values and dreams, they recognized that there were enough common interests for them to move forward together. They had something deeper than just "chemistry."

Jewelle received a warm welcome back to the office. Heather had a million questions about what she did and her meeting with Johann. Jewelle told her she'd fill her in over lunch the following day, but she needed to spend the day reviewing files and getting up to speed. She had just sat down at her desk when Heather popped in to let her know that Marg had scheduled a 2:00 p.m. lunch in the Matisse Restaurant at the Marriott Hotel on Bloor. She was working from home and would meet Jewelle there. Shortly after Heather left, Miss Mercier stormed into her office.

"So, you made it back!"

"I have indeed. How may I help you?"

"The first series has been delivered. What pre-sales have you closed to date?"

"I have closed three—American Forces Network, TVJ and CCN TV6. This information is in the last report that I gave you," said Jewelle crisply.

"I don't remember seeing those deals in your report," snorted Miss Mercier.

"Would you like another copy of the report?" asked Jewelle.

"That will not be necessary! Please come to my office at two o'clock for a brainstorming session," ordered Miss Mercier.

"I already have a two o'clock meeting scheduled."

"Cancel and reschedule!"

"I can't do that. It's with the head of the company."

"Oh, why don't I know about this?"

"Perhaps, you ought to ask Marg why she didn't inform you," said Jewelle cattily.

"I certainly will!" Chantal said angrily, slamming the door behind her.

Jewelle was anxious to learn what the meeting with Marg was all about. She tried hard to focus on her work, but her imagination was in full flight and creating scenarios about what Marg may have discovered during her absence. Thankfully, she just had a few more hours to wait.

When Jewelle arrived at the Matisse restaurant, Marg was already there. As the waiter walked her over to the table, she admired the trompe l'oeil reproductions of some of Matisse's famous paintings that covered the restaurant walls.

"Hello Jewelle. Welcome back," said Marg warmly.

"Thanks, Marg."

"Hope you got some rest and also had fun."

"Yes, on both counts. I also got to spend some time with Thérèse. She sends her regards. The best part of the trip was that my boyfriend Anthony turned up unannounced the last week that I was there," said Jewelle beaming.

"That's wonderful. He seems like a really nice young man from what I remember from the last Christmas party. Handsome too," said Marg with a chuckle.

"I'm a little biased but I have to agree with you." Jewelle and Marg both laughed.

"I think we should order," said Marg. "Do you know what you'd like to have?"

"Yes, my favourite. The goat cheese salad with mesclun greens."

"Is that all?"

"Yes. I'll spoil myself with a nice dessert!"

"Well, I'll need something a little more substantial. A steak with frites and a good glass of wine should do the trick," said Marg. She signaled to the waiter. "Are you sure you don't want a drink," asked Marg.

"I'm sure. I try not to drink during work hours. It makes me sleepy," replied Jewelle.

"Can't say that I have that problem," quipped Marg.

The waiter took the order and said he'd be back with Marg's wine and Jewelle's sparkling water.

"I'm sure you are wondering why I have called this meeting and why it is outside of the office. Well, as we both know, confidentiality is a real problem at TV3. The walls seem to have eyes and ears," said Marg.

They both laughed.

"You cannot breathe a word of what I'm about to share with you. Not even to Heather. We understand each other?" said Marg in a serious and heavy tone.

"I understand and will not betray your confidence."

"First, I'd like to apologize for not having taken your miseries with Chantal more seriously. I kept asking you to provide proof but did nothing to assist you in getting it. Frankly, I thought that you and Chantal were simply competing against each. I couldn't imagine it was anything more than that," said Marg pausing for a minute. "After my laptop was stolen and your personnel file went missing, I had an outside company install a camera in my office. I also managed to get receipts for all the purchases she made to decorate her office. These receipts had also vanished into thin air. Well, suffice it to say that I now have all the proof I need to put a stop to Miss Mercier."

"Marg, I don't know what to say except my prayers have been answered," said Jewelle smiling broadly.

The waiter returned. "Wine for you, and water for you," he said as he placed each drink.

"While you were away, I've been working from home to give Chantal more access to my office. I have gathered enough information that clearly reveals Chantal's plans to push me out. She almost succeeded because she had the support of her sugar daddy, the chair of the board. You have no idea how angry I am that this upstart tried to push me out by sabotaging me. I have dedicated over twenty years of my life to TV3 and I'll be damned if I'm going to allow Chantal and Mr. George to show me the door before I'm ready to leave," said an enraged Marg.

"So, what is your next move?"

"Tomorrow afternoon, I will be meeting with Chantal and Mr. George to negotiate a deal," said Marg with a wicked smile.

"Ladies, I hope you are hungry," said the smiling waiter as he served each meal. "Enjoy! Let me know if you need anything else," he said before walking away.

"Bon appétit", said Jewelle.

As the two women enjoyed their lunch, they exchanged stories about their lives. Jewelle told Marg all about her mother Adele. Marg advised her to be patient with her and to make time to call and visit, as it would lessen Adele's anxiety and loneliness. From her vantage point, she could clearly see that Adele had suffered many important losses—her husband, her marriage, her family, and children, who no longer needed her as they did in the past. She may feel she was no longer important to them.

When they parted, Jewelle hugged Marg tightly and thanked her for her kindness and her words of wisdom.

Sixteen

Showdown at TV3

Jewelle and Marg arrived at the office at the same time.

"Good morning," said Jewelle

"It is indeed a great morning," said Marg winking. Jewelle pushed the elevator button, and the door opened immediately. As the elevator climbed to the seventh floor, they exchanged small talk about the weather. The showdown hung in their midst, but not one word was spoken about it. They went to their respective offices and got down to work. Marg had managed to find two sponsors for two smaller events. The profit from these events would cover the shortfall created by Chantal's extravagance. She had drafted the contract and was now finalizing it so that the Chair could review and approve it.

The new company hummed its usual tunes, the sound of phones ringing, the fax machine whirring, the clicking sounds of keyboards, and careless whispers conveying half-truths and speculations about the future of the organization and the people within it. In short, it was a typical day. However, the frenzy of the last six months seemed to have waned. Yes, the sales team was still working hard but there was a shift of some sort. Jewelle attributed this to a change in her attitude and outlook. She was learning to value people more and unbridled ambition less. Jewelle was anxious about the showdown that would take place between Marg, Miss Mercier and Gregory George. As she was sworn to secrecy, she could not share this information with Heather. Besides, it wouldn't be long before Heather and the rest of TV3 would know all the sordid details.

In defiance of Miss Mercier's ban on personal phone calls during office hours, Jewelle called her mother.

"Hello Mother," said Jewelle softly. "How are you?"

"Jewelle, what a pleasant surprise! I am fine. Is everything okay with you?"

"Yes. Everything is good. I got back from Paris over the weekend. You are never going to guess what happened," said Jewelle excitedly.

"No, I can't guess, so you better just tell me."

"Anthony paid me a surprise visit in Paris. Can you believe it?"

"Yes, I can believe it. That young man loves you. I hope you will do right by him," said Adele softly.

"Mother, I promise I will. I must go now, just wanted to check up on you. I am going to visit soon, and Anthony is coming with me," said a giddy Jewelle.

"That's really nice to hear. It will be nice to have the two of you in Montreal. Bye for now, Jewelle."

When Jewelle hung up, she found herself crying. She wasn't sure why, but she felt like a weight had been lifted from her shoulders. Jewelle dried her tears, checked the time, and got back to work. The next couple of hours flew by. She was in the zone, her fingers flying across the keyboard knowingly, words presented themselves as she needed them. Emails and sales letters got composed effortlessly. She turned to look out the window and to give her eyes a rest from looking at the computer screen when Heather rushed into her office.

"Jewelle, Chantal and Marg have just gone into the boardroom. Something's happening. Do you know anything about it?"

"No," she lied. "But I'm sure we'll soon find out. You know there are no secrets here."

"True enough," said Heather.

A few minutes before two o'clock, Gregory George, the chair of TV3's board walked into the Sales Department. Before heading to the boardroom, he popped his head into a few offices to inquire how staff members were doing. When he arrived at his destination, Chantal and Marg were already seated there. Marg sat at the head of the long, polished table, surrounded by ten chairs. Chantal was sitting to her immediate right. Marg asked Mr. George to sit on her left.

"Before I get started, would anyone like a bottle of water," asked Marg.

They both declined.

"I am sure you are both wondering why I have asked you here, so let me get right to it. For many months now, Chantal Mercier has waged a campaign to sabotage the work of her colleague Jewelle Joseph. She has also taken credit for Jewelle's ideas. When Jewelle came to me with her concerns, I did not take them seriously and asked her to provide proof to back up her accusations," said Marg in a calm and steady voice. "Chantal then turned her dirty tricks campaign in my direction. My laptop, with my PowerPoint presentation of the annual report, disappeared the day before the presentation, confidential files started to walk out of my office unaccompanied. To protect my position, I had to search for proof that I was being victimized like Jewelle Joseph," said Marg pausing to take a drink of water and to give them time to absorb what she had just told them. "Now, Chantal, do you deny anything I have said so far?" asked Marg.

"All of it! I plan to take this matter to HR as soon as we are done here," Chantal blustered. Mr. George remained quiet.

"You are fully entitled to do so, Chantal," said Marg with steel in her voice. "But before you do, I have prepared a package for each of you to review."

Marg reached into her folder and pulled out two stacks of paper stapled together, handing one to each of them. The blood

BLINDED BY THE BRASS RING

drained from Mr. George's face when he saw the cover page of him and Chantal kissing in a restaurant. With each page he turned, he became more shaken. Halfway through, he stopped looking. He found his voice.

"Marg, what do you want?" he said in a quiet resigned tone.

"Before I answer that question, I'd like to give Chantal a chance to complete her review," said Marg deliberately.

They waited until Chantal had looked at the last page. She looked at Marg defiantly.

"So, Gregory and I are seeing each other. That's not a crime, is it? As for the emails, so what! The receipts for the furniture and the special events, Gregory was fully aware of all this," said Chantal smugly.

Gregory sputtered and started to cough.

"I guess you could use that bottle of water now," said Marg, handing one to him.

"Miss Mercier, the only thing I will admit to is that we have been seeing each other. And as of now, that's over! You are solely responsible for it all, and I mean all the other misdeeds!"

Chantal went white.

"Gregory," she started before he cut her off.

"Mr. George to you," he said pompously.

Chantal collapsed in her chair. Gregory had thrown her under the bus.

"Let me ask again, what do you want, Marg?"

"Not much really. I would like to fire Chantal without any challenges from you, and I would like to promote Jewelle Joseph to the VP of Sales and Distribution position. The job should have been hers in the first place. In exchange, all these documents will be destroyed, and this meeting never happened," said Marg, taking back the stack of documents from each of them.

"Marg, we have a deal. I'm truly sorry about what you and Jewelle have gone through. Please accept my sincere apology," Mr. George said meekly.

244

"You, lowlife coward," growled Chantal. "I should have known better!"

"Chantal, I would suggest you not say another word. This meeting is over!" said Mr. George sternly.

Chantal clammed up. Marg remained seated and allowed them to walk out together. Mr. George bolted from the department, and Chantal returned to her office where she collapsed in a tsunami of tears.

After they made their exit, Marg called Jewelle and Heather to the boardroom to tell them Jewelle had been appointed the new VP of Sales and Distribution and that she'd not have to go through another interview. Jewelle and Heather were elated. They hugged each other and jumped around like two schoolgirls. Marg asked that they keep the news to themselves until she had a chance to take care of the paperwork with HR.

When Marg got back to her office, she found Chantal sitting there waiting for her.

"What do you want, Chantal?" asked Marg gruffly.

"I am asking for a second chance. Please don't fire me. I need my job," she said quietly. All the bravado displayed during the meeting had vanished.

"Why should I give you another chance when you tried to destroy my career and my life?" thundered Marg.

"I'm asking your forgiveness. I *need* my job. My parents are in difficult circumstances, and I am their main source of financial support."

"Well, I hope you can forgive yourself for the havoc you created in this department. I don't forgive you, but I suspect that Jewelle might. If she does, you may keep your job."

Seventeen

Celebration

Excitement filled the air of Jewelle Joseph's downtown condo as she and family members got ready for the evening's big event, Jewelle's birthday party and promotion fete that Anthony had arranged for her. Her sisters Cass and Deeana, her mother Adele, brother Ryan and his fiancée Keisha had arrived from Montreal the day before. Her "girls" were staying with her and Ryan and Keisha at the nearby Marriott hotel.

When the girls started to chatter about their outfits, this was Ryan's cue to go check out the downtown scene. Oooh's and aahh's followed each dress and the accompanying accessories as they were displayed. This went on for some time before Keisha said good night and headed back to the hotel. They all rolled into bed shortly thereafter.

Bob Marley's "Survival" was playing in the background, and Jewelle joined in on the chorus, "We are the survivors, the black survivors," she sang as she walked down the hall to the powder room carrying a handful of hair pins.

"Here are the pins Cass," said Jewelle as she sat down in the chair facing the mirror. Cass had agreed to spruce up her locks.

"Thanks, JJ."

Jewelle started moving her body slowly to the reggae beat.

"Stop jigging about," said Cass, inserting a few more hair pins into the elegant chignon she had created with Jewelle's dreadlocks.

"Have to move when I catch a vibe," replied Jewelle.

"Well, vibe this. I'm done. There are enough pins in there now to hold everything in place."

Jewelle stared into the bathroom mirror turning her head from side to side to admire Cass's handiwork. She was pleased with her reflection.

"What do you think?" asked Cass.

"It looks fabulous! Girl, you are a genius with hair. Let's go see what Mother and Dee have to say."

Jewelle and Cass walked quickly down the hall to the guest room where they found Deeana and Adele. Jewelle entered the bedroom, just ahead of Cass, spun around a couple of times like a model, then asked, "Well?"

"You look beautiful, Jewelle, an ebony princess," said Adele.

"You mean one of your three ebony princesses," added Dee.

"Yes, Deeana, you are all my princesses," said Adele, silently giving God thanks for her girls and her one boy child.

"That's the truth!" said all three girls in unison, exchanging winks. Jewelle looked over at the clock radio.

"Mercy! It's six forty-five already. Mother, we've got to hustle if we are going to get over to Bernie's for seven thirty. Cass, you and Deeana had better get started if you are going to be *on time*," said Jewelle.

"My hair is already done. It won't take long for me to put on a little make-up and get dressed," said Adele as she took her suit from her garment bag. She then headed out the door and down the hall to the powder room.

As soon as Adele left, Cass and Deeana looked at each other and rolled their eyes.

"Here we go again," Cass whispered to Deeana. "Is JJ ever going to give this *time* thing a rest?"

"Not any *time* soon. She certainly internalized Daddy's lessons on punctuality," said Deeana chuckling.

"Guess I tuned them out," sighed Cass.

Adele soon returned wearing a black silk suit. The jacket had a fitted princess line bodice with a peplum and was accessorized with a large rhinestone brooch in a sunburst pattern. The skirt was long and narrow with a *bare as you dare* slit on the side.

"Mother, you're showing some serious leg," teased Cass. "You look great. Très chic."

"Thank you, Miss Cass. The legs are still holding up. They're not Tina Turner's, but they'll do," joked Adele. "You two had better get moving, you know what your sister is like—better an hour early than a minute late."

Deeana and Cass looked at each other and burst out laughing.

"What's so funny?" asked Adele.

"Nothing, Mother," answered Cass, still smiling.

Jewelle rushed into the room. "Mother, we've got to go. Aunt Constance is waiting in the limo downstairs. Do you have everything?" asked Jewelle.

"Yes," replied Adele. "You look lovely."

"Thanks, Mother," said Jewelle giving Adele a hug. Jewelle and Adele were already out the front door, but Adele gently pulled her back inside.

"I'd like to say a prayer before we leave," said Adele.

"It's *got* to be brief," said Jewelle

"Deeana and Cass, please come out here for a minute," called out Adele. When the girls arrived, Adele asked them to form a circle and join hands.

"Dear God, thank you for having brought us safely to Toronto once again and for your many, many blessings. As we head off to this evening's event, I'd ask that if it be your will, please bless the evening and everyone who has contributed to it. She has worked so hard. I know I don't need to tell you, but I am anyways. We ask these things in your son's holy and precious name."

"Amen," they said in unison.

"Okay, we *really* have to go now. Bye Cass, bye Dee, I will see you both at eight sharp," said Jewelle. Dee and Cass exchanged glances and again rolled their eyes.

"Don't forget the limo will pick you up at seven forty-five. Keisha and Anthony will meet you in the lobby," said Jewelle as she hurried Adele through the door.

"JJ, our ears do work, you know. We'll get there on time!" said Cass.

Jewelle and Adele headed down the hall. When the elevator doors opened, the chauffeur was there. He held open the front door, then quickly walked over to the white stretch limo, opened the door, and helped them into the car.

As Jewelle settled in the soft leather seat, she leaned back, inhaled deeply, and exhaled, emitting a soft sigh. Adele reached over, took her hand and stroked it gently.

"Are you nervous?" she asked.

"A little."

"Nothing to be nervous about, Miss Jewelle. You are amongst family and friends who are happy that your hard work has paid off."

"Even though I used to give you a hard time, you know I mean you well," said Aunt Constance warmly.

When they arrived at the entrance of Bernie's luxury condo building, there were other guests arriving at the same time. At the main entrance, men clad in sharp suits and women in little black evening dresses and glittering jewelry spilled out of cars. It was Jewelle's big night. She looked regal, dreadlock chignon neatly in place, silver and crystal chandelier earrings contoured her long, graceful neck and an elegant black bias-cut silk cocktail length tunic skimmed her slim figure.

Jewelle, Adele, and her aunt Constance were among the first to arrive. They were warmly greeted by one of the smartly dressed young men who pointed them in the direction of the elevators that would take them to the party room.

From the condo's lobby they crowded into an elevator with residents of the building. Some people smiled politely at them, some cast sideway glances, and others stared vacantly into the mirrored elevator walls. On the fifteenth floor, the elevator doors slid open, and they walked down the hall to the party room that had been transformed. It was dotted with round tables draped in black and white linen. At the center of each table there was an exquisite floral centerpiece of orchids, pink roses and greenery, a silver candelabra with two white candles, surrounded by white place settings, silverware and the appropriate crystal drinking glasses. Each table displayed a number, and some were "reserved."

When they walked into the room, Radcliffe was already seated at one of the reserved tables. As they walked over to join him, Jewelle whispered to her mother and aunt, "Ladies, best behaviour." They smiled knowingly. When they arrived at Radcliffe's table, he hugged each of them and complimented them on their appearance before pulling out the chairs so they could be seated. Adele enjoyed his attention even though she would not admit to it. Soon, the other members of the Joseph family filled the empty seats.

The table next to the Joseph family was occupied by Anthony's parents Franklyn a.k.a. Frankee and Verna a.k.a. Little (Franklyn's pet name for her), his brother Marvin, a committed bachelor, his two best friends, Cedric and Marvin, with their glamourous-looking dates, and his aunt Stella, the family's know-it-all and tell-it-all. Glancing around the room to see who was there, Franklyn's eyes landed solidly on Adele's and held her gaze. He smiled brightly and nodded at her gallantly. She acknowledged him with slight turn of her wrist. This was all the encouragement Franklyn needed to propel his diminutive frame from his seat. He stood up, puffed out his chest, walked pompously behind Verna and slowly eased out her chair. Firmly taking her hand, he helped her up. Verna's towering and thick body hovered above him. "Little, I think we should go say hello to Adele and Radcliffe," he whispered turning up his mouth in the direction of her ear. With Franklyn clutching her and leading the way, they made a beeline to Adele's table. As they drew closer, Adele and Radcliffe got up from their seats to greet them. Franklyn and Verna exchanged pleasantries with the others seated around the table. He, however, kept one eye trained on Adele's exquisitely exposed thigh. Franklyn bear-hugged Radcliffe, stepped back, surveyed him from head to toe then pronounced, "Boy you is sumting else! Not ah ounce ah fat on yu. No wanda dem young women won't leave you alone. Adele, yu didn't hear dat," chuckled Franklyn, gently rubbing his round belly.

Before Adele had a chance to respond, Verna chimed in. "Adele, don't mind Frankee. Yu know his filter done vanish long time now. Anyhow, good to see you again," Verna chirped in her singsong Trinidadian accent, reaching out to embrace Adele.

"We all very proud of Jewelle and you must be too," she gushed while concealing her shock at the naughty split on Adele's skirt.

"Thanks Verna. Her father and I are very, very proud. Happy that her hard work has finally paid off."

"Jewelle isn't the only one who should be proud," said Franklyn smiling roguishly before exclaiming, "Here nuh, Mary Brown can no longa claim to have the best legs in town."

Cass and Deeana rolled their eyes. Constance emitted a loud kiss teeth, and muttered under her breath, "Wha wrong wid dese blasted men!"

"You might be on to something," chimed in Radcliffe, giving Franklyn a devilish wink.

"Adele, don't mind Frankee, ah can't take him anywhere. And Radcliffe, don't encourage him. Yu know how he does get on. Anyhow, ah tink we should get back to our table before Frankee put his awtha foot in his mouth. All ya, enjoy dis special evening." Verna took the lead, gripping Franklyn's hand firmly like a child being disciplined.

Jewelle's posse was seated at a table nearby. The women looked ready for the cover of Vogue Magazine. Camilla's fashion forward dress was the perfect balance of daring and interesting, a hit. Jewelle warmly greeted each of them.

"Bernie, I know you were the ringmaster who gathered the crew together to pull this off! Thank you, thank you, thank you," said Jewelle fighting back tears.

"Don't bother with the waterworks you'll spoil your make-up," said Joy.

"I don't think the Alice Cooper look suits this occasion" added Maxine. They laughed heartily.

"Alright, go finish your rounds so that we can get this party started," commanded Bernie.

"Aye, aye captain," scoffed Camilla, giving Bernie a sharp salute.

"Please don't wind her up," pleaded Joy.

This was Jewelle's cue to move on. She quickly made her way to the table where Marg, Heather, and other industry colleagues were seated. She greeted each of them with a warm hug. Just as she was about to return to her seat, she felt a gentle tap on her shoulder. When she spun around it was Johann with Thérèse beside him. She let out a squeal, hugged one and then the other. Anthony and the posse had managed to keep this too hidden from her.

When everyone had arrived, Anthony took to the stage to welcome and thank family and friends who were present to celebrate Jewelle's promotion and hinted that he had another surprise of his own. With that said, Anthony walked off the stage, with the cordless mic, to where Jewelle was seated. He got down on one knee, took a small ring box out of his pocket, and spoke into the mic, "Jewelle Joseph, will you marry me?"

For once, Jewelle was speechless. It was her aunt Constance who spoke up. "Di young man waiting fi an answer!"

Everyone in the room erupted into laughter. When the room grew quiet once again, Jewelle gave her answer.

"Yes Anthony Brown, I will marry you."

This time, the room erupted with applause, whistles and some people shouted out, "Congratulations." Anthony placed the ring on her finger, stood up, helped her up from her seat, kissed and hugged her tightly. People left their tables to come over and wish them well. This went on for a while until Bernie took the mic and said, "Am I the only one in here who's hungry?"

Some people answered, "No!"

"Since we are keeping it real, will somebody say grace so that we can eat!"

Eighteen

A Fresh Start

Marg left it up to Jewelle to decide Chantal's fate. It was a tough decision. She had discussed the situation with her parents, the posse and Anthony. Apart from Joy, all the members of the posse felt that she should kick Chantal to the curb. Jewelle was conflicted until she talked it through with Anthony. He agreed that what Chantal had done was awful. However, he felt that she should be given a second chance. If she messed up again, then she should be shown the door. Jewelle agreed with Anthony.

The day after her appointment, Jewelle had suggested to Chantal that she take some time off so she could reflect on what she had done and why. One rainy afternoon they met for lunch. It got off to an awkward start but as they talked more, the tension eased, and they spoke more openly. For the first time, Jewelle learned that Chantal was a small-town girl who left home to find greener pastures. Life in the big city was rough, and she used any means necessary to get to where she wanted to go. She knew right from wrong but was so blinded by the brass ring, that she felt everything was fair game while she reached for it. The more she rationalized and justified her behaviour, the more "normal" it became.

The more Chantal spoke, the more Jewelle thought about her own battle for success. Even though she did not employ dirty tricks, she was often inconsiderate. Without exception, friends and family members overlooked much of what she did. They did not want to endanger their relationship and she was forgiven.

"Jewelle, there is no excuse for what I did to you. Like I told Marg, all I'm asking for is a second chance to show that I am not a monster. Please give me a chance to prove this to you, Marg and Heather, who I treated so badly."

Chantal aroused Jewelle's sensitive side that allowed her to summon up compassion and empathy. However, that did not change the fact that she was now responsible for leading a team that had to generate significant revenues. It was this reality that influenced her decision. Whatever she might think or feel about Chantal, many clients who were fond of her, regularly licensed programming from her, and TV3 needed the revenue. Moreover, the new company would not have to start from scratch with a new hire costing a lot of time and money. Of course, Chantal would have to prove that she deserved Jewelle's forgiveness. And Jewelle's handling of the problem would be a leadership lesson for the staff.

"You know Chantal," said Jewelle, "I have also done things that hurt others. I think if we live long enough, we all do. I am prepared to give you a break, but know this, the first hint of any power moves or other shenanigans, you will promptly be walked out the door."

"Jewelle, thank you, thank you. You will not regret it," said Chantal with gratitude.

"All that I would ask Chantal, is that as you move forward, you remember this day and do the same for someone else who needs a second chance. Take the rest of the month off and let's start fresh in ten days." Jewelle added, with a smile, "Go spend some time with your parents."

On the second day of the next month, Jewelle called a meeting with the entire sales team. She thanked everyone for their hard work and contribution to TV3 Sales and Distribution Inc. and let them know that her management style was one of collaboration and partnership, and this day marked a fresh start. Her door would be open to everyone who wanted a listening ear or had ideas that they wanted to share. She asked each of them to think about their current territories and any changes they'd like to make. The meeting ended with Jewelle suggesting that they all take a listen to Nina Simone's "Feeling Good."

When the meeting ended Jewelle went back to her office and called Anthony. He picked up quickly.

"Hey JJ, what's up?"

"I just had a really good sales meeting and I'm feeling fine," she said. She gave him the details about her meeting with the sales team.

"You are going to make a great VP; you know that don't you?"

"I think so. I am going to make every effort. Thanks for your confidence in me," she said softly.

"Jewelle, I know talent when I see it!" He laughed softly at his comment. "Go get them, JJ! I love you," said Anthony warmly.

"I love you too. I will be home by seven. What would you like for dinner?" she asked playfully.

"Surprise me!"

Nineteen

Riviera Dreaming

Inside the futuristic departure hall, Jewelle looked at the board for her connecting flight. The space-age electronic chime sound and a detached voice cautioned against unattended luggage over the public address system. Men and women clustered around tall tables absorbed in their newspapers, quaffing strong coffee or chatting noisily on their mobile phones. In need of a pick-me-up, Jewelle ordered a *café au lait* and a croissant at the bar and relished the way true French pastry melts with buttery richness. She missed that about *La Belle Province*, the Quebec of her youth where good food is as much a religion as in France.

She watched the people, so different from Toronto. How else could one describe the French, she wondered, but *chic*? The easy stylishness, how a scarf was tied just so, a sweater draped over the shoulders, women clicking along in unapologetically high heels and men openly admiring them with a glance as they clicked by on the marble floor of the terminal. She smiled to herself and nibbled on her croissant.

A few hours later, the little Airbus descended over the mountains, preparing to land in Nice. Towns slid past under the wings as the plane followed the coast. Marinas and yacht clubs were jammed with boats, villas dotted the hillsides, cars sped along the roads and Cannes came into view.

Down and down the airplane dropped, the sea getting closer; a windsurfer scudding past over the waves, and then suddenly the tarmac appeared and the squeal of wheels hitting the runway announced their arrival.

Amid the soulless glass and steel of the terminal the unmistakable odour of France permeated, an exotic blend of cigarettes, coffee, baked bread and diesel fumes. Jewelle inhaled, sighing happily, absorbing the comforting smell of a country that had given her so many good memories.

The electronic sign noted the baggage belt for her flight, and she searched among her coins leftover from the previous trip for one to liberate a trolley. She hung back from the conveyor. Others crowded forward in the vain hope their luggage would emerge first. People can be such sheep! she thought, as the throng vied for space to watch the parade of bags pass. After fifteen minutes, a lifetime for the anxious and impatient, a mere moment in the normal languid pace of the Riviera, the suitcases snaked along the conveyor and were quickly snatched up. The crowd thinned.

Jewelle cast an eye across to the belt every few minutes, still sleepy from the long trip until she and two back-packers were the only ones waiting. The conveyor stopped. No luggage. A door opened out to the tarmac, and a baggage handler carried in two large plastic bags, putting them down on the floor next to the belt. One of the backpackers ventured over, checked the contents through the clear plastic, smiled and picked them both up. Jewelle abandoned the trolley and approached the Air France baggage counter. Two staffers were locked in an important personal conversation. She attempted to grab their attention in vain.

"Oui Madame," one woman finally said with a bored indifferent tone now that she had finished speaking with her colleague.

"Bonjour." Jewelle launched into a query about her luggage, pulling out the claim sticker with her boarding passes and ticket.

"One moment, Madame," the agent said, tapping her keyboard, a pensive look passing over her face. "Ah, yes, your bag did not make it onto the flight. It is still in Toronto." She smiled, the mystery obviously solved.

"Toronto! How did that happen?" Jewelle cried, incredulous.

"I don't know, Madame. These things happen sometimes." The agent shrugged with the aloofness of someone practiced in giving bad news.

"Will it come on the next flight?" Jewelle asked.

"It should," the woman tried to assure Jewelle.

"It's rather important, I'm here on a business trip, I have documents, samples, I need my clothes!" Jewelle insisted, hoping to express some urgency, fighting the anxiety building within her. Thank goodness she had put an emergency outfit in her carry-on.

"Yes, Madame. I will make a note of it." The woman typed on her keyboard.

"I need more assurance than that. I need to know that my suitcase will be here tomorrow!" Jewelle raised her voice.

"Madame, I can only put a priority message on the system. I cannot snap my fingers and make it appear, comme magique!" The woman bristled, sitting up straighter in her chair, and thrusting her chin forward.

"I understand that, but when I asked if it would be on the next flight you told me 'it should,' and that's what I need to be more certain, you see?"

Jewelle tried to recover her poise recognizing that no amount of arguing would change the situation. After all, she was in France where workers had their own rhythm and ways of "managing" things. She'd just have to pray for a miracle and trust that her luggage would be found and delivered to her in a timely manner.

"Madame, when the luggage arrives here in Nice, will someone deliver it to my hotel?" she asked.

"Are you staying here in Nice?" the agent asked.

"No, in Cannes. I'm here for MIP-COM," Jewelle explained.

"Cannes?" the agent said, a glimmer of life flickering across her face. "We don't usually deliver luggage."

"Well, I'm sure that Air France doesn't usually forget to load passengers' bags onto the plane either," Jewelle retorted, her annoyance beginning to flare. "But seeing as this is all rather unusual perhaps you could make an exception," she said, barely keeping the Mandinka in check.

"*Pleeze* give me your address in Cannes. I cannot guarantee before 10.00 a.m. tomorrow, Madame." The agent relented, handing over a form and pen for Jewelle to complete.

Ten minutes later, she walked out of the arrivals hall into the warm Mediterranean sunshine, a meagre €50 in emergency cash in her pocket courtesy of the airline "for essentials," the agent had said. Determined to not let the episode sour a beautiful day, Jewelle caught the express coach to Cannes, and contemplated what Didier might have on his table d'hôte this evening at La Cigale. The warm sun coming through the window and the hum of the coach's engine made her drowsy. The billboards advertising the newest Peugeot, a promotion on garden furniture, an upcoming concert in Monte Carlo became a blur as her eyelids drooped shut. The coach sped on toward Cannes.

In this moment of relative peace and calm, she felt truly blessed and was filled with gratitude as she thought about her many likes and dislikes of Cannes, a place that she had grown to love.

Her likes: The language, the Mediterranean Sea, the pink tinged evening sky of the Mediterranean that Cézanne and his contemporaries loved, the evening symphony of les cigales, the old stone houses with clay-tile roofs, the clothes, the cuisine, the pastry shops, the language, the *brocanteurs* selling their treasures—silverware, porcelain, depression glass, the impressionist style water colours, furniture from another time that still maintained their charm, weather-beaten leathery old men playing boules in the park, the mature plane trees, the vibrant garden beds along the *Croisette*.

And her dislikes: Their "soon come" and "island time" approach to things. Jewelle often marvelled at the similarities between French public servants and those she had encountered in Jamaica. For both, any request for service was received with annoyance, if not outright contempt, withering looks of dismay that you dared to interrupt whatever they were doing, in many instances office gossip. Boozy and breezy chatter. Garish overdesigned jewelry with outrageous price tags and overpriced designer clothing that people with common sense and bit of courage would call out as ugly and impractical. But for many rich tourists and market executives, these brands were the ultimate symbols of success. Reckless eyes devouring the female form often resulted in the proclamation of an *oh là là*. In Jamaica, the equivalent would be *cho*.

As she faded in and out of sleep, Jewelle thought about her life and all that she had experienced over the last five years—career, friends, and family. Periods of turbulence had taught her some valuable life lessons. It was now clear that in the days ahead, she'd put first things first—Anthony, family, friends, and career in that order. She now understood that perfection in a relationship was not something to be pursued. Rather, a deeper love and understanding that would allow her and Anthony to journey from *me* to a place of *we* while still being able to grow and mature individually. Anthony would never be and should never be an extension of herself. And, her family, she'd resolved to love each one as they were and no longer try to "fix" them or anyone else for that matter, including Chantal. She knew there would be setbacks in her efforts to keep things balanced because old habits did not readily surrender their place to new ones.

She fell into a deep sleep with a smile on her face.

Acknowledgements

This book is dedicated to my late mother, Mrs. Adassa Scarlett, a.k.a. Dassy, my late aunt Florence Anderson, a.k.a. Flo, and Roger McTair.

Mother's fearlessness, unwavering faith and the love of God and family were an inspiration to me and all who had the good fortune to know her. I miss her every day but am thankful for the many years we journeyed together. You are forever in my heart.

Roger McTair, a.k.a. Raja, brilliant writer, storyteller, story editor and filmmaker, has been a loyal mentor, colleague and friend. Whenever I have asked for help, he always said "yes." Without Roger, *Blinded by the Brass Ring* would have remained just an idea. I am truly blessed and thankful to have Roger in my life as someone who has lived through the challenges of "the biz" without becoming bitter.

I'd also like thank the following individuals who made it possible for me to have a career in film and television: Kris Gilbert, Cindy Galbraith, Pat Fillmore, Susan Nobel, Louise Charbonneau, Antoinette MacDonald, Marie-France Picart, Robin Welch, Ditta Cuzy and Horst Bennit.

Special thanks to my friend and colleague Winston Mattis, whose daily encouragement helped me to cross the finish line and my multi-channeled friend, Maurie Alioff, who beamed in from his private planet to read and edit the novel. My siblings, Maureen, Hugh, and Doreen, who have stood by me through thick and thin. And my husband Gerard, and son Alexander, who have weathered all the storms that threatened to topple us.

Glossary

ACRONYMS

LCBO: Liquor Control Board of Ontario

TTC: Toronto Transit Commission (Company that operates the buses and trains in Toronto)

PAL (Phase Alternating by Line): A broadcast format used in Europe and other parts of the world. PAL television images consist of 625 lines unlike the North American TV Standard (NSTC) which consists of 525 lines.

FRENCH

L'addition, s'il vous plait: The bill, please

Au revoir: Until we meet again

À bientôt: Until later

Bien, merci: Well, thank you

Bonne nuit: Good night

Boule de crème glacée à la vanille: Scoop of vanilla ice cream

Ça va: It's well

Café au lait: Coffee with milk

Le chocolat chaud: Hot chocolate

Deux: Two

Dors tard demain matin: Sleep in tomorrow morning

Est-ce que tu seras libre, le 15 à 13 h 00 pour une réunion et 20 heures...: Will you be free on the 15th at 1:00 p.m. for a meeting and at 8.00 p.m. ...

Êtes-vous prête à commander?: Are you ready to order?

La Belle Province: The Beautiful Province (Quebec, Canada)

La famille est très importante: Family is very important.

Marché aux Puces de St-Ouen: The Clignancourt Flea Market

Non. Toujours pareil: No. It's always the same

Oh là là: Oh my

Oui: Yes

Pâtisseries: Pastries

Pichet de vin rouge: Pitcher of red wine

Salade verte: Green Salad

16th arrondissement: 16th borough (Paris is divided into 20 boroughs, some on the Left Bank and some on the Right Bank)

Tarte tatin: Apple tart with caramelized apple

Très bien et toi?: Very well, and you?

JAMAICAN PATOIS

A rahtid lick: A hell of a slap

Mawga: Skinny

Mahnaz: Manners

Mek mi see wha yu going do now!: Let's see what you are going to do now.

Nerves nuh sell a shop: Nerves are not sold at the store

Now, we going to mek you bow!: Now, I am going to make you bow.

Oh, so you tink you can ramp wid big man!: So you think you can play with a don.

Tek dat!: Take that!

We run tings, tings nuh run we: We are in charge of things and not the other way around.

About the Author

Patricia Scarlett's stories reflect contemporary Black life in Canada and explore the intersections of race, class, and culture through a Caribbean-Canadian lens. Over the span of her career, Patricia has comfortably worn many hats, including those of serial entrepreneur and consultant. Her newest venture, Media Business Institute, is a Toronto-based TV training and production company. Her early experience in television began at TVOntario where she worked primarily in international sales. Looking to the many journals she has kept over the years about the inner and outer workings of the domestic and international TV industry, Patricia wrote her first novel *Blinded by the Brass Ring*. Patricia regularly attends industry trade events such as MIP-TV & MIPCOM in Cannes, France. She is the recipient of the 2020 Afroglobal Television Media Award.

Also from Baraka Books

FICTION

Full Fadom Five
David C.C. Bourgeois

Almost Visible
Michelle Sinclair

Foxhunt
Luke Francis Beirne

Maker
Jim Upton

Things Worth Burying
Matt Mayr

Shaf and the Remington
Rana Bose

Exile Blues
Douglas Gary Freeman

Murder on the Orford Mountain Railway
Nick Fonda

The Nurse Linton
and Detective Bellechasse
Mystery Series by Richard King
A Stab at Life
Banking on Life
Serving Life

NONFICTION

Keep My Memory Safe
Stephanie Chitpin

The Legacy of Louis Riel, Leader of the Métis People
John Andrew Morrow

After All Was Lost, Resilience of a Rwandan Family Orphaned on 6/04/94
Alice Nsabimana

The Great Absquatulator
Frank Mackey

Montreal and the Bomb
Gilles Sabourin

Cities Matter, A Montrealer's Ode to Jane Jacobs, Economist
Charles-Albert Ramsay

Mussolini Also Did A Lot of Good, The Spread of Historical Amnesia
Francesco Filippi

Waswanipi
Jean-Yves Soucy

Printed by Imprimerie Gauvin
Gatineau, Québec